CW01646440

THAT SUMMER IN NAUTILUS COVE

JULIE HOLLAND

hearts and minds art

Copyright © 2021 by Julie Holland

All rights reserved.

No part of this book may be reproduced in any form or by any electronic or mechanical means, including information storage and retrieval systems, without written permission from the author, except for the use of brief quotations in a book review.

CHAPTER ONE

MARNIE SQUINTED at the heart shaped fridge magnet: What do you pack to pursue a dream, and what do you leave behind?

She snorted. You don't pack anything. You study, work hard, try to be a good parent and juggle everything in between. You give ten years to a job to have it taken away due to a department reorganisation by an external consultant with a flashy PowerPoint presentation. Marnie's demise from the coveted marketing role at a top private girls' school had come out of left field. Reasoning with the principal over the following days had fallen on deaf ears, so in the end Marnie had stood up, rebuttoned her suit jacket, and stated, 'I loved my job and met all expectations. You said as much year after year, but you can stick it.'

Professional – no. Satisfying – yes.

It had been over a year but her sense of worth had been shattered – 'lower than a snake's belly,' her dad would have said. As devastating as it had been, Marnie was relieved she hadn't been restructured via a Zoom meeting; she had decided to draw a line through the events and stumble away.

But it had been impossible to separate herself from what had happened next. The car accident, and its escalating fallout between herself and her daughter Claire, sat heavily on her shoulders. Marnie hadn't been able to draw any lines through that ghastly event. And now she was to mind her sister's house. At least Libby would be away. Marnie didn't think her patience would survive being that close to her for so long.

'Why are you glaring at my fridge? Oh, that photo. I kind of like that photo.'

The trilling voice behind her made Marnie jump. It was only then that Marnie noticed a fading photo below the magnet.

Two tanned, skinny youngsters with big smiles and floppy hats stared back at her. The sisters stood knee-deep in water, the beach out of camera range, the horizon and all it had to offer their futures in the background. Aged ten, Marnie had to stoop a little to allow their arms to loop across each other's shoulders. Their hair, like salty seaweed, sat plastered around their summer holiday faces. Marnie was smiling broadly while Libby, three years younger, pulled a face. But then Libby had always been the quicker spirit in all things.

'Remember those bathers?' Libby laughed. 'Mum used to tie the straps together with a ribbon at the back because we didn't have any boobs. Hilarious!'

Marnie did remember that hot Melbourne day but now, forty-six years later, recalled that she had found it more embarrassing than funny.

'Just after Dad took that photo a wave came and totally flattened us,' she said.

'Really? I thought you pushed me over. You being the big sister and all.' Libby roughly nudged her sister.

'Good lord, Libby. I've only just got here. And remember, I'm doing you a favour so don't start, okay? I was actually reading your silly daydream magnet.' Marnie pointed at the purple words.

'You know, you are going to have to chill a bit. Big City attitude doesn't cut it here. This might be the "go-to" place for all you southern tourists to escape to, but we do like to keep it friendly and personal. And the magnet isn't about daydreaming, it's about dreams. There's a difference.' Libby shrugged as she held aloft a chilled wine bottle.

'Let's open this cheeky little chardonnay, sit out on the deck, and I'll fill you in on life in Nautilus Cove, and I have to introduce you to Beebs. Oh, that's my phone.' Libby shoved the bottle at her sister. Condensation was already dappling its sides, leaving wet patches on Marnie's shirt.

As Libby whispered into the phone, one arm waving like limp spaghetti to emphasise a point, Marnie took their filled glasses outside onto the deck. Two white Adirondack chairs faced the turquoise river as if they were just waiting for someone to plop into their deep seats. The soothing *click, click* of an outdoor fan circled lazily beneath the overhanging roof. Sloping lawns led down to a low rock wall, a timber jetty cutting through it and leading out into the river. At the end of the jetty was a lone light, its globe large and round like a full moon. One-hundred-eighty-degree views took her eye along the length of the Nautilus Cove River where a smattering of solar lights began to blink on along other properties' boundaries. The setting sun reflected orange prisms across the water's surface as giant pelicans glided home.

Marnie's shoulders relaxed gently. It looked like the cover of a romance novel; all that was needed was a hunky male to wander out onto the jetty next door, glance her way and say g'day. It seemed her sister lived in paradise.

It was late October, still spring in Australia, but Marnie

had underestimated how warm it would be compared with Melbourne. A gentle breeze rustled the surrounding foxtail palms, urging her to gather her pile of wavy hair off her neck into a high ponytail. She'd been surprised to see Libby's short pixie cut, but it made sense in the subtropical climate. The view was certainly beautiful but Marnie couldn't settle, fidgeting in her tailored trousers and shirt. She kicked off her black ballet flats.

'Watch your glass!' Libby called from inside the house, her cell phone still pressed to her ear. Marnie swept it out of harm's way as a black mass rounded the table, a sweeping tail connecting with everything in sight.

'Sit, Beebs, sit! Sit!' Libby had given up on her phone call and was in pursuit of the dog.

'You said your dog was ten years old!' Marnie exclaimed.

Libby ruffled the dog's ears, directing her answer to Beebs. 'You are, and aren't you gorgeous. Black Betty Bamalam, this is my older, much grumpier sister.' Libby laughed as she gave Marnie a comic wave with one of the dog's front paws. 'You can call her Beebs.'

Marnie let the 'grumpier' comment slide as she took in the writhing black Labrador. She loved dogs, but this one was clearly short on training and long on enthusiasm. Beebs rolled over onto her back, all four legs in the air, and beckoned Marnie with pleading brown eyes.

'Oh, she loves you. Give her tummy a scratch, you lousy thing. Just remember that she will eat anything in sight, so no overfeeding. I should have called her Hoover. Anyway, here's to us.'

Libby slid into the other chair, raised her glass, and glanced sideways at Marnie. 'Welcome to Nautilus Cove. I really do appreciate you offering to come up, Marnie. I just didn't want to put Beebs into a kennel and I'll only be gone a couple of weeks. Anyway, you can't complain about the accommodation, can you?'

'No, it's a gorgeous spot. You seem to have landed on your feet.' Marnie hoped none of the jealousy she was feeling showed.

'It's taken a lot of work, I can assure you, as you would have known if you'd visited before now.' Libby waggled her glass at Marnie. 'Yes, yes, I know. You were too busy running the education department. Oh, don't get all thin-lipped!'

'I'm just surprised you could afford to buy your own place.'

She turned away, cross at herself for shuffling onto shaky ground so soon.

Libby had plastered an instant smile over her frown, instead gesturing to a platter of cheese and biscuits, quince paste and nuts. 'Try this goat's brie. It's from Benardo's, a fabulous deli not far from here. I'll show you where it is. Anyway, more about my little shack.'

Marnie registered she hadn't actually inquired about Libby's house, but she took a welcome sip of wine and settled in for one of her sister's ramblings.

'When I first bought the cottage it was in need of love in every sense of the renovator's word. I did a bit of an extension and put in a terrific new kitchen, reclaimed the wood floor and gave it a lick of paint and look at it now. All the old musty glass windows in the bedrooms were replaced with plantation shutters to let in the glorious southerly breeze. And I didn't even use a designer which is contrary, I am sure, to your city beliefs, but there you go. Nowhere near the "look at me" architecture of the mansions along the water here, but I love my little space.'

Marnie had to agree. It certainly had Libby's chic boho stamp on it. She glanced back through the floor-to-ceiling glass windows, taking in the soft tones of Hamptons dove grey meets Noosa China blue. An army of scattered pillar candles came as no surprise. Libby was always the queen of the candles. Subtle French pear, woody bergamot or heady lemon myrtle had always betrayed whichever phase Libby was in at the time. A beautiful mobile hung near the doorway. Libby had given it a gentle touch as she passed, making it slowly turn, its glass hearts sending prisms of light across the deck.

Libby continued. 'Apparently the house was the guest wing or summer boathouse or something for next door's McMansion before they subdivided it. There's a bit of work in the garden to be done but hey, maybe you could turn your hand to that while I'm in Hong Kong.'

'Very funny. You know I can't even keep an African violet alive,' Marnie retorted. 'You may remember Melbourne has more roses and lavender than pandanus and frangipani.'

Marnie glanced along the river, taking in the lush green trees and shrubs. Melbourne was already turning brown, having had little rain over winter. This richness was a welcome change, although she wasn't prepared to admit it to Libby. 'Don't you miss autumn with all those rustling leaves and changing colours?'

'We have falling flora, don't you worry about that! It's just that they're giant palm fronds. You can cut them up and put them in the bin which takes forever, get one of the dozens of gardening services in, or ask my neighbour's cute, well-muscled gardener to take them away. I choose the latter.' Libby smirked. 'Speaking of which, have you met anyone since Philippe?'

The question had come out of left field. Marnie's foot paused on Beebs's stomach. The Lab looked up, panicked that this new person could even think of stopping the attention.

'Why your neighbour's gardener would remind you of Philippe I have no idea, Libby. It's over a year since the divorce came through and I see no reason to keep in touch, so I don't know or care how he is. We communicate about the house and the kids see him of course. Ollie more than Claire, I think.'

'And Claire? Is she okay?'

'Yes, she is, apart from her back spasms.' A frown creased Marnie's brow. She had never gone into great detail about the accident, not wanting to be burdened by her sister's unwanted advice. 'You do know that the accident wasn't my fault, don't you? I mean, I was driving but the old man came through a Stop sign on my left. There wasn't anywhere for me to go.'

'Of course, of course. It was just unfortunate for Claire that she was in the passenger seat. Thank heavens she is, um, on the mend …'

Marnie turned her attention to the river and the ripples that had suddenly appeared. Except for a hovering mosquito, the air was silent with expectation.

'Do you want to talk about it? Share?' Libby sipped her wine, eyeing her sister over the rim.

'No. It's all fine.' Marnie focused on a bug struggling in her wine glass, feeling its pain.

'Right. Well.' Libby slapped her knees, then stood up. 'Topic obviously closed. How about a refill? The wine gets warm quickly here. Do you want a condom?'

'What?' The dog jumped up and raced around in circles at Marnie's shocked tone.

Libby laughed. 'For your glass. You know, one of those foam wraparound things you get from the souvenir shop.

Mine have poinsettias on them. Ghastly, I know, but they do keep the drinks cool.'

'Ah, no. They sound most attractive but I'll be okay. In fact it's been a long day. It was quite a drive in peak-hour traffic to the airport this morning, then hours on the rambling Sunny Coast Bus from Brisbane. I'm bushed. It must be the heat too. I think I'll go to bed.'

'I told you to fly in to our local airport,' Libby replied. 'It would have saved the dreaded trip up the highway. That half hour in the middle alongside the pine plantation is so boring.'

'Well it was cheaper to fly into Brisbane,' Marnie justified. 'The part settlement hasn't left me a millionaire, and I still pay a mortgage until I find somewhere I can afford to live when I go back.'

'Okay, okay, just saying.' Libby held up her hand. 'So, tomorrow we'll visit the shop and I'll introduce you to Laila Wilson. She has her moments but I have to rely on her. All you have to do is check in a couple of times a week to make sure she has enough coin, carry bags and such.

'What kind of *and such*?' Marnie asked, aghast. 'You specifically said *house and dog minding*. Nothing about the shop.' She hooked her fingers to emphasise the phrase Libby had used to convince her to journey north.

'Like I said, Laila is okay but no business is as good as when you are there yourself. It would be so helpful if you could keep an eye on things for me.'

Libby's sudden pleading tone didn't wash with her sister. 'Libby, I know nothing about retail. Nothing. Except what is good service and where to buy the best white T-shirts. And that's online.'

'Wash out your mouth! Your sister here has a bricks and mortar store, and a fabulous one at that, so the online word is never, ever mentioned.'

'Mmm. Maybe you need to get a bit more up to date. Surely online is where it's all at. Actually, Whimsy doesn't have an online store, does it? Why is that, because your rents must be huge here?'

Libby frowned. 'I have Facebook and Instagram that I post product onto and sell through queries from those. Because most of our items are one-offs, it would do my head in to constantly have to update a website. Like you said, you know nothing about retail.'

THE COOL SHOWER water felt heaven-sent as it ran over Marnie's face and body. She sighed with pleasure as it washed away the day's clamminess and frustrations. *Why do I always pick a fight with Libby?* It was nowhere near the first time in her life she had asked herself that question. Libby had a touch of gypsy in her, whereas Marnie was more of the conservative/dinner party type. Whilst growing up Libby had easily moved from one relationship to another, whereas Marnie had locked herself away, dissecting each conversation and possible reason for her various breakups. While Libby had backpacked around Europe post-school, Marnie had quietly taken a brief trip to Central Australia. They had been different personalities their whole lives.

And then came the family breakdown over money that had plunged a knife deep into the sisters' relationship. It remained as an underlying scar that itched whenever they came in contact.

Rolling her stiff neck from side to side, Marnie grudgingly admitted she actually envied Libby's outlook and her apparent ability to thrive in a messy life. But she certainly didn't envy her sister's apparent ability to move on with little regard to the debris left in her wake. In recent times Marnie had tried to be more of a risk-taker, a believer that anything is possible – she had never seemed able to pull it off. If she was honest with herself, she knew her attempts had been more just dipping in a toe than taking a full leap into that unknown.

'Give it to reliable, conscientious Marnie, she'll get it done' was a phrase she'd often heard. From organising the fete when Claire and Ollie had been at school, to the tennis competition roster; from fine-tuning large charity events to Education Department expos. Having to learn on the spot or just bluffing was how she had got through on many occasions, often surprising herself. She always took great satisfaction in a job well done, but it had been exhausting. She stuck to the rules whereas Libby took chances.

She tried to ignore the heaviness weighing down her body and her thoughts. What was the point though – when push came to shove it wasn't always the hardest worker who receives the accolades or promotion. Nor was it the most attentive parent who was always included in a daughter's world.

Marnie flicked the taps off abruptly. No more moping!

Fluffy, sand-coloured bath sheets greeted her as she stepped out of the shower; bowls of floating frangipanis an added welcome. As Libby had predicted, a gentle breeze blew through the shutters bringing with it the heady scent of the sandalwood incense burning on the deck, a hopeful deterrent to the evening mosquitoes. Her sister seemed to think she lived in Bali.

As she dried off and slipped on a silk slip, she could hear Libby's renewed phone conversation.

'.... well at least Beebs has taken to her. No, she's here the whole time I'm away. Just do a drive-by every day or so to make sure she hasn't self-combusted and the cottage hasn't gone up in flames. Only joking. It's good to have someone minding the house, but it will be marvellous to be on the plane …'

The ceiling fan rotated slowly as if low on energy and interest in the room's occupant. The cottage didn't have air conditioning but Libby had assured her the fans did the job of circulating the air and keeping the rooms cool. Marnie wasn't so sure and turned it up a notch.

She offloaded the mountainous pile of rectangular and European pillows stacked on her bed, pulled back the lightweight quilt and crawled between cool cotton sheets. Gazing at the ceiling, Marnie acknowledged that Libby was right: *I am a grumpy old woman. Well, fifty-six isn't old-old, but she was right about the grumpy.*

It made Marnie nervous that everything seemed to annoy her. Her heart raced all the time; she seemed to be balancing on tiptoes, just waiting for someone or something to set her off.

'You feel deserted and left out' was how her friend Dee had summed it up. Dee loved being the amateur psychologist. 'Your husband has gone, your children have left the nest and your day job has, well, ended. You feel out of balance, with an underlying fear of nothing to do. But that's no reason not to get on with life, my friend. In fact, it's an excuse to try something new, go somewhere different, have a fling.'

'I don't want or need to have a fling, Dee. Good lord, I wouldn't know where to start.'

'I know, believe me. You have to keep your legs waxed one hundred percent of the time.'

'What are you talking about?' Marnie had gasped. 'You and Sam have been married forever. Don't tell me you're having an affair.'

'No, of course not. Way too exhausting. But I read the

magazines about what's expected, and anyway, we have our romantic moments … "On a blanket on the ground."' Dee had guffawed as she sang the line from an old song.

'Now I do feel ancient,' Marnie had laughed. 'I'd never get back up. Maybe I should go back to yoga and stretch all those bits that haven't been stretched for ages.'

'And try to shrink back all the stretched bits that shouldn't be stretched.' Dee had winked and nodded as though she was the authority.

Ignoring the dating advice, Marnie had put herself back on the jobseeker list. She had been snapped up by a major winemaker, Pettigrew's, for a short-term contract position. It had been a thoroughly enjoyable time, and she had done well but it hadn't managed to shake her grudge against Manning College.

It seemed that everyone was moving on with their lives, whilst she remained despondent and unemployed. It was as if there was a hole in her heart and no matter how many grains of hope she poured into it, the emptiness never went away.

Her bedroom door creaked open. Marnie heard the click of paws as they padded across the floorboards, then a wet nose nudged her hand. At the sudden touch Marnie had to squeeze her eyes shut as silent, lonely tears slid down onto the pristine white pillow.

CHAPTER TWO

LIBBY PUFFED a sigh of relief when Marnie's bedroom light flicked out. She had been surprised at her older sister's appearance. Goodness, so corporate and stern, like she had packed for a two-week conference in Sydney, not a break in southern Queensland. And were those bags under her eyes? Marnie's discreet inspection of her candle collection hadn't gone unnoticed. *She'll imagine I think I live in LaLa Land.*

Libby had presumed that time away from Manning College followed by a stint working at some winery would have mellowed her. Her sister had been full of the dramas of life, seemingly having lost all sight of a sense of humour, as if no one else ever faced obstacles in their life. It had all been too negative, particularly when Marnie's ex-husband, Philippe, was thrown into the mix. He was a tosser, but had come in handy when she needed some financial advice about Whimsy.

Where had Marnie been when her marriage to Drew had crumbled? In the wings, presuming she knew all the facts, that's where.

'You overcommitted, Libby,' Marnie had said. 'Emotionally and financially and now you've taken other people down with you.'

The echo of those words still stung. This invitation to Nautilus Cove wasn't exactly an olive branch; more of a cushion to break the fall if or when the truth ever came out. She needed someone to help out while she was away, but perhaps inviting her sister to Nautilus Cove had been a mistake.

Libby had kept up her own contact with Claire and Ollie, making sure they were weathering their mother's apparent ups and downs. Libby had never regretted her decision not to have children; the timing had never quite been in her favour. But the opportunity to be an aunt to Marnie's children was a bonus, one she surprisingly enjoyed. Whenever Claire, in particular, had needed a sounding board or a confidante, Libby had always been there. She sighed and wished on a star that her sister never would know that she had been the first person Claire had called after their car accident.

Libby had to acknowledge that she and Marnie were similar in that they both always had to look at both sides of an issue. Although Libby didn't go at it like a science experiment. She was proud of being more of a big picture, 'let's just have a happy ending here so we can all move on' kind of gal.

Well Big Sis is here now, tucked up in bed nice and early! Libby pulled her feet up under her slim figure, relishing her plans of heading off overseas. She figured she was long overdue for an adventure.

'I am off to Hong Kong for sights, shopping and sex, and not necessarily in that order,' she informed the dog, her toes curling at the thought of Rob. 'I am taking a well-earned break away with that handsome fellow I met at the trade fair. I told you about him, remember? You have to keep your sweet little eyes on your new mistress, Beebs. I'm not confident she's quite ready to relax in paradise.'

CHAPTER THREE

THE SISTERS SAT in the dappled shade of a giant Moreton Bay fig tree. Libby had warned Marnie that Queensland was experiencing an early summer, but Marnie still felt like a lobster on simmer. She fanned her perspiring face with the menu, mentally rejecting the clothes that still sat in her suitcase. The heat hadn't dampened her appetite though; she was ravenous, having eaten only snacks during her travel the day before. She gave her order of savoury corn fritters with tomato and cucumber relish to the tanned young waitress whilst Libby ordered acai muesli with fruit salad.

The Pier Café overlooked a small, picture perfect bay. On one side, pristine, golden, sand ran down to calm water which was dotted with an array of colourful dinghies. On the other curved a marina and entrance to Nautilus Cove River. Marnie was finding it hard to get her bearings, presuming the river must be long and meandering. A bit like how her life was turning out – all twists and turns with nowhere to pull in and reflect.

Ducks and pelicans bobbed amongst yachts and cruisers of all sizes. Between the river's passenger ferry and a luxury houseboat nestled a wooden boat. Marnie squinted against the piercing reflection of sun on water to read its name: *Starlight. Wouldn't it be peaceful just to sail away in that little boat*, Marnie dreamed, before being drawn back to her breakfast.

'This is delicious.' She bit into a crispy strip of bacon. 'And they make a good coffee.'

Libby raised her eyebrows. 'Not all good baristas live in Melbourne and Sydney, you know, and trust me, you will never starve in Nautilus Cove. We have a terrific range of cafés and restaurants. I'll leave a note as to which ones are dodgy but on the whole they are fab.'

'It seems to be pretty dog friendly.' Marnie watched the group of canines around the deck, including Beebs who was intent on licking up something foreign.

'My girl loves coming here. You can walk from the house, have a coffee and a chat with other dog lovers, give Beebs a paddle in the water down there and be home in a couple of hours.'

Marnie ignored her sister's hint. Like that was going to happen.

A call from Laila at Whimsy distracted Libby for a few moments, then with an apparent sigh of frustration, she hung up.

'So, what are you going to Hong Kong for again?' Marnie asked.

'There's a huge Homewares Trade Fair thing. Rob, one of my suppliers, is exhibiting and suggested I go. I don't usually buy at trade fairs. I prefer the more unique items, hence why I don't stress about not having an online store,' she stated pointedly. 'Who knows, I might just pick up something different though and it's a good excuse for a break. The Asian Art Fair is nearby too, and it will be so stimulating to expose myself to what other artists are doing. Maybe next year I'll participate.'

'Really? Those fairs are pretty expensive to exhibit at, aren't they? And what would you put in?' A twinge of creative jealousy flitted across Marnie's abdomen.

'A bit of encouragement would be good, you know, Marnie. Maybe I've started painting again, and maybe I'm getting a good response, and maybe I thought I could promote myself through the business by having an exhibition next year. Anyway, I need a break.'

From what? Running a shop can't be too difficult, surely. 'Okay, okay. I didn't know you were painting again. Good for you, I guess. It's a hard industry …' Libby's steely look silenced her.

'Don't tell Mum and Dad,' Libby said. 'I don't want to hear their negative thoughts too. Where are they at the moment, by the way?'

'What, didn't you get the map and set of pins to track The Great Trip? You must be too irresponsible.' Marnie bit her lip. She hadn't intended anything by the comment, but Libby hadn't reacted so she continued. 'I was presented with a huge map of Australia with their itinerary written on it, plus thumbtacks to stick in where they're staying for more than a week. Dad put magnetic squares on the back of the map so it can go on the fridge.'

'So, the Great Carmichael Caravan of Courage Trip, or rather the Motor Home of Courage, is staring at you every time you go for a wine. Hilarious! Oh wait, do you have a fridge?' Libby stifled a giggle.

Marnie slapped her hand over her mouth, her eyes wide. She could see that her sister wasn't sure if this was forbidden territory, but it did stir up memories. 'Oh yes, I remember. You wanted to buy finger puppets for your African sponsor child and we walked the St Kilda markets for hours in the rain …'

'And you were getting madder and madder and in the end said, "Just buy him a fridge magnet", and we felt awful for the rest of the day when we realised he wouldn't have a fridge to put it on. I felt so guilty I sent a special parcel to him every week for ages.'

Marnie relaxed, watching the *Starlight* bobbing on the water. She hadn't thought about that day for a long time. Deep down she knew there had been many other memorable days with her sister that she should revisit. It felt good to let in a little of the past to remind herself of the good times in her life. It was like a beam of warm light.

Libby doused the light with an abrupt change of subject. 'I suppose Mum and Dad were full of advice about your accident.'

'Something about me not appreciating all the dangers of being on the road was mentioned, unfortunately.'

'Seriously though, where are our parents? Gawd, you didn't bring the map with you did you?'

Marnie shook her head. 'They are happy and healthy and in Broken Hill, thank heavens, and probably driving all the other grey nomads crazy. Trust me, Libby, you continue to be the newly appointed Golden Haired Child after my divorce. You know how they loved Philippe and could see no wrong with him. The split was all my fault, as well as the accident, apparently.'

As Libby took another call from Laila, Marnie sipped her coffee and thought about Hong Kong. She and Philippe had had a wonderfully romantic week there a few years back. Who knew the upheavals and betrayals that were around the corner? They had become adventurers. She clearly remembered the overwhelming sounds and pungent smells when scampering up old steps to find the traditional Luk Yu Tea House, Philippe laughing as he gently pushed her up steep alleyways in the rain. Pockets of solitude had been enjoyed together on the nearby islands as they hiked then relaxed at one of the many seafood cafés. How they hadn't ended up with some stomach bug she didn't know; neither the water nor tanks appeared to be particularly clean but it had been fabulous. She still had, somewhere, the little jade bird he had bought her in a dusty antique shop on Cat Street on the way back to the hotel.

'Penny for your thoughts,' Libby interrupted.

'I was remembering Hong Kong. I loved it so much. Philippe always used to say I must have been Chinese in a previous life.'

Libby nearly choked at that gem but Marnie ignored her and continued. 'No, really. I felt as though I belonged as soon as I got off the plane. It's changed so much recently that some of the places I knew have probably gone. See if you can still visit Aqua. It's an amazing bar high above Victoria Harbour where they tailor make your gin cocktail, and then there are all the independent fashion designers squirrelled away in tiny little rooms in Kowloon high-rises. The street art is unexpected and …'

'Hi, Libby.' The sisters turned around, Beebs leaping to her feet in excitement.

'Caroline, come and meet my sister,' Libby called.

Pure Queensland Coastal would be the way Marnie would have described the approaching slim but curvy vision in Versace-style white and gold. Marnie could sense the appraising glare she was receiving from behind large, stylish sunglasses, and she sat a little taller in her chair. As Caroline approached, a smile of perfect white teeth broke across her tanned face. Marnie noticed she gave Beebs a wide berth as she tucked bleach blonde hair back into her perfect high ponytail.

She double air-kissed Libby. 'Caroline, this is Marnie. She's visiting from Melbourne.'

'I love Melbourne. We pop down as often as we can. Any friend or relative of Libby's is a friend of mine.' Caroline instantly turned back to Libby.

'We were just discussing my trip to Hong Kong,' Libby said.

'Another shopping mecca. Well, it used to be. Louisa and I always shopped there for our new season outfits.'

Marnie stifled a laugh. She had been lusting after Hong Kong dumplings.

'Actually, Libby, I'm just on the way to Whimsy. Do you have those shibori cushions in yet?' Caroline was obviously back to business, friendly but firm.

'They're due next week, Caroline. Laila has a note to call you as soon as they come in. She's always there before nine o'clock to let customers know if their orders have arrived.'

'Lovely, darling. She can drop them to my home, or maybe Marnie will be able to. You must visit and have a glass of bubbles.'

'Oh, I'm not …' Marnie stumbled. She was cut off as Caroline whisked out her phone, the sun glittering off the Swarovski cover like a million little flashbulbs. She sauntered off, ponytail and attitude swishing.

'She's a big spender in the shop, and rather nice too once you get to know her,' Libby said as Marnie rolled her eyes. 'No, really, she is. Like a lot of people up here, she's ex-city.'

'Great. You could "freeze ice on her ass" as they say in the movies.'

'*Pretty Woman,* right?' Libby laughed.

Marnie nodded as her own phone rang, the screen showing it was her daughter, Claire. She quickly answered.

'Claire! How are you, sweetie? I'm sitting here with …'

'Mum. I can't believe you left before I had a chance to go through the house. Dad says you've packed everything into boxes and put them into storage. You know I've always loved those retro glass pieces Dad bought you in Sweden.'

Marnie's grip tightened around the phone, disappointment arrowing through her body. Did every twenty-four-year-old daughter think mainly about themselves? She glanced at Libby, sure that her sister could hear Claire's clipped voice. She could picture Claire sitting in a trendy outdoor café somewhere, her eyes looking heavenward.

'How are you, Claire?'

'I'm fine. Please don't ask me that every time we speak.'

A few more grains fell through Marnie's heart. 'It does seem a little odd to be talking about Scandinavian glass.'

'I just think you should …' Claire interrupted.

Marnie flicked her eyes towards Libby before turning slightly away.

'Firstly, the glass is mine no matter who gave it to me, and I'm not dead so I guess it is still mine. Secondly, I was under pressure to start to organise everything. Contrary to what your father thinks, the contents are not packed up yet, and it's none of his business anyway. I am still living there, you will remember. Some help would have been great but both you and Nick couldn't so …'

Marnie took a deep breath. She didn't want to have yet another disagreement with her daughter, let alone so publicly. 'When I get home we can go through some things then okay? Perhaps you could keep an eye out for a snazzy new house for me and email photos of anything you think might suit.'

'I am a little time poor, Mum. Anyway, Dad said you didn't know how long you'd be away.'

'Well maybe your dad doesn't know what I'm doing.' *What does Philippe care anyway? Bloody hell.* 'Would you like to say hi to Aunt Libby?'

'Hasn't she left yet? I thought it was this week. The fair sounds amazing.'

Marnie handed her cell phone to Libby, wondering how Claire would know when Libby was leaving for Hong Kong and about the fair.

All at once the ferry horn blasted and a group of tourists chose to laugh and chat beside their table. Libby moved away to better hear Claire.

A tight ball of not keeping everyone happy rolled and swelled in Marnie's stomach, any family warmth quickly evaporating. For so long she had strived with her heart and soul to be a steady centre, happy to work hard so her children could safely thrive around her. Not for the first time she wondered if that had been the right thing to do for them and for her. It was so hard to achieve a satisfying balance for everyone, but wasn't it natural to expect some kind of recognition in return?

'Fiery' would be how she would describe her relationship with Claire. Philippe had indulged their daughter from the day she was born, whereas Marnie had had to choose her battles carefully to keep the constant dramas at bay. And now she was on the outs again, their mercurial relationship completely collapsing after the accident. Marnie could only presume she was being blamed for Claire's ongoing physical pain. She glanced quickly toward Libby, who was still chatting animatedly. Surely her sister would tell her if there was any other problem with Claire.

Beebs looked up at her, wagging her tail as if reading Marnie's troubled thoughts. Marnie stroked her head.

'Lovely to chat to her,' Libby enthused, handing the phone back to Marnie.

'I've never been very good at just chatting with Claire. Apparently I'm always in the wrong.' She glanced away, suddenly feeling vulnerable to be speaking about the relationship. She hoped her sister didn't hear it caught between her words.

'Nonsense. I'm sure you were always there for her. I just think the whole divorce thing made her feel a bit displaced and angry. You were the unfortunate one who was front and centre to receive the fallout.'

Marnie stared at her sister, stunned at her insight and apparent support.

Libby shrugged. 'We exchanged a few emails, but she seems to be coming along well.'

Marnie thought it was an odd comment and was about to ask her if she was just referring to the divorce when Libby cut in, 'Okay, let's go and introduce you to Whimsy and Laila. Laila used to work at Posh Pit. It's farther down Figtree Street. There have been a few, umm, moments of conflict, shall we say, between me and Posh Pit's owner, Rachel. She has been trying to switch our suppliers to her shop, spreading rumours that Whimsy is going bust, as well as a few other things.'

'Don't you have territories or something?' Marnie probed as they got into Libby's old Golf. As soon as Libby started the ignition Marnie turned up the air conditioning, directing the vents onto her glistening face.

'Everyone's different but I have a rule that if we stock an item, then it can't be sold elsewhere on the Coast. It's too small an area and I try so hard to be different. Anyway

Madam Rachel ordered the very same bracelets that I had, but through her other store in Brisbane, then she put them into Posh Pit here. The maker didn't even know until I rang her.' Libby nodded across at Marnie as though she had a million other stories of skulduggery in the retail industry. 'Laila says she doesn't see Rachel anymore, but I've got to keep on my toes.'

Libby turned to Marnie. 'Relationships are about balance, aren't they? Husband and wife, employer and employee, parents and kids.'

Marnie turned her attention to the passing streetscape, not prepared to be counselled by her younger sister.

CHAPTER FOUR

WHIMSY SAT ON FIGTREE STREET, which curled lazily around picturesque Lantana Bay. The busiest street in Nautilus Cove, Figtree catered to the many holidaymakers and tourists; boutiques, cafés, restaurants and resort hotels all jostled for their attention. Outside of the holiday peak times came the baby-mooners looking for a quiet break before the onslaught of parenthood, the wedding market, the retirees looking for investment properties, and the grey nomads, who spent very little in dollar terms, apparently, but did spread the word about how glorious the area was. Then there were the young couples looking for a chilled environment and nature lovers who could surf or walk the nearby national park.

'This seems to the happening place for a business, Libby.'

'There you go again, Miss Retail, but I agree. We have a wide range of quality shops, mine included, I dare to boast. There are so many different reasons to visit Figtree Street.'

They wandered from the carpark onto the bustling sidewalk right outside Whimsy. Marnie stopped in surprise, the photos she had received from Libby not having done the little store justice. It was gorgeous. Whimsy's double frontage was open, its lemon exterior paint happy and welcoming. Whimsy sat as the last shop at the end of the street, set back slightly on a concrete veranda. A black-and-white striped awning gave the store a quaint but sophisticated edge as it leant out over Libby's pots of cut flowers.

To the left of Whimsy spread a small park where a family of magpies hopped happily around the lush lawn. A path, shaded under tall palm trees, meandered around the corner following a pointer sign to the beach. To the right of Whimsy were resort-style clothing boutiques, a jewellery store, then a little café called Nest. Opposite sat a small square between a shop called Threadz and Lickity Split ice-cream parlour.

Marnie skipped up onto the veranda, surprised at her eagerness to see inside Whimsy. Giant wooden fans slowly rotated, circulating botanic scents that came, presumably, from the scattered soaps and open diffusers. Whitewashed wood floors led to a large beech counter, the front displaying Whimsy's dandelion logo.

Marnie had always been a shopper and could instantly see Libby's unique touch sprinkled over the displays. Why did that surprise her so much? She should have paid more attention to her sister's Instagram posts.

A pile of coffee table books caught her eye. As she flipped through one on the Amalfi Coast her heart sank, wondering if she would ever visit other countries again. Time and dollars certainly seemed to be working against her at the moment. She missed travelling, particularly when she had her camera in one hand and someone special in the other.

'Oh, here's Laila. Were you in the stockroom? Did that scarf turn up by any chance?' Libby directed her questions at a woman who was shuffling out of a back room.

Marnie caught a slight hitch in Libby's voice, recognising impatience. Perhaps the assistant wasn't as efficient as Libby hoped she was. Marnie tried to ignore the scattering of crumbs strewn across Laila's exploding bust as she extended her hand. 'Hi, I'm Marnie, Libby's sister.'

'Oh, Marlee from Melbourne,' Laila replied as she flopped on the side of the counter. She didn't introduce herself. 'Libby said you were due. Taking a break after being laid off, Libby said.'

'It's Marnie.' Marnie forced a smile. 'I wasn't laid off. I decided to leave my position after a reshuffle some time ago.' She turned away, smarting at the comment, and pretended to take an interest in a range of silver earrings. Laila pursed her lips and went behind the counter to serve a young couple.

'Really, Libby.' Marnie hissed as her sister approached. 'Do you have to discuss my life with your employees?'

'Laila won't tell a soul, don't worry. More importantly, what do you think of my baby?'

Marnie stood in the centre of the cool store, calming her annoyance. 'I like it, Libby. I really do. There's something peaceful about it.'

'Well, it's actually a bit light on stock right now. I have a lot of fabulous product deliveries due over the next few weeks. Here it is late October and people are already doing Christmas shopping.'

'Really? It's way too early. But I guess as soon as the big stores get their Christmas stock in there must be a pressure for everyone to follow suit or you'll miss out on buyers.'

Libby nodded, distracted. 'Laila, can you change that awful music? It sounds like a nightclub in here. Maybe Melody Gardot please.'

'I heard you say you've misplaced a scarf. It hasn't been shoplifted, has it?'

Libby shook her head. 'No, I don't think so. We actually don't lose much to shoplifting I'm pleased to say. It must be the positive vibes. I ticked it off the delivery docket last week and put it in the stockroom but can't find it now. It's a bit of a worry because they are gorgeous – hand-dyed silk and felting made by a lovely woman in central Queensland. All soft muted colours.'

Libby led Marnie through a back door to a large storage area. 'Gosh, this is marvellous. At least you have somewhere to store all your stock. And empty boxes. I've never seen so many.'

Libby sighed. 'Hopefully Laila will flatten them when she has a moment.'

Marnie wandered around Whimsy as Libby helped another customer. Laila had disappeared again. A wide range of cards and journals were displayed beside locally crafted ceramic dishes and bowls, in turn nestled next to jewel coloured jugs and glasses. Large wooden tables overflowed with Nautilus Cove candles, funky tote bags and tea towels depicting Australian flora. No foam condoms here, Marnie noted.

Through an archway Marnie could see an enticing range of children's books and nursery room decorations. All of Whimsy's walls were hung with an eclectic range of artworks, from quirky pen and wash illustrations to vibrant works on canvas. Libby was right, only the most appealing original artwork made it into Whimsy.

'Who does your merchandising?' Marnie asked, still unsure if Libby's talents ran to such eye-catching displays.

'I do,' replied Libby. 'Ugh, that music! I'll change it myself. Laila's playlist is different to mine, obviously. I'll just tidy up the flowers out front, then let's grab a coffee at the new café down the way.'

NEST'S INTERIOR was as delicious as its window display of pastries. Glossy green palms in large earthen pots were reflected in little copper nests suspended from rafters above the cake cabinets. Lazy jazz filtered through the buzz of conversation.

'Hi, we haven't met,' Libby said to the woman behind the counter. 'I'm Libby. I own Whimsy at the end of the street. This is my sister Marnie.'

'It's lovely to meet you both. I'm Eleanor. We haven't been open long so I haven't got around to meeting the neighbours.' A lovely wide smile spread across the owner's face, interrupting a maze of freckles. 'Now what can I get you today? I bake all these mouth-watering cakes myself, and the sandwiches are made from local ingredients. We have lots of gluten-free options too.'

The café quickly filled with hungry customers as the sisters enjoyed their coffees and raspberry macarons. Marnie noticed a neat little man sitting in the corner, smiling to himself as he read the paper and sipped his cappuccino. A huge slice of what appeared to be carrot cake was half demolished on his plate. Libby was unusually quiet, seemingly more interested in watching the comings and goings of the new café than having a chat. That suited Marnie. She was enjoying being in her own space; her shoulders dropped an inch, her spine softened. She hadn't thought about house hunting or Claire for a couple of hours.

Looking through the café window she was already filing away potential subjects for her photography. The light was so different from the southern state – clearer and higher somehow. As they made their way back to the car Marnie began to imagine enjoying this break after all. She couldn't explain why that unsettled and excited her at the same time.

CHAPTER FIVE

LIBBY INSISTED on taking Marnie for a quick tour around the edge of the bay. 'This road takes us along to the national park. It is so divine. There's a map at the park's entrance that sets out the distances for all the different walking tracks. You can take one that goes inland through the bush to the other side of the hill, but I like the coastal track better because you get a lovely onshore breeze. Wear your swimsuit, Marnie, take a towel and dip down into the coves and you'll see dolphins and turtles and stingrays. I guarantee it.'

Swimsuit, swimming? Marnie didn't think so, although she had to admit that the openness of the shoreline was truly beautiful. Even at a distance her sunglasses were no match for the glare that spiked off the waves, but she couldn't drag her eyes away from the sweeping water views.

Suddenly two red Vespas zoomed around the curve toward them, ducking back into their lane at the last minute. Two young tanned fellows in shorts and flip-flops waved apologies.

Libby laughed. 'You have to watch out for the

backpackers on scooters, or as we call them, Nautilus Harleys.'

'Very Positano.' Marnie nodded, trying to calm her heartbeat.

Libby shrugged. 'Yeah, whatever.'

'All the surfers head out here,' she said, continuing her travelogue. 'There was a huge surf culture in the Cove in the '60s, apparently. This hill used to be one big banana plantation right up to the lookout. Wouldn't that have been good to own; you'd be sitting on a fortune now. Do you still like photography? Because the local library has some great old photos if you're interested.'

Marnie didn't get the chance to nod or reply before Libby prattled on.

'It's real estate porn at its best too, with the dollar tags to match, I might add. There are holiday rentals, permanent homes and private holiday houses for Brisbane families or expats escaping the Dubai summers. You won't believe how busy it gets here at Christmas.'

The passing vista had held Marnie's attention, Libby's voice drifting farther and farther into the distance. Now, Marnie suddenly spun to face her sister. 'Christmas! I won't be here at Christmas, Libby. I'm here to mind your house while you are away, then I have to get back to my life. I have to sell the house and find another, get a job and, you know, reconnect with routine.'

'Reconnect with routine? Reconnect with routine?' Libby exploded with laughter, slapping the steering wheel with her palms. She quickly pulled a straight face when she registered Marnie's hurt expression.

'Well really, Marnie. I know it's been tough for you over the last year or so, but maybe now is a good time to live life a bit more. You have two great kids, you're healthy and look good for your age, and I presume you are okay financially. It's probably better if you lighten up a bit though. You should be out finding a new man …'

'Oh please, not you too.'

Libby appeared to miss Marnie's annoyance. 'Which reminds me, I have to call in to see an artist while we are out this way. This guy is a sculptor and uses metals, concrete and wire. I'm hoping I can be a source for decorators and customers wanting something a little different. Apparently, he works his magic somewhere else but has an open studio here as well. Oh, here we are.'

THEY HAD CURLED their way around the cliff-face, high above the waves and rocky outcrops. The many surfers below were specks now, the approaching waves like milky moustaches skimming across the turquoise bay. Thick tropical foliage had given way to sparser vegetation; still a luscious range of greens, but more spindly. Libby turned onto a private narrow road as Marnie wondered if this visit was the true reason for the drive.

A sculpture depicting a school of copper fish arced their way over the driveway, swimming from one bluestone pillar to the other; the afternoon sun bounced off their silver, aqua and golden scales. Marnie loved it and peered through the windscreen for more. She could just glimpse a couple of metal birds – herons? – hidden amongst the trees. They had to be at least head height.

'Aren't they a bit big for your shop?'

As the car emerged into an open gravel courtyard Libby turned to her sister with a cheeky wink. 'I'm trying to convince him to do some smaller works just for Whimsy. They'll be expensive but worth it.'

Directly ahead of them sat a low rough-hewn bunker. It was the style of building that the home improvement TV show *Grand Designs* would feature – unpretentious yet beautifully constructed. An old, open-backed van with a surfboard jutting out of the back was parked to the side. Not so *Grand Designs.*

The scent of eucalypt trees was heady as Marnie stepped out of the air-conditioned car into the still, humid air. A kookaburra took up its laugh, interrupting the eerie silence. Not even a hint of a wave could be heard. The studio's front door was slightly ajar.

Libby knocked her car keys against the wide metal straps that clutched across the door's large slab of wood. They could hear the sound echoing across the gallery inside but received no response. She pushed the door open farther and called out. 'Harry? Hi, it's Libby Cherry from Whimsy.'

The music must have been between tracks as Amy Winehouse now interrupted the silence, promising not to go to rehab. Marnie followed her sister as she set off into the studio.

'Oh wow!' Marnie stopped in her tracks as she rounded the expansive foyer and took a step down. She gazed around the room that opened before her. Glass windows formed a giant curve across the opposite end of the studio, only interrupted by pillars of shale stone that extended to the ceiling. In front of each pillar stood a tall, thin waterbird made from intricately twisted wire. Beyond the glass was endless sky, tickled by the tips of swaying gumtrees. She wandered over, drawn to the world beyond. Down below, dappled through the bush, was the ocean – all 180 degrees plus of shimmering blue.

Marnie was mesmerised. She leaned into the view, her hands against the glass. If it all gave way, she would simply float out and glide above the trees like an eagle leaving its eyrie. She closed her eyes, hearing the kookaburra's call, jealous of its freedom.

'If your nose gets much closer I'll have to charge you window cleaning fees,' a rough voice announced. Marnie quickly turned, embarrassed.

'Harry, there you are,' Libby trilled. 'We did knock.'

The fellow turned away toward Libby. Marnie could now only see his back, his wide shoulders shrugging away her sister's comments. 'No problem. It's a studio, it's open.' He angled back to face Marnie, fixed her with open curiosity and quietly enquired, 'Have we met?'

'I don't think so. I would remember. I mean I have a good face, um, you have a good face. I mean I have a good memory for faces.' Marnie could feel the heat rise in her cheeks as she became more and more tongue-tied.

Libby dashed forward. 'This is my sister, Marnie. She's from Melbourne. She's jetlagged.'

'Jetlagged from Melbourne?' His eyes danced. 'Did you come via some far-flung continent?'

'Well, we're not in Kansas now, are we.' Marnie's attempt at humour fell horribly flat. Libby raised a questioning eyebrow, giggled, then led the still smiling Harry off to view his latest works.

Marnie watched them go. She let her eyes wander over the retreating figure; the faded Bahamas board shorts, the loose, white linen shirt with sleeves rolled up to the elbows. Tanned, muscled limbs extended strongly from both. Buff loafers finished off the image of a shambolic, but finely tuned she suspected, creative spirit. *He's very tanned for someone who works inside. Building things. Maybe he surfs. Yes, he must, look at his hair, dark blond and a little bleached, with a promise of grey at the sides.* Marnie presumed he must be the owner of the van and surf board. Right up Libby's alley.

Her appraisal was halted when Harry stopped and turned. Marnie glanced back up his body only to be caught out by clear blue eyes, their corners crinkled with amusement. She quickly turned away from his unsettling yet kind stare. A little ripple of pleasure rose through her chest. Her attention landed on the reception desk, a beautiful table resting in its own space. Its high clean lines lent it an almost Danish appearance except the colours were dovetailed tans and rich reds. Each piece of wood had been expertly polished and integrated. Behind it, recessed into the wall, was one word in cursive copper: Pocket. Marnie presumed it was the studio's name and nodded to herself in approval. Pocket – simple, but kind of nice.

'Hello?' a mellow voice said, more as a question than a greeting as a recessed door opened behind the counter. Marnie could just glimpse an office behind the slender blonde woman who emerged. She was so perfectly put together that Marnie was scared to breathe too hard in case a hair wisped out of place. Pencil skirt, white shirt, a large pewter gallery-style necklace and high heels. Marnie couldn't help but categorise her into a mental box: more Sydney than beachside. Fortyish, but looks thirty and obviously spends more time in the gym than in the sun.

'Hello.' Marnie tried to gather her own elegant genes together.

The woman flicked her eyes across to Harry and Libby. 'Harry, here are the keys you had misplaced.'

Harry beckoned to the woman. 'Samantha, come and meet Libby Cherry from Whimsy. You know, at the end of Figtree. And Marnie, Libby's sister.' Samantha smiled to

Marnie as she glided to take Libby's hand, and the trio commenced their chat about what pieces had sold recently.

The office door remained slightly ajar and Marnie noticed how orderly and squared away it appeared. Like Samantha. Surprisingly, behind the minimalist wooden desk sat an old club chair, its beaten leather that had once been a mahogany brown sporting wear marks and scuffed studs. It looked homely and out of place in the pristine room.

Marnie sauntered around the gallery space, studying the various sculptures – solid bronze magpies and galahs sat atop plinths, schools of shimmering copper fish swept across the side walls, a beautiful vine of rusty roses tiptoed up a wall and weaved its way across the corner of the ceiling. But it was the delicate works in wire that Marnie was drawn to; suspended at different levels from the ceiling hung various birds in flight. Marnie stood transfixed as intricate pelicans and seagulls swayed noiselessly above her. Each one had a character of its own, each one heart-warming and uplifting. This guy was talented and so lucky to be able to use this stunning space to showcase his pieces.

'That might be the owner now,' Samantha said as a soft ringing summoned her back to the office, her heels silenced by the closing door.

'Harry, they're all amazing. Do you actually make mistakes? Do you have any that never see the light of day?'

Marnie heard Libby's question and wandered over to the pair. She tried to be included, to make up for her earlier Kansas remark.

'Creativity is allowing yourself to make mistakes, and art is knowing which ones to keep. I can't quite remember who said that originally,' she said. Silence. 'What? What's that look for, Libby?'

Libby was staring at her. 'You never cease to amaze me. But I do like that saying. Now Harry, about these pieces …'

Marnie, embarrassed, turned away. She saw a line of little brass turtles, half buried in sand, and couldn't resist leaning over for a closer look.

'So, do you have a favourite?' a warm voice enquired behind her a moment later.

Marnie swung around. 'Oh, I'm not buying …'

'I didn't ask if you were buying.' Harry frowned. 'I asked if you have a favourite. They are all slightly different.'

'Oh, they are, aren't they. No, I don't …'

'Okay, well. Sorry to disappoint,' he said quickly, digging his hands into his pockets. Harry nodded, then strode back to Libby, who greeted him with a light touch on his arm as she handed him one of her business cards.

Marnie watched him go, registering how many times she'd done just that in the last hour. Possibly her 'not buying' comment had offended him, but more likely he was the prime example of a moody artist. She did like his little turtles though; they moved her. Like making a new friend.

CHAPTER SIX

THE FOLLOWING day Marnie tried to stay out of the way as Libby became a whirlwind catching up with friends and trying to finalise loose ends for Whimsy. Marnie declined the farewell drinks but did offer, reluctantly, to drop off a couple of orders to clients. As Libby left for a pedicure at a local spa, Marnie remained in Whimsy. She presumed Libby would want the shop in order before she left, so offered to help.

'Laila, can I unpack these candles for you?' Change the CD from Meatloaf? Make you crack a smile?

'No, I'll get to them.' Laila waved her away.

'But I was just noticing that there aren't any Coconut & Lime out on the counter, so I could replenish them.'

'I said I'll do it. Why don't you go for a coffee, Marlee. I'm perfectly capable here on my own.'

'Right. Well, it's Marnie, not Marlee, and I wasn't inferring you weren't capable, I was just …'

Laila turned her back on Marnie to shout across the store, 'Can I help you ladies? Just looking? Well, can I suggest …'

Marnie retreated to the stockroom to retrieve her handbag. She had to fight her way through the forest of empty boxes and would have offered to flatten them but Laila obviously didn't feel comfortable with her around. Marnie overheard the customers whisper, 'Let's go, that woman won't leave us alone.'

Marnie was still thinking about the comment as she entered Nest. Eleanor smiled at her. 'Marnie isn't it? Would you like a moment to choose?'

Marnie couldn't help but register the difference as she checked out the delicious range of cakes. 'A latte and one of the melting moments please, Eleanor.'

Marnie collected a glass of water and, gratefully, sank into a seat. She couldn't pinpoint if her lethargy was a reaction to Laila's negative attitude or Queensland's unseasonal humidity. There was also an underlying simmer with Libby that she couldn't shake. The sooner her sister boarded the flight the better, then unspoken issues could remain exactly that.

As Nest's cool interior wove its magic, she gazed around, noticing the same gentleman in the corner tackling his cake. The little café was bustling with Eleanor and her staff so welcoming to everyone who walked in. There was a steady stream of takeaways and turnover of customers, so Marnie hoped it boded well for the new business. It reminded her of the local café at home, the favourite kind of place you headed to for a comfortable chat with a friend, or escaped alone to read the paper or just to sit with your own thoughts.

When she and Philippe had first separated Marnie rarely ventured out on her own. It was easy during the week as there was so much to do at work, then she would come home and start again on the housework, paperwork, the kids' needs and trying to sort out her future. It had taken time and a few false starts for her to be comfortable on her own in a café. She'd take out her phone and flick through boring online sites or pretend to go through her diary. But gradually she had learnt to enjoy her own company and realise she didn't have single/divorced stamped on her forehead. She had even gone to a movie on her own. Some ghastly chick flick comedy, but she had still been quite proud of herself asking for a single ticket. It was ridiculous in hindsight.

She picked the last melting moment crumbs off her plate, choosing to ignore how many calories were in each one. The buttery biscuit was delicious but, as always, she had managed to crumble it everywhere. She was just about to check it wasn't spread around her face when she heard a familiar husky voice.

'Hi.'

Marnie looked up, straight into Harry's smiling face.

'Oh, you've got a little ...' He flicked his finger across her cheek, accidentally dropping his keys.

As he bent to scoop them up, Marnie took a quick look in the wall mirror, appalled to see what seemed like half the melting moment sticking to her skin and lips. She hurriedly brushed it away, quickly running her tongue along her teeth at the same time.

'Don't you just love melting moments?' she joked.

'I can't go past an apple muffin on a good day,' he said.

'Coffee, Harry?' Eleanor called across the counter.

'Hey, darlin'. Yep, to go, please. You know how I like it.'

Darlin'? He was obviously a quick worker if Nest hasn't been open long. But then again, maybe they're childhood friends. That's it. Friends who were born, educated and still live in the same state. Predictable. *Who are you kidding Marnie – that's your life's journey too, you know.*

'Marnie?'

'I'm sorry. What did you say?' Marnie stuttered as she realised Harry had been chatting away above her and she hadn't heard a word; she had been lost in her own useless mind games again.

'Not to worry,' he replied good-naturedly. 'Thanks for the coffee, El.' He dropped his change into the Donate to our Farmers Tin and with a wink across the counter, he was gone.

LIBBY RACED AROUND THE HOUSE, calling out instructions for Marnie's growing to do list and throwing extra clothes into a bulging suitcase. Finally she was ready to leave, only then realising she had forgotten to book her bus pickup. Marnie offered to drive her to the coast's local airport for her connection to Sydney, then on to Hong Kong.

Marnie's heart was in her mouth as she made her way around yet another roundabout, a honking horn warning her she was in the wrong lane. Flashbacks to her car accident were never far away.

'I always get nervous before going away. It's not the flying part, that's a breeze. I don't know what it is; the whole build-up, I guess, but a few glasses of bubbles on board will help.' Libby slouched in the passenger seat, holding her stomach. 'You don't drink on flights? Obviously not by the look you just gave me.'

'So where are you staying in Hong Kong?' Marnie asked, annoyed at her transparency. 'I presume I call you on your cell number if I need you?'

'Yes, the same number but I think it's cheaper on WhatsApp. I'll be at The Intercontinental in Kowloon. Pretty swish, I believe. I'll have a couple of days sightseeing and then get stuck into the fair. Oh, you can turn into the airport here.'

There was a touch of mini-Miami about the little airport

as palms lazily swayed overhead and casually dressed travellers strolled around looking for their hotel connection or a taxi. The car rental companies only took up three rows in the nearly empty carpark opposite the terminal. One way in, one way out. Simple.

'This is kind of cute. I much prefer this to the large hectic airports. They do my head in,' Marnie said.

'I did say you should have flown into the Sunny Coast …' started Libby before dropping the topic. 'You don't have to stay until my flight goes. Thanks for coming, Marnie. I mean it. Take the time to chill out a bit, will you, and try to leave all that Melbourne shit behind for … a while.'

'Well, that's easy for you to say, Libby. Take care and text me a photo of you in Honkers.'

Libby unloaded her suitcase from the boot and wheeled it into the terminal. Marnie waited for an over-the-shoulder wave goodbye, but the doors slid closed without a backward glance from her sister. For the second time in a few days she wondered when her own next overseas adventure would be.

A VACUUM of loneliness hit Marnie, as if the world was revolving without her. She breathed deeply and clutched the wheel, trying to slow her heart. She was now on her own with two long weeks stretching ahead of her. Ever since the Qantas tear-jerker ads, she hadn't been able to farewell someone at an airport without a heavy heart. Like when Claire had set off on the compulsory post-Year 12 trip years earlier. Marnie had smiled and waved and put on a mother's 'I'm so happy for you' face, but inside she'd already started to miss her daughter. No more loud music, no more giggly sleepovers. She had sniffled all the way home from the airport.

As Security urged her to leave the drop off zone, she pulled out and turned on the car radio. Sam Smith's 'Stay with Me' wasn't what she needed at that moment so she flicked around the stations, one eye on the next roundabout.

A mounting sense of fraying around the edges fingered her heart – like a length of string, normally perfectly fine and strong until a little nick starts the unravelling. Marnie realised the ache was all too familiar, that the airport scenario was not totally to blame. It had been the same when she had left Manning College. The circumstances were quite different but an idea of what to do next was just as cloudy.

Her fingers tapped nervously on the steering wheel, as they had done on the surface of the massive boardroom table. Marnie relived the queasiness in her stomach, the unnerving sense of not being in control of what came next.

The words 'comfort zone' came to mind as the Queensland bush whizzed past her window. That was the common thread – her comfort zone. There was no backup of a job, no responsibility to fulfil or a project to see through. In fact, nothing to do in a place she wasn't familiar with. What was that phrase that should be on one of Libby's fridge magnets – Don't pass over the present in a race to the future. Marnie had always found that easier said than done.

The garage door glided open, then down behind her, firmly locking out the world. Marnie shook off her bubbling fear and breathed deeply, acknowledging that it was time to regroup. She had successfully put herself out there before, and she would do so again. She would rediscover the shape of her life.

CHAPTER SEVEN

JOGGERS WERE ALREADY POUNDING the pavement when Marnie made it out at six the following morning. It seemed that in Nautilus Cove early to bed and early to rise was the norm. Whether it was due to the early sunrise, to beat the day's building heat, or the fact that everyone had something more to do with their day than she did, she didn't know.

Libby's suggested one-hour circuit took her along the glistening river where patient pelicans waited for the fishermen to return with scraps, past mansions that sat serenely silent behind trimmed hedges, and down to the dining precinct. Setups for the day were already starting with pavements being swept and tables and chairs being unstacked noisily. Trendy little takeaway coffee carts with names like Hi-Tide and Francis Bean were doing a roaring business.

Marnie stopped at the water's edge and watched a distant plume of smoke curl its way into the soft, milky sky. She overheard someone say that back burning of heavily treed areas had started in the lead-up to summer, so she presumed this was one of them. The river was wider here than at

Libby's house; she would need a map to work out what was on the other side apart from the odd house visible through the bush.

Several ducks skimmed across the smooth water, then waddled across the sand and through tufts of grass. Picnic tables sprinkled the lawns, together with a few exercise equipment stations, which Marnie ignored. A tai chi class caught her eye, the participants' silent movements like birds stalking the peaceful shadows. A short distance away, young mums stood chatting, jiggling their prams in a way that became second nature to a parent. Marnie couldn't help but glance into the prams, then she was on her way again.

Rows of large jacaranda trees formed an avenue down the road, raising her spirits. Libby had told her the dry Queensland spring had brought on the trees' flowering, a stretch of purple haze the stunning result. Marnie regretted not having brought any money with her as another coffee shack beckoned, so she headed for home.

A few hours on the computer catching up on her emails only added to her restlessness. In the afternoon she set out again, with Beebs on the lead. The dog proved to be her social accessory as people stopped to pat the happy Lab, then continue to chat. A group of older ladies propped around one of the picnic tables beckoned her over, a biscuit extended to the dog. They almost looked like a human jigsaw puzzle in the dappled light. A game of Scrabble was set on a gingham tablecloth between a china teapot, cups and plates of cakes. Marnie smiled as she pictured her parents probably playing cards with new friends in an RV park somewhere.

A slim woman, urged on by her Arnold Schwarzenegger personal trainer, jogged in the opposite direction. Marnie upped her pace past the yacht club, then back along the side streets to the cottage. What else was there to do?

The following morning she left Beebs behind and ventured all the way along the river into Figtree Street. Perspiring but strangely invigorated, she continued on around Lantana Bay – she figured she could catch the river ferry back to a stop near the cottage if she ran out of energy. The boardwalk was windswept, fine wisps of sand dancing across its surface, the onshore breeze cooling her down a few degrees. Through the sun's glare she could make out silhouettes of surfers sitting on their boards at The Point, waiting for the next big wave. The national park formed a backdrop to huge boulders lining the secluded coves. She peered at the cliff, trying to pinpoint where Harry's studio was, but the bush provided an excellent camouflage.

The beach fanned out in front of her. Families spread along the shoreline like sprinkled coconut. Marnie watched dads swinging their toddlers safely above the waves, the children's shrieks warming her heart with memories of her own childhood. A sand sculptor was well on his way to completing an intricate multi-tiered castle, complete with moat and dragon. Older couples in their baggy swimsuits and caps strode into the water for their daily dip, and the Surf Lifesavers were setting up their flags for the day.

The whoosh of waves across the clean sand soothed Marnie's thoughts. Unbeckoned memories surfaced of the trips she and Philippe had taken to the southern stretches of France and Italy. The colour and novelty of it all, not to mention the utter confidence of beachgoers of all shapes and sizes as they strutted in only G-strings, had captivated her. Even the pebbly beaches were like being on another planet after Australia's great expanses of sand. Marnie had found it amusing to have to pay extra to sit in the shade, but Philippe had only scowled. She had soaked it all in. Somewhere there were photographs to prove she had been there, but it seemed like another life to her now.

She kicked off her walking shoes, curling her toes into the narrow strip of cool grass which abutted the sand. A multitude of little white shells had been abandoned at the high tide mark as if they were too fragile to continue on their journey. Delighted, she scooped a few into her pocket, leaving the rest to find their own new home.

Marnie couldn't explain the shift in her mood even to herself, but suddenly she couldn't help smiling, almost giggling. She used to laugh a lot. Yet it was now, on a sunny beach in Queensland, that Marnie felt a growing and unexpected sense of belonging. She turned her face to the morning sun and breathed in the salty air. Stretching her arms above her head she stood still, enjoying the moment. Just in case she couldn't find it again.

The beach front cafés already had queues of holidaymakers wanting to experience the signposted 'breakfast with a true Nautilus view'. No doubt the tables would rotate to accommodate 'lunch, cocktails or dinner with a view' as the day wore on. Marnie cut back up a walking track, through an arcade full of healthy food outlets and out onto Figtree Street, then turned right towards Whimsy.

The street earned its reputation as one of Australia's finest tourist precincts. She had read that it had gone through hard times with financial downturns, airline troubles that for a time were slow to bring visitors to the area, and rising rents, but it had survived and sparkled. Now, it seemed to buzz with self-satisfaction.

The sandy shells jiggled in her pocket, sharing a sudden sense of freedom and joy. Marnie wasn't dawdling or just filling in time; she had purpose again. She had no idea what that purpose was, just that she was excited by something.

Window-shopping her way along the street fuelled the buoyant mood. Big name designers and exclusive jewellery stores mixed with surf, souvenir and sunglass retailers. As enticing as they all were, Marnie realised what set Whimsy apart – Libby had created something tantalisingly different, like a little oasis amongst the expected.

She crossed over Figtree Street to check out Threadz children's wear store, but as she neared it was clear it was also possibly haberdashery. Is there such a word these days?

An embroidered long-stitch sign labelled the charming window display as The Family Threads Collection. Marnie ran her finger along the glass, mentally caressing the items she saw. A bunny rug delicately embroidered with pink, green and grey flowers; a pair of little ballet shoes propped against a Degas cross-stitch; a tooth fairy box, the lid a mass of thread knots depicting a fairy's garden. 'So beautiful,' she murmured.

She spotted another embroidery of a beautifully framed Tree of Life, its branches and intricate leaves the olive, orange, gold and greens of autumn. Across the bottom, in burnished thread, was intertwined 'Therese-Rosalie-Nathalie'.

'Good morning.' A young girl grinned across to Marnie whilst opening the store's doors. 'I will be open in about ten minutes. I just have to set a few things up, then the owner, Nathalie, will be in.'

'No problem.' Marnie headed back across the road, pleased to see Nest was doing a roaring early business. She stopped at Whimsy's window, not having been in since Libby left for Hong Kong. It was dark inside, despite it being right on nine o'clock. There was bubble wrap piled on the desk and unpacked boxes strewn across the floor.

Marnie frowned, uncertain why the shop wasn't open.

Hadn't Libby mentioned Laila always arrived by nine? How much nicer would it look if there was a window display or was at least tidy.

Mind your own business, Marnie! But she couldn't help it, her professional hat was firmly back on her head. She propped on a low fence at the entrance to The Woods to see how the day might begin for Whimsy.

At 9:05 Laila arrived, a piece of toast between her teeth. She dumped down a huge basket full of magazines and what looked to be a thermos, and unlocked the door. By the time she had turned the lights on, opened the doors and brought out the external displays, it was past 9:30. Once again, Marnie told herself to mind her own business and slipped away.

Back at the cottage she poured herself a large glass of water, sat on the deck and phoned Claire and Oliver. She missed her children and their life updates, and now Marnie wanted to share some of what she'd been up to. She knew they were hardly life-changing events, but she was keen to let them know how she was getting on 'up north'. Claire's number went to voicemail. Disappointed, Marnie left her daughter an edited version of life in Nautilus Cove and a request to return the call for a further chat.

Oliver answered with a sleepy hello. Marnie could just picture him, all rumpled and probably hungover from a late night now that the university year had ended. She did most of the talking, getting grunts and yeps in answer to her questions, but she persevered.

'Ollie, we can have a better catch-up when I get home. Let me know what days you're working and we'll book in a breakfast at Church Street Deli. Okay?'

'Well, they want me to work at the pub pretty much full

time up to Christmas, Mum. I've got to save a lot more money for next year so I'll have to wait and see.'

Oliver's voice had suddenly become very clear and precise. Marnie's Mother-of-All-Warning-Systems kicked in as she wondered what her son was referring to.

'I've decided to defer Uni next year. I want to travel. You know, have some fun.'

Defer? Have fun?

'Ollie. This is the first I've heard about this. Did the exams go okay? Have you decided on another course?' She knew she had to calm down if she was to learn any more and decided to bring up something he may not have considered. 'Do you realise how many people don't go back to study after deferring?'

'I've already decided, Mum. Davo is coming with me.'

Fabulous. Ollie was travelling who-knows-where with Dave Deblin. More-dollars-than-sense Davo.

'The exams were a breeze, and of course I'll go back to finish the course later on. I'm just not quite sure when. Anyway, Dad thinks it's a good idea. He said it'll be good to see what's happening in design around the rest of the world.'

Marnie stiffened at the mention of her ex-husband. She knew how hard her son had worked to get into his university course in the first place – she was quite sure Ollie and Dave would not be spending any time chatting with designers once their feet hit European dirt. She took a moment to think how best to approach his unexpected news. She needed to show him she was open to discussing his life with him with no judgement.

A pelican flapped slowly across the sky as she drummed her nails on the glass table. 'You've obviously made up your mind, you're an adult, so I guess what I say doesn't really count. But I'd like to talk about it more with you, Ollie.'

'The trip will be great, Mum. I'm really looking forward to it.'

Shit. 'I'm sure it will be a great adventure.' Marnie could feel a catch in her voice, so ended the conversation with her normal 'Love you, see you soon.'

Feeling deflated, she immediately dialled Dee.

'Well, my friend, I actually can't see the problem. Good on Oliver. You don't want him sitting around Melbourne all his life, do you?'

'No.'

'There you go. It's a break, not a lifetime. And if it becomes a permanent thing, then so be it. He's a big boy wanting to explore the world. You just make sure you can WhatsApp him so you can see he's looking healthy and that he's registered on Smartraveller. And make sure you have all the embassies on speed dial.'

Marnie sighed. 'And of course you're going to be just as happy when William wants to do the same thing.'

'Oh no. He's not going anywhere,' Dee replied.

The two friends laughed. 'You never stop being a parent, do you, Dee? I just want him to be safe.'

'Naturally. But you've got to let go too. Heavens, it's not as though he's off to a foreign boarding school with no local language and an admissions officer who hasn't a clue. We both know how difficult that must be for some kids!'

The giggle in Dee's voice reminded Marnie of a time early in their friendship when they were both finding their feet in careers, yet when life seemed so much simpler. Dee had asked Marnie to fill in for her whilst she was on leave, as Admissions Officer at one of Melbourne's universities. Her role involved welcoming overseas students and settling them into the foreign university world. Dee had assured her everything was in place with no new families due to arrive;

Marnie just had to assist those already in residence. On Marnie's first day she had arrived to find an entire Indian family waiting in her office to enrol their daughter. No one spoke English. Then she had been informed she was hosting the boarders' cocktail party that evening – she had had no idea what she was doing but no one was the wiser. Fake it until you make it! Dee had found the near disaster hilarious, but knew she had owed Marnie big time.

'We've always said we would give our kids more freedom than we ever had, remember? It's a different era. How is Claire?'

'Don't speak to me about Claire.' Marnie sighed. 'I think I'm on the bottom of her list of favourite people. Apparently mothers aren't allowed to go away or have a life of their own if it interferes in said daughter's plans.'

'I'm sorry for how Claire has treated you. It's strange, but believe me when I say this friction you have with her will pass.'

'I just feel so hurt, but I promise I'll be really patient. I think that's why I didn't go off the handle about Ollie's plans. I don't want to cut him off like I've somehow managed to do with Claire.' Marnie felt some of the weight of guilt fall from her shoulders, already feeling better after a heart-to-heart with her long-time friend.

'Good. Now, how are the bright lights of Nautilus Cove? What are the locals called anyway – Covians, Nautilusers?'

'I've no idea. You know, Dee, I have to admit I'm a bit surprised. Remember when Libby first moved here, we all warned her against it? We thought it was made up of surfers and over-sixties dropouts. What I see are people with small businesses working really hard. They're fighting for the tourist and local dollar, all the while praying a major retailer doesn't move in next door. And they really care for their environment as well. I don't know, maybe it's the same everywhere.'

'You just can't take off that business hat for a moment, can you?' Dee said, not unkindly.

Marnie laughed her off. 'There you go then. I haven't gone all tropical yet.'

'Lovely to chat as always and I look forward to more Covian news bulletins, but more to the point, I look forward to your return. Goodbye lovely.'

'Bye, Dee. Thanks for the advice.'

MARNIE HAD BEEN LOOKING FORWARD to unwinding on the cottage's deck, a glass of wine in one hand and a black Labrador under the other. Her camera sat on the table, waiting for the perfect moment to catch the latest spectacular sunset. She had noticed there wasn't a true twilight, the sun setting quickly in a blaze of glory as if it had somewhere else to be.

She was mulling over how best to capture the various shades of tangerine when music curled toward her from farther along the river. Plus, the tantalising aroma of a barbecue and snippets of muffled conversation. It sounded like a family gathering. Marnie had loved the early years of her marriage, when the children were young and they gathered together for a huge winter roast or summer barbecue. But then things had gone a bit lacklustre as the children had grown older. Philippe was regularly away with his work or she had been at school meetings, then Claire had had a brief spell of being a vegan and Ollie often had to leave for basketball practice. Everyone was suddenly doing their own thing and the barbecue sat idle.

On reflection, it had been hard to say exactly when she

and Philippe had started doing their own thing too. Probably long before either of them recognised it. Separate timetables, different interests, drifting along – whatever name is given to it, the result was the same. They simply fell out of love with each other. Philippe had stopped referring to her eyes as baby blues or calling her by her nickname Moo. The slow disappearance of their sex life had instilled a fear that perhaps her husband had a health issue, but it was his admission he had 'lost interest some time ago' that had been a sledgehammer to Marnie's heart. Some time ago? She had felt foolish for not having picked up on his lack of enthusiasm and obvious excuses. It was the nail in the coffin of any true intimacy between them. And then came the affairs.

Philippe had brought it all to a destructive head, having met someone else. He wanted to leave them. To leave her. Marnie waited to be relieved, grateful or excited at a new beginning, but instead it was betrayal, loneliness and fear that she felt at what lay ahead. The fact that Philippe had fallen in lust with one of the newly single mothers at Manning College rubbed salt in the gaping wound. Apparently they had hit it off at one of Marnie's fundraising balls – as she was introducing the guest speaker, Philippe was introducing himself to the ex-Mrs Jayce.

Dee's thoughts on the whole affair had been insightful, if not bloodthirsty. 'Just think, Marnie, those women haven't finished procreating. Philippe could be a middle-aged man with a baby. End of freedom. Finito! You've got to admit that's kind of funny.'

Marnie hadn't found it at all amusing. She knew her friend was only trying to make her feel better but it hadn't helped. She had been gutted and spent endless nights weighing up the predictable allocation of blame. She knew she wasn't faultless, but bitterness whispered that a chunk of her life had been deemed worthless. She had hoped that her growing lack of agency in the marriage hadn't been evident to Claire and Oliver, and she'd turned her attention to making the split as painless as possible for them. Thankfully, the gut-wrenching butterflies brought on by such memories had slowly subsided. She had strung up a veil, dividing the then and now, and could usually look back on that stressful time from a protected distance.

Marnie wandered inside to start Libby's Spotify, smiling when Xavier Rudd's cruisy 'Follow the Sun' drifted around the room. She grabbed another sandalwood incense stick on her way back out, having already felt the sting of an unwanted mosquito. As she flicked the glass mobile, Marnie couldn't ignore the fact that her current relaxed lifestyle was only temporary.

'Beebs, I'm going to miss you but time is ticking. There are major things to cross off my list, the first biggie being the sale of the house and finding a new one. If only I knew what I wanted.'

Something like Libby's cottage would be great. Not too large but stylish with no work to be done; maybe down along the Esplanade with sunset views across the bay. *I should be able to afford that if I'm careful.* Marnie nodded. An apartment? No, too soon.

A faint humming sound caught her attention as a small boat motored past the bottom of the garden. It was *Starlight*, the cute wooden boat she'd admired at the marina. A woman was sitting in the rear, her bare arms stretched along the back of the seat as she watched the man at the wheel. They pulled alongside a jetty a few properties down from Libby's cottage. Because of the river's bend Marnie was hidden but could see them quite clearly through the foliage. Soft laughter floated along the water as the fellow tied up the boat and held out his hand, helping his passenger onto the jetty. She wore a long, softly flowing teahouse dress and held aloft a pair of sandals, the jetty light catching their myriad of sparkles.

Marnie recognised Harry in an instant. There was no mistaking the outline of his body, his untroubled yet strong stance, the way his hand swept back his hair. Marnie slunk deeper into her seat, although the pair's attention was only on each other. The woman leant in and whispered into Harry's ear as he took the tips of her fingers and followed her up towards the house.

CHAPTER EIGHT

AT THE SAME time Marnie was spying on her neighbour, Libby was wandering through her hotel suite, trailing her palm across the luxurious furniture. She inspected her reflection in the suite's window and, for once, liked what she saw. Her fingers fluffed up her radically short haircut, the deep red tones accentuated by her soft tanned skin and fine features.

Half-hearted thoughts about home came and went. Libby knew she really should call her sister to see if she was okay. She wondered if Marnie had spoken to any locals yet, hoping that it might lighten her up a bit. Marnie had asked what she thought of Hunky Harry after their visit to his studio, but Libby doubted he was her sister's type.

There had been no contact from Laila, so presumably Marnie hadn't dropped in on Whimsy. She knew too well that her sister had to keep busy, to be on top of everything. She and Laila should get on just fine. Libby nodded, resolving to call soon for an update.

Libby's thoughts quickly reverted to herself. Hong Kong was proving to be so much more fun than she had anticipated, particularly with Rob's knowledge of Kowloon, Hong Kong and the surrounding islands. He had even booked her into the hotel's spa as a treat. She wasn't used to being so spoilt but knew she could get used to it very quickly.

The trade fair had proved to be a bustling metropolis of product, services, suppliers and noisy hawkers. It wasn't as large as previous years due to political unrest, but Libby had still felt like she was drowning in information. The sheer volume of available product was overwhelming.

'Check out the catalogue, highlight what you are interested in and just take a section at a time,' Rob had advised after the first day.

'I have found a few new possibilities, but I just don't want to have what everyone else is ordering. I think I'm more comfortable just interacting with my chosen artisans from an armchair in Australia,' Libby had answered, not in the least confident of what she should be doing at the fair. 'Rob, I have to admit this experience has taught me to think a bit more globally though, so when I get back I might revisit some gorgeous ceramics I saw on a Cornwall site. Most likely the transport costs to Australia would be horrendous though.'

'It only takes an email to find out. Maybe they have a distributor in Australia already,' Rob had suggested.

After so many years having to make decisions on her own, Libby was finding it reassuring to use Rob as a sounding board. As he leant across to refill the champagne glass on her bedside table, she trailed a finger across his bare chest. 'I am so excited at the prospect of the art fair. Thank you, Rob, for setting up some introductions for me.'

Rob was proving to be a bit of a surprise in other areas too. He was single, pretty good-looking, fun to be with during the day and more than she'd anticipated after dark. He didn't ask endless questions about her past marriage, nor did he need to offload any of his own emotional baggage.

Over dinner some weeks earlier Rob had said he had admired her. Libby had nearly choked on her wine.

'You're kidding, right?'

'Come on, Libby, take the compliment. You seem to me to be able to combine a kind of boho attitude to life, yet you run a successful business. Either you work very hard at putting on appearances, or you're not as calm underneath as you seem.'

Libby had stiffened, replying, 'Rob. One thing you don't get with me is *putting on appearances*. I have had first-hand experience of how destructive that can be.'

That comment replayed in her mind later when he suggested they visit Macau. When Libby read the brochure on how much land had been reclaimed to build the gaudy Vegas-style casino strip, she had insisted they tour the island's historic Portuguese areas instead.

'Casinos are as bad as horse racing. When the betting gets out of control it can ruin your life.'

'I guess you're not interested in a night at Hong Kong's Happy Valley racecourse then?' Rob had asked, obviously puzzled.

In her own head she excused him: He wasn't to know that she had endured a husband who had considered keeping up appearances a life skill, even with his wife. His gambling problem had come so close to losing her life savings on Horse 5 in Race 3. Never again.

CHAPTER NINE

IT HAD BEEN a restless night with hazy images of Harry and her neighbour dodging in and out of Marnie's dreams. She didn't seem to be able to get the man out of her head, the phrase 'mental stalking' coming to mind as daylight streamed through the shutters.

A quick glance along the deserted river satisfied her curiosity that the *Starlight* was no longer there. Not that it was any of her business. Marnie knew the only cure for her fuzzy head was to get in an early walk before the day heated up. Not for the first time she wondered what high summer must be like in Nautilus Cove, convinced she would never survive its temperature or humidity. Having hoovered down the dog food at great speed, Beebs was turning herself inside out sensing another walking adventure.

'Okay, let's do the circuit to the marina and back. No, it has nothing to do with Harry. I just think it's good to try out some of Libby's suggestions in case she asks,' Marnie told the dog.

In fact, Marnie had hoped Libby would have called by now. She wasn't sure who this Rob fellow was, but he seemed to be securing a lot of her sister's attention. All she had received were a couple of texts saying that the gift fair was fabulous and she had found one new supplier for Whimsy. She prayed it wasn't for any more hanging wicker decorations and wondered what happened to the unique product policy.

The river was sparkling in the morning sun as if a trillion little stars had fallen along its surface. Everyone nodded good morning to Marnie as they walked or cycled by, with many stopping to chat about their dogs. Huge Moreton Bay fig trees towered over the meandering path, providing shade but also a curtain against any breeze. It was sticky and Marnie, although she enjoyed the chats, started to think she had attempted too long a walk.

The marina was quiet except for the chinking of masts and the soft thudding of boats against the timbers. Marnie sank into a seat at the café and nudged their dog bowl of water closer to Beebs. *Starlight* was bobbing at its mooring with no sign of Harry.

Marnie took in the peaceful surrounds. She found it interesting that Libby had made a life and business in a small coastal town. Her sister had been one of the cool kids growing up, the life of the party and centre of any crowd. There had always been a boyfriend in the wings, before she had fallen heavily in love and married her apparent soulmate Drew. They had moved to Queensland to expand Drew's successful boat building business and, together, sailed catamarans back down the coast to Melbourne for wealthy clients. Libby had always said they worked hard to keep the rich afloat.

At the time Marnie had been tied up in her own world of raising Oliver and Claire, being there for Philippe and building a career, and she had assumed she knew how her sister was faring generally. When Libby's sobbing call had come through announcing she and Drew had split, it had come out of left field to the whole family. Their parents had rushed to her side. It was a gesture not extended to Marnie when her marriage ended – apparently there was more suspicion and blame to place when a husband wasn't happy at home and there were children involved, as was her case. When finally it was Philippe who left, they had been horrified. Her father had taken her aside one day and said sternly: 'Marnie, you need to think carefully about this for the children's sake. After all you aren't getting any younger. Who is going to take you on in their life?'

She had cried and cried. Marnie could never understand her parents' reaction and had since closed a door firmly on their attitude – all she had wanted and needed was some support from her family. She continued to hope for what Dee called 'a second growth spurt' and to rid herself of the initial fear that she would be alone forever.

Despite Marnie's probing and being sisters, Libby had never talked about what had caused the breakdown with Drew or why there had been no children. Marnie would have welcomed the opportunity to have a brief sisterly chat and offer help but 'It's just one of those things' and 'I have my reasons' were the only hints Libby had offered. Then the news that their business had folded spectacularly, and Drew had set off to charter yachts around the Cote d'Azur. Marnie had been staggered to hear Libby had purchased a cottage in Nautilus Cove and managed to secure a lease in the coveted Figtree Street.

Where had the money come from? Libby had pulled the shutters down on any further discussion – it was only through an innocent conversation with their mother that light was shone on the true path Libby had taken.

'We'll have to be careful with our savings now, of course,' her mother had said, flicking Marnie a sidelong glance. She seemed nervous.

'Why?' Marnie had asked.

'Well, we did have a little investment in Drew and Libby's business, but that's all gone now.'

Marnie had dropped the cup she was washing at her parents' kitchen sink.

'What? I didn't know that. How much, Mum?'

'I'm not going to discuss figures. And now, of course, Libby is going to need a little extra to get back on her feet.'

The dishcloth had nearly been ripped to shreds in Marnie's hands. How had Libby managed to persuade her parents into giving her money? Twice. Where had their offer been when she had fallen on hard times, when her marriage had broken down, when school fees were due? But then she had never asked. She tried so hard not to be jealous. Libby had built a seemingly strong business, so good on her. Yes, good on her.

Money was the root of all evil, they say. Marnie didn't accept that, but she did know how easily it could drive a wedge through a family.

The sun's rays were starting to bite and a refreshing shower was beckoning. But Beebs had other ideas. As Marnie knelt to pick up the lead, the Lab gave a yap and took off as if her life depended on a quick escape. Marnie stumbled, half holding the lead, clutching the table, her chair toppling backwards. Beebs hurtled after a small fluffy white vision, the lead flailing behind her.

'Beebs! Beebs!' Marnie yelled. Labradors loved water, didn't they? She could launch herself into the water at any moment. She chased the dog across the deck, around the side of the fish shop, and straight into a firm body coming the other way.

Harry braced himself, holding onto Marnie's upper arms.

'My dog!' she exclaimed, although half her thoughts were on her sweaty skin sliding under Harry's hands.

Harry half turned, gave a shrill whistle and slapped his knees. The four-legged traitor came instantly, dropping at Harry's feet. Panting, she looked up at Marnie as if to say, 'What? Is there a problem?'

Marnie gathered the lead, pushing her sunglasses back up her perspiring nose. 'Thank you,' she mumbled.

'Excuse me, madam, but you didn't pay for your breakfast before leaving the café.' A waitress had followed Marnie and was now thrusting a docket under her nose.

Marnie blushed. 'I can assure you I never leave without paying. My dog …'

'I'll leave you to it.' Harry gave her a cheeky wink, gave Beebs a final rub behind the ears, then wandered off toward *Starlight*.

It had all happened so quickly. Marnie was unsure if Harry had actually recognised her from the studio visit and melting moment cookie scenario. She retraced her steps to the café and apologised, but the waitress's raised eyebrows showed she wasn't convinced it had all been an embarrassing mistake.

The walk home was long and hot, like a tour of duty. Marnie directed her frustration at the dog as she summoned some energy. 'You don't understand. I'm perfectly capable of handling situations and people. I've started to relax, to let my guard down, and look what happens. Now I'm going to have a shower, get dressed and head into Whimsy to put myself to use. And you're not coming!'

CHAPTER TEN

'I'M PERFECTLY capable of running Whimsy, Marlee.' Laila jammed her hands on her hips, barring Marnie from putting her handbag into the storeroom.

'It's Marnie. Yes, I'm sure you are, Laila, but I would like to help. What about all the deliveries that Libby said were due? Have they arrived?' Marnie craned her neck, trying to see beyond Laila's imposing figure. She was trying to whisper, to keep their conversation away from the browsing customers, but Laila had no such concerns.

'Look. *Marnie*. Why don't you just go and do coffee. You look at bit frazzled in the heat. You're obviously not used to it.'

Marnie inclined her head toward a couple waiting to be served. As Laila heaved a sigh and went to the counter, Marnie slipped into the storeroom and was immediately horrified at the mess. Unpacked boxes were piled high, like cardboard Leaning Towers of Pisa. Paper carry bags had toppled off an overloaded cupboard and lay exactly where they'd fallen. A half-eaten sandwich sat on a stack of greeting cards – with onion, judging from the smell.

Marnie grabbed a Stanley knife and sliced off the delivery docket from a random box. It was a large supply of notebooks from Satchels, a stationery supply company. She knew Libby had been waiting on them, eager to fill the gap on the shelves. The next box's docket was for a stylist's order Marnie had seen on Libby's 'To follow up' list – ceramic bowls to be included in an imminent advertising shoot for a local wedding venue. She presumed the large tube propped in the corner contained an aerial print that was supposed to have been couriered to the framer the previous week. Laila!

Marnie swept up her cell phone and strode past Laila. By her shocked expression, Laila hadn't known Marnie was still there. Anyone could have been helping themselves to stock out the back, not that they would be able to find anything.

It was late morning in Hong Kong and Libby picked up on the third ring. 'Marnie, is everything okay? I was just thinking I should …'

'No, it's not. I have just called into Whimsy.'

'Oh, good.'

'Libby, listen to me. Your orders are arriving and are just being stacked in the storeroom. The shop is a mess. That woman is rude to your customers and arrives late to open. And she keeps calling me friggin' Marlee!'

'Marnie, she can't be that bad. She filled in for me when I went to Port Douglas a few months back. There was a bit of a backlog when I got home, but I had to keep the doors open. It's too expensive to have someone permanent even for one day a week when I'm home and I don't have anyone else in the wings. I'm sure she's doing the best she can. Maybe my notes weren't clear enough.'

Marnie could feel herself hyperventilating. She told herself that she had no attachment to Whimsy; she was reacting because she couldn't abide laziness and mismanagement. 'Libby, I am only going to ask this once. I am happy to come in and sort the deliveries and do some visual merchandising, but you will have to speak to Laila to let her know that I am not intruding. I am doing this for you, not her.'

'Visual merchandising? Since when do you visual merchandise?'

Marnie could hear the snort of laughter all the way from Hong Kong. 'That's not the point, but I'll have you know that I organised many photo shoots for Pettigrews and exhibitions for Manning College. I can tell you now that anything I do will be better than what's happening in Whimsy now, or not happening, more to the point.'

'I know it wasn't pristine when I left but I'm surprised it's that bad in such a short time.' A slight pause sat in the airwaves. 'Have you really done merchandising?'

A stab of disappointment pierced Marnie, that her own sister had no appreciation of her skills. She decided to stay with Whimsy's problems. 'Yes, it is that bad. Product you paid good money for is getting damaged. Your greeting cards have been jammed into the holders every which way and are bent, the silver jewellery hasn't seen a cleaning cloth in who knows how long, and the artworks are stacked against each other along the floor.'

Marnie just couldn't understand why Laila didn't take more pride in her job. She took a deep breath and continued, 'Anyway, it's only until you return and you can reorganise it all if you don't like what I've done.' She didn't add, 'Who knows how high the boxes will be by the time you get back if Laila is to be counted on.'

'Ah, well actually, Marnie, I was going to call you about that.'

Marnie's shoulders sagged, wary of Libby's words. In this whole wide world, how can two sisters be so different?

'Do you remember me mentioning Rob?'

'And what, Libby? Spit it out.' Marnie cast her eyes to the heavens, waiting.

'Well, the thing is we are getting on reeaally well. He has a few art contacts in Asia and has offered to introduce me to a couple of outlets. We were discussing it just now.'

'This is for the paintings you haven't done yet, right?' Marnie tried to go lightly with the sarcasm; she needed Libby to return home. Her fingers tapped rapidly against her thigh.

'Marnie, I was hoping for a bit more encouragement from you. And yes, it is for my future creativity to find a home.'

Oh please.

'So I'm staying a little longer. An additional few days.'

'Libby, you have a business here that could self-combust at any moment.' Libby may have answered, but Marnie was distracted by Laila, who was scowling at her from the store's doorframe. Why didn't she put herself to use – trim the flowers that were wilting in front of her, at least.

She tried a different angle. 'I know how much you care about Whimsy. Do you want all your efforts to be ruined in such a short space of time?'

A shard of flint sat below Libby's tone as she replied, 'It's only an extra week. Maybe. It has been so good for my soul to have a break and to know everything is okay at home. I'm trying to plan ahead for me and for Whimsy without, you know, the present pushing itself in to cloud my thoughts.'

Libby's voice mellowed. 'Please, Marnie. Please can you stay and mind the house and Beebs? Beebs needs you.'

Marnie knew that was extremely doubtful, but she had to acknowledge everyone yearned for space to think and create and plan. She groaned. At a point when Nautilus Cove had begun to work its magic and she had started to unwind, her sister once again had caused ripples in the pond; it had been the same their whole lives.

She sighed, wondering why people seemed to take advantage of her. Only yesterday she had received a brisk email from Claire asking why she hadn't left her car keys on the kitchen bench. Didn't Marnie know Claire's car was getting serviced that week and she needed to borrow her mother's car? Marnie had deleted it, without replying – she'd rather not put Claire and cars together in the same thought.

She had to think about herself and what was best for her. What was in Melbourne for her at the moment anyway – house-hunting and a fractious daughter were the only answers she could come up with.

Marnie knew Libby was waiting patiently for the answer she wanted. 'It's lucky I haven't already booked a return flight. On one condition – that you have a word with Laila. I am going back in there now to sort out the storeroom before a family of mice take up residence.'

Marnie could picture Libby reclining somewhere, waving the phone around in the air, pretending to listen to her older sister rant and rave. 'Are you listening? I will not be ridiculed, sworn at or in any way made to feel in the way. I will pass Laila the phone now and you explain to her that I am here to help. Okay?'

'Sure. No problem.'

Marnie retraced her steps across the road and handed the phone to Laila. 'Libby would like a word.'

A fellow strolled into the store as Laila pursed her lips and plopped onto the bench at the front of Whimsy. She turned toward the street ensuring Marnie couldn't hear the conversation.

'Can I help?' Marnie asked the customer before she knew it.

'Ah, yes, actually. Do you gift wrap?'

Glancing behind the counter, Marnie hoped she hadn't said 'Oh dear' out loud, but then she spied rolls of gorgeous gift wrapping, multi-coloured ribbons and patterned bellybands. 'Absolutely,' she replied. She gave the young man a hesitant smile.

'Great. I need a present for my mum's birthday. It's today. I'm meeting her for a coffee now so I'm in a bit of a hurry.'

'Okay. There are some lovely necklaces here, as well as soaps.' Marnie quickly glanced around the shop, searching for a great gift that would suit. 'These soy candles are made locally, I think. And, somewhere, aah, here they are, are scarves. Scarves are always welcome and not always something that you would buy for yourself.'

'Great! She does wear scarves. That pink one with the tasselly things looks like her. Can you wrap it? Quickly?'

The chatty atmosphere evaporated as Laila strode into the shop, a look of thunder on her face. She perched like a large vulture, watching as Marnie took off the price tag and started to wrap the gift.

'Laila, could you please fix up this payment? The gentleman is in a bit of a hurry.'

'Can't you use a register?' Laila asked sweetly, her raised eyebrows reflecting her inner cynicism.

'No problem with the EFTPOS, but I am wrapping at the moment so just put it through please.' Marnie didn't drop her smile as she turned to her customer. 'Do you need a card to go with that?'

'Oh thanks, I forgot. This one with the flowers on it is good.' He quickly took the gift card from the counter box.

Marnie wrapped the scarf in embossed white paper,

adding a rose-pink bow to finish the look. She offered a pen for the fellow to write on his card, then tied it to the gift and wished her first customer a good day. A smile crept across her face as the Rowan Atkinson gift wrap scene in *Love Actually* came to mind. Only without the potpourri.

Laila sniffed. 'Libby tells me you are going to be here to unpack and sort the product. I'm off in an hour or so. See what you can get done by then.' With that she stomped out to the bathroom as Marnie rewound and put away the ribbons.

Despite the shop's air conditioning and fans, the storeroom was stuffy and Marnie was soon perspiring. She could hear Whimsy's comings and goings through the louvered door but was yet to hear Laila give any kind of customer service. She wondered where Libby had found her, particularly when she heard Laila suggest that a customer try Emporium down the road for a different fragrance of soap.

Marnie was making great headway as she unpacked boxes and cleared the space of rubbish to a recycling bin at the rear of the shop. Handcrafted ceramic bowls now nestled next to funky vases, trinket dishes stacked alongside presentation platters. She cleared a safe area for spare pieces of jewellery and their display busts before they toppled off more empty boxes. There was no sign of Caroline's shibori cushions – Marnie dismissed the possibility that Laila had already delivered them.

The sound of slamming doors lured Marnie into the shop. Sure enough, the racks of Nautilus Cove tea towels and other displays had been brought in from the front deck, and Whimsy was closed for the day. It was ten minutes to five. It would be safest to restock the shop after Laila had left.

'Doesn't the shop close at five o'clock?' Marnie tried to sound innocent.

'I get paid until five and I have to balance the takings and close up inside yet.' Laila slammed the counter drawer shut.

Marnie had handled worse personality conflicts than this, so she decided to give the conversation another shot. 'Laila, I'm happy to turn everything off when I go. I still have a couple of things to do. The register automatically does a day's total, doesn't it? Just tell me what else needs to happen and what to do with the cash, and you can be on your way.'

Laila glanced guardedly at her, obviously checking for any tricks. Her apparent eagerness to leave overcame any job responsibility and she quickly went through the end-of-day procedure. With an earnest shuffle to retrieve her handbag, via a quick stop to moisturise her hands with the store's Sea Mist tester, she was gone. Marnie noticed she had left one of the bird mobiles hanging outside and quickly brought it in.

'Here we are, Whimsy. Just the two of us.' Marnie turned off the music, eager to potter around Whimsy on her own. The little shop seemed to settle around her as if grateful to be rid of the earlier negative vibes.

The courier's number was easy to find so Marnie quickly rang them before their office closed, organising pickups for the next day. She then texted the stylist to say her props would be delivered in the morning, immediately receiving a grateful return message. The next hour was spent filling Whimsy's patchy shelves and slightly altering the displays where needed. Cleaning up leaves, dead mosquitoes and ants from under the tables took another half hour. She even found a customer's empty water bottle tucked behind some signage.

The shop's incredibly messy counter beckoned with every discarded paperclip and bleached rubber band. Marnie's eye fell on a solitary book that sat tucked at the back of the bottom shelf. She blew the dust away from the surface, revealing it to be a Baby Journal: A Keepsake of the First

Twelve Months. She ran her hand over the dirty cloth cover, then randomly opened it to a page. A little envelope invited the first lock of hair to be held safely, forever. Snapping the journal shut, Marnie blew out a long, shuddering breath. She had completed such journals for both her children; now she just hoped Claire in particular would still be speaking to her when the time came to pass it on.

Keen to head home, Marnie scanned the store, hoping she hadn't forgotten anything. She wasn't sure if the overhead fans stayed on or not so she turned them off with the lights. As the fans slowed, a gentle silence fell over Whimsy as if all the products had gone to bed. She smiled at the memory of taking Claire to see *The Nutcracker Suite* ballet; how they were both mesmerised by the toys as they came to life. Marnie missed those innocent mother/daughter outings and promised herself to invite Claire to see the latest Melbourne Theatre Company play, with dinner at Federation Square beforehand. It would be a real bonding evening, an olive branch.

With the doors closed, fragrances from the soaps and diffusers mingled tantalisingly with the woody scents of the furniture. Soft light glowed from several stunning small arc lamps that would remain on overnight. With the row of white bud lights strung across the rear wall, the store offered a truly magical reflection of its moniker. Marnie realised, a little guiltily, that she had never bothered to ask Libby how she had come by her business's name.

She smiled, feeling surprisingly satisfied by everything she had achieved in a few hours. But then she always had been the list keeper of the family, loving every time a job could have a line drawn through it, completed. It had always annoyed Philippe. Inflexible, boring, detail focused were a few of the names he had thrown at her at various times.

Ironic, seeing as he was the accountant. Nobody bemoaned his endless spreadsheets; apparently they had been vital for the family's future, or so he kept harping. Her own lists had definitely saved her on more than one occasion during hectic times at Manning College. Fundraisers, huge annual fetes, art exhibitions and open days all had Marnie's Lists as their foundation and a hardworking band of volunteers to thank for their success.

She hadn't thought about her old job for weeks but welcomed the possibility that she was finally chilling, breaking the monotonous habit of being wound up like a spring. It was as if the salty air was acting like a filter to offer peace in the north.

A blurred shape on top of an old bookcase near the back door caught her attention. Was it a sculpture? Arching out of a marble base was a copper rod. Sprinkled along the rod sat a galaxy of stars: some small, some larger, some sitting at the end of little antennas. A crescent moon hung a third of the way along. She thought it was stunning, simple yet so adorable, and she suspected she knew exactly who the maker was.

Tucked under the sculpture was a piece of paper, a note in Laila's writing: To be returned to H ASAP. It was dated the day Libby had left.

Marnie carefully placed the sculpture in a carry bag, resolving to take it out to Harry's studio herself the next day. She didn't leave a note, firm in the knowledge that Laila wouldn't even miss it. Realising the baby journal was still firmly clutched under her arm, she dropped it down the side of the bag.

CHAPTER ELEVEN

MARNIE WAS LOST. She had been so mesmerized by the amazing views of the bay she hadn't noted exactly where Libby had driven along the cliff road. So she just pointed the car towards the headland and kept the water on her left; it had to be the right direction.

Another turn, another dirt road, another anonymous gum tree appeared as she nosed the car around the meandering roads. She flicked up the air conditioning. And then out of the bush appeared a familiar private driveway; farther along the arcing fish and a small brass sign beckoned. Pocket. Marnie slowed, the only sound as the car crawled forward was the crunching of tyres on gravel. She emerged into the empty clearing. No car, no music. Just stillness, and a sudden summery eruption of cicadas. She parked the car and approached the studio's entrance, hoping the door would be ajar.

Confronted by a locked studio, Marnie was unsure what to do, if it was safe to just leave the sculpture at the entrance. She wandered around the corner of the building, taking care to avoid the giant spider webs hovering to snag the unwary.

Small lizards scattered as she approached, but she couldn't venture far. The land fell away, exposing the rough underside of the cantilevered studio. Marnie marvelled at how the building quietly reached out, eager to be a part of the natural canopy. She could now understand the overwhelming sense of floating amongst the bush she had felt when held inside, behind glass.

Small birds dived and flicked, snapping up insects. The intertwining scrub stopped any wisp of a breeze relieving the heat and heavy humidity. Marnie, her T-shirt sticking to her back and hair plastered onto her neck, retreated back to the entrance. She knocked again, an echo the only reply. There wasn't even a sign of the well-heeled Samantha.

Marnie withdrew to the car and its air conditioning, surprised that disappointment seemed to be outweighing frustration that the studio was empty. Perhaps she hadn't been as intent on delivering the sculpture as much as seeing the sculptor? She flicked the notion aside, deciding to return another time. Marnie glanced in the side mirror to reverse the car when a half-hidden timber railing caught her eye, possibly a staircase leading down to the beach.

Temptation won in the hope that she'd find a cool breeze and some great photos at the bottom. Marnie reached into the back seat, retrieving her trusty Nikon. Philippe had always said 'the world is divided into Nikon and Canon users' and had promptly bought himself the latest Canon. She had never seen him use it and presumed it was still sitting in its box somewhere with a dozen new lenses.

Accepting that she was no Annie Leibovitz, Marnie had persevered with her early love for photography. She had been accepted into several professional development courses over her career, improving the craft then exploiting it further at Manning College. Small details appealed to her rather than broad landscapes – close-ups of hands around a test tube, an abandoned row of gym shoes, a junior girl's expression as she waited to go on stage. Since leaving her job she had taken herself off on a couple of photographic excursions. An overcast day in the city had produced some shots she was particularly happy with – crowded alleyway cafés, rusty shingle signs, dusty windows in the old garment industry buildings, vibrant graffiti. Urged on by an artist friend, she had uploaded them onto an online site, thrilled when a couple had sold during the first week.

It had been months since she had taken up the camera, but Nautilus Cove was reigniting the urge. Her excitement built with each cautious step down the steep wooden steps. But two flights down without seeing anything but scrub and feeling only sticky perspiration, Marnie began to regret her decision. The climb back up was going to be worse – hot and vertical. As her enthusiasm faded, a long boardwalk appeared to her left. She could hear waves shushing in and out of the shore as her skin welcomed clean air that filtered through the foliage. The boardwalk dropped down another flight, then ran straight again, interrupted only by a little viewing platform. Suddenly there it was: Lantana Bay spread out below her. The stunning panorama reflected the view from Harry's studio, just as she had suspected. Several stand-up paddle boarders were gently working their way around The Point as if they had all the time in the world, which they probably did. Marnie looped the camera over her head and faced the refreshing onshore breeze, closing her eyes. The tang of salty air felt good.

Her vista shots were turning out pretty well, but they weren't the images she wanted. Another flight of stairs led down to rocks and silver sand. Carefully she changed lenses, glancing down to where she needed to be. She was surprised and pleased to see the beach below was deserted except for a lone seagull looking out to the horizon.

Lizards of all sizes dashed back into the prickly scrub, their basking interrupted by Marnie's arrival. She looped the camera case over the railing, tossed her shoes to the base of the stairs and jumped onto the sand. It was warm and soft under her feet, powdery between her wiggling toes. As Marnie picked her way between scattered stones and over smooth, shiny boulders her shoulders dropped, and a smile crept across her face. The gentle breeze caressed her neck as it tried to take away wisps of her hair like a bird gathering threads for its nest. She slowly stretched to meet it, raising her arms to the so-blue sky, and breathed deeply. She wandered on, squatting every so often for close-up shots of a broken shell white against the steel-grey rocks, of a small reddish starfish, and the tiny bubbles that floated in the rock pools. Translucent crabs scurried out of sight, either from her intrusion or from the circling seagulls. Little ripples spread silently across the pools' crystal-clear surfaces as if the larger sea was sending secret messages in Morse code.

The wet sand, so clean and white, sucked at her toes; the cool water lapped around her ankles. She felt so alive, it took her breath away. Marnie gazed at the horizon, listening to the rolling waves and squawking gulls … and the squeaking of footsteps in the sand.

She turned, squinting at the approaching figure.

'Hi, I saw you from the boardwalk.' Harry waved his hand lazily over his shoulder toward the path. 'Marnie, right? Am I interrupting?'

'No. I was wanting you. I mean I was actually at your studio.' Marnie could feel her feet sinking into the sand as the water receded. 'I was returning a sculpture I found in the Whimsy storeroom. But the studio was closed, and I saw the stairs and thought I'd take some quick shots.' She waved her camera as if to back up her statement.

Marnie hoped her sunglasses shielded her eyes as she drank in this attractive man. His wet hair was slicked back, his T-shirt stuck to a very impressive chest. She realised she must look windblown and sandy and totally out of place.

He scanned along the beach. 'No wayward dog today?'

That answered whether he remembered her outside the café, when Beebs escaped from her. Marnie shook her head. 'It was a spur-of-the-moment decision to come down to the beach. A side trip.'

Harry nodded at her camera. 'I'm a Nikon man myself, actually.'

'I just dabble, but I do believe you should take as good a shot as you can at the outset. Rather than, you know, Photoshop it to hell later.' Marnie stopped, fearing she sounded like a photography lesson.

'Yep. Totally agree.' Harry squinted over her shoulder. 'Did you get the pandanus over there? That's a typical Nautilus Cove scene.' He moved closer, tilting his head to look at her shots.

'No, just the pebbles and these gorgeous little rockpools. Close-ups, actually.' He was standing right against her now, the shifting sand unstable under their feet, their shoulders rubbing with every wave. Marnie switched the camera so he could view the gallery of images.

He leant in, his damp hair brushing the side of her face as he lifted his glasses to look closer. 'Ah, a details girl.'

Marnie laughed. 'Ha, yes. That's me.'

He turned slightly, a questioning gaze bearing into Marnie's eyes. 'These are really nice. May I?' Harry took the camera from her. 'Whoa, look out!'

Marnie didn't jump quickly enough to escape a small

rogue wave as it flattened to shore. As she toppled out of the way, she felt Harry's hand grab her and saw his other arm shoot into the air to protect her camera from the foaming crest. His tanned, muscled legs and arms braced them against the swirling water as their bodies propped against each other.

Marnie gasped, feeling her legs being tugged as the water swept out again. She was relieved to have her hand in Harry's firm grip. Amidst the spray and chaos, she felt a scraping along her arm and caught sight of a cluster of knotted strings around his wrist, presumably Buddhist love or luck knot bracelets. They partly hid a small tattoo which Marnie couldn't quite make out before Harry loosened his grip on her.

'Well, I didn't see that coming. Thank heavens it wasn't any bigger,' she said, pressing a hand to her chest.

'As long as the sun rises in the east and sets in the west, the waves will come. So they say.'

They both laughed self-consciously, although Marnie was relieved to hear she wasn't the only one who shared favourite quotes. Harry's had come naturally, as if the rolling sea was a major part of his life.

'The tide must be coming in. Come back here a bit.' Harry still held Marnie's camera as he kept her hand in his and guided her back to the stair. He dropped her hand, passing her a blue and red striped towel that was draped next to her camera case. He replaced the space with his sunglasses.

'It's my towel,' he assured her as she flicked the wet sand off her legs. 'This is private access, so no one else comes here.'

'Oh, I didn't know. How can it be private when it's a public beach?'

'I meant the access is private, not the beach. A technicality of easements.' He shrugged.

'Well someone is lucky,' Marnie responded. 'Is that the owner of your studio? He must be pretty smart with planning regulations. Or she.' As she bent to rub the towel over her feet, she just caught what looked like a sparkle of amusement in his eyes.

'It's a he, and I believe he has a background in planning and development.'

'I hope the planning and development isn't too widespread. The bush really is so raw and natural here, in a prickly kind of way.' Marnie shook her hair, trying to get rid of the sand and embedded wayward twigs. Her skin tingled with the slight zephyr, bringing a coolness she knew wouldn't last.

'Yes, it is. In a prickly kind of way.' Harry held her gaze, as they exchanged towel for camera. It gave her the chance to enjoy his eyes which were almost like blue sea glass in the light, and to appreciate Harry-in-close-up – older than she had thought, maybe late 50s, with a handsome Australian beach style. Dee would have said he was in excellent shape. Marnie's body gave an unbidden shiver that had nothing to do with the breeze.

'Well, this climb is likely to take me several hours so I'd better get started.' She packed her camera away as Harry swooped to pick up her shoes. 'Thank you. I would have forgotten those.

'Don't mention it. I'm always forgetting or losing things.'

They headed up the stairs, Marnie conscious of Harry climbing just a few steps behind her. She glanced back at him, then scrutinised how far she had to go. 'Do you want to pass? I could be a while.'

'Nope. All good here,' Harry replied.

Without having to turn around fully, Marnie could hear

the amused lilt in his voice and sense his smile. The cheeky fellow seemed to be enjoying this.

'Damn it. Speaking of forgetting things, I've left my sunnies at the bottom,' he said. 'You keep going, and I'll catch up.'

Marnie amped up her pace to move ahead as far as possible, but it took him no time at all to reach her. By the time they got to the top of the staircase perspiration was trickling down Marnie's body, pooling around her waistband.

'I should be wearing the silly Fitbit my parents gave me last Christmas,' she said, as she collapsed against the railing.

'I'll grab a couple of bottles of water,' Harry said as he headed to the studio.

Marnie opened the car doors, an almost visible wall of warm air bursting onto her face. A quick glance in the mirror confirmed she looked as wild and red-faced as she feared. The old van, Harry's presumably, was parked to the side under the trees. Had he seen her scoot down the stairs earlier?

They stood in the shade which was dappled but welcome. Each sipped the water and rubbed the chilled bottles across the backs of their necks. Marnie handed Harry the carry bag. 'I really like this piece, Harry. It's sort of magical. I'm sorry it wasn't returned promptly.'

'No problem. It's only a sample. I wanted to see if Libby was interested in stocking a couple. I do need a name for it though. What do you think? Moonlight? Stargazing? Starlight?'

'Not starlight. That's the name of your boat.' Marnie winced when she saw Harry's surprised response. 'Um, isn't it? I saw it at the marina.'

'Yes, it is, but starlight can mean many things, actually,' Harry said slowly, his eyes not leaving her face. 'You are a details girl!'

Feeling oddly pleased that he had asked her opinion, Marnie gave it some thought. 'How about calling your sculpture … *Under the Milky Way*?'

Harry nodded. 'Perfect. You know, you should come and look at my workspace some time.' His eyes crinkled. 'You should see the look on your face. I said my studio, not my etchings!'

Marnie's heart was pounding but it was no longer from the climb.

'I presumed you had a workshop under the studio, Harry. But I saw how it's perched out of the hill with nothing but vegetation and rather large spiders underneath.' She knew she was rambling but wanted to prolong their chat.

'You did take a wander then.' Harry's enjoyment at her expense seemed endless.

'I was looking for you, as I said,' Marnie replied. 'So, where is this working studio then?'

Harry's response was interrupted by his cell phone. He flicked a look at the screen, then tilted the phone toward Marnie.

'Sorry. This is a client waiting on some details so I'd better take it. Thanks for bringing the sculpture back. *Under the Milky Way* I mean. Can I catch you later?'

'Oh, sure. See you.' Marnie hurried to her car. As she glanced in the rear-view mirror she could see Harry wandering towards the studio, talking animatedly into his phone as he swung the carry bag, the towel slung casually over his shoulder.

CHAPTER TWELVE

'DEE! Hi! I'm in the car, but on hands-free. How are you?' Marnie was thrilled to see her friend's beaming face come up on her phone contacts. She made a mental note to keep the bay on her right as she headed away from Pocket. She didn't want to get lost trying to find the right road again, although she knew Dee would keep her entertained.

'I'm missing my coffee partner,' Dee whined.

Marnie laughed. 'Libby seems very reluctant to return home. Honestly, Dee, how can Libby and I possibly be related? I'd be having a breakdown if I had gone overseas and left my business in the hands of someone so hopeless, but it doesn't seem to worry her. Also, there's a man involved, so you know.'

'Ah yes. Say no more. We both know Libby falls in love more than Elizabeth Taylor. But without the diamonds. Oh well, good on her.'

'What! I want to go home and I'm stuck here with a business I know nothing about and a lazy employee who snarls every time I walk in the door. I've been sweating since I got off the plane, so just a walk to the corner with the dog is exhausting.' But the exercise was welcome in such a beautiful location.

'Oh nonsense, Marnie. Nautilus Cove is paradise and you know it. Just enjoy it while you can. It's freezing down here despite it nearly being November.'

'I'll be back by Melbourne Cup. Have you organised our annual betting'n'bubbly girls' outing?'

A few seconds of silence warned Marnie that perhaps Dee hadn't been able to arrange time off work.

'That's part of the reason for my call,' said Dee. 'I feel really bad about this, but I've been asked to go to the Cup as a corporate guest. A swish media event with all the trimmings including a pass to all areas – you know, a full luncheon in the grandstand right on the finish line, even betting coupons.'

'Of course you must go.' Marnie was pleased for her friend but disappointment wrapped around her like a wet, smelly towel. The Melbourne Spring Racing Carnival was always great fun and a chance to really frock up. Neither of them was interested in going to the horse races at any other time, but the season was one of the city's events of the year. Posh marquees, amazing fashion and millinery, fun each-way betting and champagne were hard to say no to. The prestigious Melbourne Cup race was always held on the first Tuesday in November.

'I tried to get an extra pass for you …'

'Don't be silly. It's okay.' Marnie tried to brush aside Dee's explanations. 'Good on you. You've obviously kicked some goals to get invited. But you owe me! When my prodigal sister finally returns and I get back, you can buy me endless coffees and biscotti.'

'Biscotti?' What happened to apple cake and cream? Anyway, so sorry luv.' Dee sounded relieved to have shared the news. 'I'd better get back to work. Take care and we'll chat soon.'

Marnie slumped in the car seat. She had looked forward to the Cup for months and had searched high and low in advance for a new dress and hat, finally falling in love with a Stella McCartney outfit. She had justified the cost by promising herself to wear it to a couple of the carnival's days. But something else saddened her – this was a further example of why she needn't return to her life in Melbourne in a hurry. It seemed that everything and everyone was getting on just fine without her. She was pleased for Dee and her corporate success, but it only reinforced her own feeling of inadequacy.

A QUICK DETOUR to the cottage for a shower and change of clothes set her back on track. She decided to head into Figtree Street to check where Caroline's cushions were. Libby had emailed to say her customer was complaining they hadn't arrived, and could Marnie follow it up? Marnie had agreed, stopping short of asking the whereabouts of her supposedly reliable assistant. After Dee's phone call, Marnie was in no mood for a confrontation with Laila, but she had promised her sister that she would find out what she could. She found a parking space but still couldn't face Laila, so she ducked into Nest.

Always ready with a cheery hello, Eleanor took her order and ushered her to a seat in the café's window. Locals and tourists sauntered by as Marnie watched them and sipped her coffee; teenagers weighed down with backpacks, young families slowly wandering with ice creams in hand, older couples window shopping.

Marnie idled over her second coffee, visions of Harry

playing havoc with her thoughts. She could just see across the road to the window of Threadz and contemplated heading over to distract herself. Marnie waved goodbye to Eleanor and set off across the road.

Threadz's window was tantalising, showcasing beautiful handcrafted pieces in an array of gelati colours. She couldn't escape being drawn inside the store. Rows upon rows of coloured threads, wools and other yarns were like a rainbow along one wall. Racks of handcraft kits of every kind were displayed below stunning examples of finished items, from intricate cross-stitches to embroidered bunny rugs. Soft chatter came from the back of the shop where a couple of ladies were enjoying a sewing class.

A flier on the counter caught Marnie's eye: Salute to the Sun Yoga on the Beach. Daily 7 a.m.

As Marnie took a copy, the attractive lady behind the counter smiled. 'I've been thinking of doing that class too. A bit of relaxation under the palms would be good, don't you think?'

Marnie was surprised and embarrassed to notice her hand holding the flier was shaking a little. She presumed she had had one too many coffees and hoped it wasn't the reason for the woman's comment.

She was still waiting. 'Can I help you with anything today?'

'Maybe some wool to make something that would probably be full of dropped stitches by the end. Heavens, it took me seven years to finish a Nantucket pull rug, so I don't know what I was thinking.' Marnie paused. 'I think you're right. It looks like yoga is exactly what I need at the moment, although I'm very rusty.'

The woman blushed. 'Oh, I didn't mean *you* specifically. I think everyone could benefit from it, and I hear the instructor is a lovely fellow. It's just taking the first step to actually go and do it, isn't it. That's the hardest part, for me anyway.' She reached out her hand in greeting. 'I'm Nathalie. Have I seen you over at Whimsy with Libby?'

'Yes. I'm Marnie, her sister, and it would seem the caretaker of Whimsy whilst Libby is away.' They shook hands. If appearances counted for anything, Marnie thought Nathalie looked the perfect owner of Threadz – kindly with a pretty face. Comical little earrings dropped below her short blonde bob; silver knitting needles on one side and a gold ball of wool on the other.

'Libby is lucky to have you. It's so hard to get away as a store owner, and Libby does so much extra for the community as well. I know there is another lady over there but I haven't met her.'

'Laila. Actually, that's why I'm in the street today. I need to catch up with her for Libby, so I'll have to come back another time. Nice to meet you, Nathalie. Your window is beautiful, by the way.'

WHAT HAD Nathalie meant by Libby's community work? Marnie wondered. But her attention had refocused on the confrontation with Laila, which couldn't be put off any longer. She slipped into Whimsy. The store was busy and she couldn't see Laila at first, but then spied her at the back of the shop, her phone pinned to her ear. Marnie caught snatches of a private, chatty conversation as she approached the wayward assistant. Seeing her approach, Laila didn't hang up as Marnie expected but turned and walked into the storeroom. Several people came to the counter so, relieved she had stopped at home to change, Marnie stepped in to help. Her eyes shot across the shop at the sound of broken china, only to see a mother ushering her son out of the front door, without a backward glance at the broken teacup left behind on the floor.

Laila finally re-emerged, raising an eyebrow as Marnie handed a parcel across to the last customer. Marnie couldn't contain her frustration.

'A teacup was broken whilst you were out the back on the phone. Perhaps you could sweep up the pieces, leave the saucer in the storeroom for Libby to see and reset the display. Please.'

Laila did as she was asked at the speed of a snail, then headed toward the back once again.

'Laila, can you come here for a minute?' With no customers in the shop, this was her chance. 'Libby has rung. Apparently Caroline Bernhadt hasn't received her cushions and isn't happy that no one has contacted her.'

'What do you mean, Marlee?'

Marnie let the name-change go. 'Have they arrived, and if so, where are they?'

Laila shrugged. 'That's probably the parcel in the storeroom. From Linen Lane? Would that be it?'

'How would I know, Laila? I don't work here, nor do I know the suppliers. I presume a note about it would be on the long list that Libby left you.' She flipped open the file Libby had put together. 'Here it is. Highlighted, so you could call Caroline as soon as they arrived.' Marnie added under her breath, 'And if you don't take that smirk off your face pronto, I am tempted to hit you over the head with this order book.'

'They're only cushions, for heaven's sake,' Laila mumbled.

'But it's providing customer service.' Marnie lowered her voice as a group of chatty women entered, oohing and aahing about the store. 'I'll check them myself.'

Marnie took the book into the storeroom, unable to believe Laila's attitude. Surely Laila appreciated that the quickest way to lose a customer was to show them neither respect nor service. In Marnie's opinion Laila was being paid to do a job and she had no excuse for her poor, in fact, appalling attitude towards Whimsy's customers.

Marnie checked the delivery against the order, then rang a very frosty Caroline to say she would deliver the cushions to her home.

CAROLINE LIVED ONLY a couple of minutes from Figtree Street, but it was an area Marnie was unfamiliar with. She knew it was in an enclave abutting the national park but quickly realised she was entering serious money territory when the bush cleared to blocks of manicured gardens, high gates and hidden driveways. The winding bitumen road casually led her up and around Nautilus Hill, then flattened into a T intersection. Ahead lay the ocean; she could smell it, hear it and sense its command, somewhat like the large stylish mansions that lay either side of her. Hamptons, Bali, Noosa, New England; all the pages from *Architectural Digest* were there. She gambled on turning right into Denisson Circuit and soon found Caroline's house.

Marnie rang the intercom on the imposing front entrance. She rather liked the double entrances favoured around Nautilus Cove; they offered a sense of mystery and privacy. The sweet fragrance of gardenias and wealth wafted around Marnie as she waited. Presuming the click of the heavy oak gate was her invitation to enter, she walked through into a dense tropical garden and across a small stone bridge. A smoky glass door sat ahead under a deep shale portico. It swung open noiselessly, revealing a palatial entry and Caroline standing, champagne flute in hand, waiting for her. Marnie told herself to act nonchalant, as if this mansion was just like her own home.

'What an amazing house, Caroline.' Suddenly Marnie wasn't interested in playing games and didn't really care what opinion of her Caroline had drawn.

'It needs so much work.' Caroline sighed as she waved away the compliment. To the contrary, Marnie thought it was stunning, if not a little too grandiose. Caroline's kitten heels clicked across the marble, leading Marnie through to a rear conservatory. A picture-perfect view spread in front of them – 180 degrees of sky expanded over water the colour of lapis lazuli. 'It's usually wonderfully wild but is on its best behaviour today.' She smiled as though nature was a child being told what to do.

As they approached the vast glass doors, a sunken terrace was revealed where several ladies reclined in oversize white peacock chairs. Even from a distance Marnie could recognise the circles that Caroline moved in, and when a couple of the blondes flicked their eyes up and away from Marnie, she knew on the spot it was a group she wouldn't be welcomed into. She was thankful in a way.

Caroline tilted her glass at Marnie, indicating she was still clutching the cushions. 'You can just pop those over there. I'll need to wait for my designer to organise them. I do like to support the little local businesses and Libby assured me the linens would be top quality.'

Marnie pretended to scan the room, stifling a laugh that threatened to escape any second. 'I'm sure they'll be perfect. The shibori indigos nestle perfectly with your other toning.' She followed Caroline's gaze as it settled on a nude sculpture nestled into a wall recess. 'Oh!'

'It's amazing, isn't it?' Caroline cooed. Cory and I usually purchase our works in Italy, but we couldn't resist getting that one commissioned from a local sculptor. She sauntered over, running her free hand down the female's back, across the buttocks. 'He got the curves just right.'

The nude was vastly different to anything Marnie had seen in Harry's studio, but she knew instinctively it was his work. It was sensual and alive and, to her, the most exquisite piece in the opulent room.

'Caroline. Come here, darling. Jacinta has some wonderful news.'

Marnie saw her cue to leave. 'Apologies for the delay, Caroline. I hope Whimsy can help you again in the future. I'll let Libby know you're happy with the cushions and ...'

'When is Libby back anyway? I'd much prefer to speak directly to a business's owner. The woman she has there at the moment is hopeless.'

Marnie was tempted to wholeheartedly agree but instead said, 'Libby will be back soon, and I'll leave a note for her to contact you. Goodbye, Caroline.'

CHAPTER THIRTEEN

'STRETCH UP TO THE SKY. Inhale. Up. Feel your core balance. Now, bring your arms slowly, slowly to your sides. Exhale and let it go. Take a moment. Bring your hands together over your heart. Hold your stillness close. Thank you for this beautiful morning. Namaste.'

The tingle of warmth on her skin and the sea breeze whispering through her hair tempted Marnie to enjoy the position a moment longer. With another deep breath she opened her eyes and blinked at the calm waters in front of her. Gentle waves lapped at the shore, dancing in and out. Never-ending.

Paulo, the impossibly serene instructor, strolled over to her. Winding his black hair into a topknot, he targeted Marnie with deep soulful eyes. 'I hope you enjoyed your first session here.'

'It was wonderful. I don't know why I let my classes go.'

Paulo shrugged, not an ounce of judgement in the gesture. 'Life gets in the way sometimes. It is up to our own hearts to work out what is best. I hope to see you again.'

Marnie gathered her yoga mat and water bottle and started

to search for her shoes in her backpack. She tried not to let any thoughts intrude just yet; tried not to start scheduling her day.

'Marnie?'

'Oh, I'm sorry. I was miles away.' Marnie turned to the woman who was standing beside her.

'It's good to see you made it. When you picked up the class brochure in my shop it spurred me on to make the effort. I should thank you for my newfound serenity.'

'Nathalie! I enjoyed it so much too.'

'Shall we go to Nest for a treat? I think we deserve it,' Nathalie quietly enquired.

Marnie was thinking she might take a walk along the beach to extend the sense of calm and strength that the yoga class had stirred in her. But she also valued the friendly invitation.

'What a great idea, but let's walk slowly this way, if that's okay. It's a bit longer but so tranquil, isn't it? The perfect location for a yoga class. I do like Paulo's style too, not that I'm any expert.'

'I think the delectable Paulo is spoken for by Rudi. He's the beach masseur.' She gently nudged Marnie's shoulder, laughing.

The two women were comfortable in their silence as they strolled along the sandy boardwalk, watching the seagulls swoop and the palm trees sway.

'Heavens, it's like a movie backdrop,' Marnie finally said. 'Or a resort on one of those awful reality shows.'

'Like when they try to get couples back together again in front of millions of viewers? I was on one of those.'

'Really? Well, I don't watch them so I'm speaking out of turn,' Marnie apologised. She sensed rather than saw Nathalie's smile.

'Only kidding, but it is beautiful.' Nathalie turned to Marnie. 'I'm still not used to it, really. I moved from Sydney a few years ago. Sydney Harbour is to die for but Nautilus Cove has just that little dollop of the tropics that makes you want to keep sighing with pleasure. I'm sure my feet have spread two sizes since I've swapped heels for flats.'

Marnie laughed. 'Well, that's something to look forward to. Not that I'll be here that long.'

They reached Nest, dusted sand from their feet, and wandered into the cool interior. 'Even without a yoga session I always relax when I come in here for some reason,' Marnie said as she eyed the pomegranate and coconut slice. 'I'm having lemongrass and ginger tea and no cake. Heavens, what next!'

Nathalie ordered the same. 'Do you always travel with a yoga mat?' she asked as they found a table.

'No. I knew Libby would have one somewhere in the house. I did bring these workout pants with me for walking and the big T-shirt is great to cover all the lumps and bumps.'

As they enjoyed their tea, Marnie went on to explain the whys and wherefores of being in Nautilus Cove. She chatted easily with Nathalie, thoroughly enjoying her humour and company.

'And look at Threadz. It's such a pretty store and you obviously know your way around a needle and thread. Is the Family Threads collection your family?'

'It was. Well, I guess it still is, in a way. But gone now. I keep the display to remind me never to take anyone for granted.'

Tears glistened in Nathalie's eyes. Clearly embarrassed, she hurriedly blinked them away. 'Gosh, the yoga must have released some hormones; I'm not usually that forthcoming about what lies behind that display.'

Marnie rested her hand on Nathalie's arm, giving her room to speak further or end the topic. She chose the latter and deflected the conversation back to Marnie.

'It seems to me like a good deal all around. Libby is lucky to have you and you're experiencing a different scene. It's always good to 'walk down the other side of the street', as my dear Grandma Therese used to say. And, excuse me for saying, Marnie … none of my business, really … but you seem to genuinely care about Whimsy. You don't think you'll stay?'

'Stay? Heavens no. I mean, this is good, great even, for a holiday, but I have a life back in Melbourne. I have children and a house.'

'Didn't you say your kids had moved out?' Nathalie raised her eyebrows at Marnie as she took another sip of tea. Marnie laughed, wagging her finger.

'Whoa, I'll have none of that in my café, thank you.' They both looked up to see Eleanor, hands on hips. 'There's way too much fun in this corner. And I did notice there were no cakes coming to this table, so it can't be from a sugar hit.'

The three women grinned at each other and, just like that, Marnie was welcomed. She felt Libby's Marnie-from-Melbourne tag slip away, to be replaced by Just Marnie, which was how she liked it.

Eleanor stayed where she was, trying to keep a poker face.

'What?' Nathalie prompted. 'Eleanor, you look like the cat that got the cream.'

'And well I might. A certain fellow was in earlier, and when a certain lady didn't arrive that fellow wrote his contact number down for this café owner to pass on when she saw said lady.' Eleanor passed Marnie a slip of paper. It had a giant H, a cell phone number and a star written on it.

'Oh,' Marnie said, startled. She still wasn't sure if Eleanor was one of Harry's ladies. 'It's nothing. I said I needed to return a sculpture to him. Which I did, and he said he would get back to me with some, um, details on something I can't quite remember.'

'Marnie, I could have made fifty cappuccinos in the time you are taking to explain one little note. If you wanted Harry's number, you could have asked me because my Dave surfs with him.'

'I wasn't looking for his number. In fact, I'm sure Libby has his number in Whimsy somewhere. He makes sculptures for her.' At her reference to a Dave, Marnie noticed Eleanor's wedding band.

'Well, he obviously wants you to have it,' Nathalie said. 'It could be another reason to stay. Speaking of Whimsy, is Laila sick? The doors weren't open last time I looked.'

Marnie groaned, all feelings of goodwill evaporating.

EVEN FROM A DISTANCE Marnie could see that Whimsy was locked and silent. She checked her phone. No messages from Laila. A young couple stood on the veranda, their faces cupped to the window, trying to see in. She grabbed her mat, said her goodbyes to Nathalie and hurried up the street. Dodging the dog bowl that had been left out overnight, Marnie approached the couple.

'I'm sorry, we've had a bit of a mishap this morning and are running very late. But we will be open shortly if you'd care to come back.' The couple nodded and walked away as Marnie dialled Laila's number. No answer, but a beep alerted Marnie that she had a call coming through.

'Libby!'

'Marnie, I've just had a call from Laila. She's not well, apparently. What's the time there? Oh, it's quite late.'

'Yes, it is. She rang you in Hong Kong? I gave her my contact number if she needed anything. I've just realised your shop isn't open and I'm standing out front trying to get hold of Laila. Libby, you have to do something about her. I get the feeling she's not sick at all. Just late again,' Marnie said, her fingers rapping against the window.

'She did say you had words with her yesterday and she's feeling very anxious. A panic attack or something. She's threatening not to come back at all. I can't deal with her from over here.'

Marnie momentarily felt a pang of guilt, but it drifted away. She assumed this was more of a payback than a panic attack. 'Well I'd open Whimsy myself, Libby, but I'm standing here in leggings and a giant T-shirt. Not work gear. Just a minute.'

Nathalie had followed her to the store and picked up on Marnie's exasperation. 'Can I help?' she mouthed.

Marnie put her hand over the mouthpiece. 'No, but thank you. And thanks for the tea 'n' company. It was great. Let's do it again?'

'Love to. Hope everything works out with you know who. Oh, is that her now?'

Laila was striding up the street. She faltered when she saw Marnie but walked straight past her onto the veranda, pulled out the shop key and stormed inside.

'Libby. I'll call you back. Laila just arrived, but something's not right.'

Laila dashed into the storeroom. Marnie manoeuvred herself to see through the crack in the door. Laila had her back to the door as she hauled something out of her shoulder bag, then quickly shoved it between some table runners on the bottom shelf. Marnie eased back to the counter and waited until she reappeared.

'Laila. I'm sorry to hear you're not well. It would have been helpful if you had called me and I could have come in.' Marnie ignored Laila's expression that could kill and put her six feet under and halfway to hell. 'But as you can see I can't stay and I am presuming that, as you're here now, you're feeling better.' In fact, Laila was dressed as though she was ready to work the day. Had she rung Libby just to complain about Marnie?

'Marnie, I told Libby I was very upset at how you spoke to me yesterday. I'm still not myself.'

'Right. We do seem to differ on a few points, but Libby has requested that if you could possibly work today, it would be appreciated. I'll come in tomorrow if you're still not feeling like your normal happy self.' Marnie nearly bit her tongue at having to grovel but she had her reasons.

Laila didn't break eye contact. Marnie stood her ground, resisting the urge to flick her eyes towards the storeroom.

'If you can open the doors and put out the front display, I'll quickly get everything ready here, okay?' Marnie said.

Laila shrugged and shuffled to the front of the store. Marnie ducked into the storeroom and quickly lifted the table runners. A scarf lay between them – hand-dyed silk and felting made by a lovely woman in central Queensland. All soft muted colours. Now crinkled and obviously used more than once.

Marnie tucked it back into its hiding place. Her shoulders slumped. She didn't know who to feel sorry for – Libby or Laila. The sense of betrayal wound its tentacles around her heart too, and she had to wonder if she was starting to feel more a part of Whimsy than she had realised. The little store was quiet as if waiting for her answer.

After Laila grudgingly agreed to stay, Marnie trailed back to her car. She tried not to think about how Laila's attitude would come across to customers. But she did have a couple of answers for Libby; she could tell her the missing scarf had been returned and where it had been. This was one of those moments when she would find comfort in her photography. To be able to transfer her attention to a magical detail in nature was always a salve to her emotions. It was as though that moment in time could infiltrate her soul; it calmed her and gave her more pleasure than anything else she knew. Well, except for a hug and some damn good sex.

She accepted that it would have to be her Nikon that would keep her company for the afternoon. But even before that, she desperately needed to do some serious shopping for new sunglasses and lightweight clothes.

CHAPTER FOURTEEN

YOGA WITH PAULO and a catch-up with Nathalie was becoming a welcome routine. A quick peek along the street showed Marnie that Whimsy was open. *Hallelujah.*

As they entered Nest, Marnie caught sight of Laila hugging a woman outside Whimsy. Marnie watched as Laila and the woman laughed.

She and Nathalie nodded in greeting to the old man sitting in his customary seat with his habitual carrot cake, then sat at the window counter

'Nathalie, who's that woman walking across the street over there? The one with the frizzy hair and black dress.'

'That's Rachel. She owns Posh Pit farther down the street.'

Marnie shivered. Wasn't that the name Libby had mentioned; the competition that Laila was no longer friends with? She tried not to jump to conclusions.

Nathalie continued. 'I don't really know her but I think she's a friend of Laila's because I've seen her in Whimsy quite a bit since Libby has gone away. Why?'

Their conversation was interrupted by Eleanor, a grin

spread across her pretty face. 'So, Marnie, have you called that number yet?'

At Marnie's perplexed expression, Eleanor sighed. 'The note. The number. Harry?'

'Um, no. What was it for?' In truth, she had nearly called several times.

'Good lord, how would I know?' Eleanor raised her eyebrows at Nathalie, who was already smiling. 'Maybe he has some sculptures to show you for Whimsy. Maybe he wants to take you surfing. Ah, probably not. Let's go with the sculpture idea.'

'Okay. I'll call him when I leave here,' Marnie assured her.

Eleanor gave her a thumbs up and wandered off behind her counter.

'Marnie. You never got the wool the other day. Weren't you going to knit something for someone?' asked Nathalie.

'No, I don't think that's on the agenda really, knowing my patchy craft background. I was just taken by your pretty shop and had to have a closer look. Have you been in retail long?'

Nathalie looked down into her cup. 'It kind of found me. The wools and stitching, I mean. My mother, when she was alive, had a great eye for sewing. When I was born her, ah, mother would send us things she'd made. Beautiful cot blankets embroidered with woodland animals and hand-sewn fairies made from the most gorgeous fabrics. She would make little smocked dresses that were quite old-fashioned in a way, but I thought they were magical.'

'And you kept them,' Marnie prompted gently, sensing there was more to the story.

'I kept as many as I could, but Mum and Grandma didn't get on.' Nathalie faltered. 'You see, my mum had been given up for adoption as a baby and wouldn't reconnect with

Grandma. But deep down, she must have felt something because I found all those gifts in a suitcase in Mum's house after she died. They were like little memories packed away just waiting to be discovered. I can still smell the camphor that flowed out of that box when I opened it.'

'Oh, Nathalie. How sad. Your mum must have been young when she died.'

She nodded. 'Cancer, before I moved to Nautilus Cove. There was a letter too amongst her things. I'm sure she wanted me to find it. From Grandma to her, asking for forgiveness and hoping that she could visit, to meet me. Mum never responded. But after she died I decided to contact her. Therese, that is, my grandma.'

Nathalie took a deep breath. It was as though they were the only people in the café, all noises and chatter falling away as Marnie listened to Nathalie's story.

'It was wonderful when we met. I was very nervous and so was she, but we recognised each other straight away. I got the impression that maybe she had watched me from a distance on occasion, which is kind of nice, really. Like a guardian angel. Anyway, she explained it all to me and I understood. She had been a teenager when she fell pregnant to a fellow who shot through from their town as soon as word spread. The pressure to adopt out a baby if you weren't married had been huge in those days, and so she had succumbed and kissed her baby goodbye. She knew Mum had found a loving home, but they had never reconnected.'

'Do you think they would have if your mum had lived longer?' Marnie asked, hoping she wasn't being too personal.

'I would have made sure it happened,' Nathalie said firmly. 'Therese said that a day hadn't gone by that she hadn't thought of her daughter, to whisper her good morning and blow her a kiss goodnight. Anyway, Therese and I saw each other regularly until she died a couple of years ago from a heart condition. Her one request was for "Somewhere Over the Rainbow" to be played as her ashes were scattered. And typical Therese, it had to be Billy Thorpe's version.'

'Well it is the best.' Marnie smiled gently.

Nathalie's eyes brimmed with tears as she nodded. They'd finished their tea, so Marnie stood, taking Nathalie by the arm and walking her outside. She steered them silently up the street without a glance into Whimsy, then through the parkland to the boardwalk.

Once they were overlooking the beach with the fresh air on their faces, Nathalie sighed. She glanced at Marnie. 'I'm okay. Really. I'm just sad that Mum and Therese never got together again and that I had so little time with my grandma. My inheritance from her enabled me to move away from Sydney and to set up Threadz here. I feel so blessed. I know she would have been proud of me and my business. In fact, is it silly for me to believe she's often in the shop with me?'

Marnie shook her head with conviction. 'Of course not. She's right there in the window as well, in your Family Threads display.'

'Therese-Rosalie-Nathalie. All joined. Because we were – are. I presume you don't have grandchildren?'

'No, but I will one day, I'm sure, and I'm really looking forward to it. We can often take our families for granted or find silly things to differ about. Libby drives me nuts, but I still love her. I'm glad you met Therese in the end though, Nathalie. What was she like?'

'My mum was rather reserved. My dad was too; they divorced when I was a teenager. Therese was different. I guess I would say, robust. Funny, with a big laugh, and she was such fun to be around. She called a spade a bloody shovel and yet could create these delicate handcrafts.'

Marnie linked her arm through her new friend's and gave it a squeeze.

Nathalie gazed across the water as if her precious memories were painted on each cresting wave. As they wandered back toward Figtree Street, Nathalie simply said, 'Thank you, Marnie.'

After they parted, Marnie sat in her car for a while thinking about families, about relationships and hierarchies, past upheavals and future wishes. She promised herself to contact and resolve unspoken issues with her children, particularly Claire, as a priority on her return – face to face. And Libby – how to address the fragmented relationship with her sister? Nathalie's story had stirred emotions in her that she had squashed for too long.

In that moment she needed to connect with one particular person. She took out the scrap of paper from her handbag and dialled Harry's number.

HER CALL WENT TO VOICEMAIL. Harrison Mitchelton's voicemail. She quickly hung up, then rang back.

'Hi, Harry. It's Marnie Fawkner here. From Whimsy? Eleanor gave me your number and …' She was timed out by the voicemail god, so she redialled.

'Marnie again. Anyway, I guess you needed to talk with me about the sculptures for the shop. I can pick up some if …' She was cut off again. Frustrated, she texted Harry her number with a 'call me if I can help' message.

Five minutes later, as she was pulling into the cottage driveway, Harry called back. No preamble, no 'Hi, Marnie, it's Harry'.

'I do indeed think you can help me, Marnie Fawkner. I

was ringing about your services. Nothing to do with Whimsy.'

She could hear the smile between the words, picture his cheeky expression.

He left the request hanging, unaware of the tingling sensation that was working its way up Marnie's body. When she didn't respond, he continued.

'Are you free for a coffee?'

She was surprised by the unexpected invitation but found herself replying quickly. 'Yes, sure.'

'There's a little place on the river next to the U-boat Hire called Jetty. Half an hour okay?'

'Yes, sure,' she repeated.

'Terrific. See you then.'

Harry hung up, leaving Marnie bewildered at what he had been hinting at, if Whimsy wasn't involved.

She hurried inside for a quick shower, grateful for her shopping trip. Her urban black-on-black range was returned to the suitcase, replaced with cool cottons and linens in tones of seashell and soft blues and greens, sheer shirts and open sandals. She swept her hair up, catching her reflection in the dressing room mirror. Much to her surprise, a slightly older, paler version of Libby gazed back. Even more surprising was the look of calm anticipation in this person's eyes. With a wink in the mirror and a treat tossed to the dog, Marnie left to meet the sculptor.

SHE ARRIVED at the quaint little café ahead of Harry and took a seat under the awning, having forgotten to bring a sunhat. She felt unexpectedly excited to be meeting him again.

'You look happy,' came a deep, slow voice.

Harry was silhouetted against the sun but she could tell he was grinning down at her. Marnie's stomach gave a little kick that he might have read her mind.

'Sorry I'm late. I dropped my keys in the bush at Pocket and couldn't find the darned things, but all's good now. Coffee?'

'You know, it's so hot. I might have an iced green tea if that's okay.'

'Got it. Muffin or something else?'

'No, I'm good, thanks.'

Harry returned with a slice of toasted banana bread, butter melting down its thick sides onto the plate. When Marnie inhaled deeply and admitted that it did smell delicious, Harry quickly cut it in two, easing a piece toward her. Their drinks were delivered and they settled back in the striped canvas deck chairs, taking in the picturesque scene laid out before them. From behind, they would look like a couple.

'So, Marnie,' Harry began, sounding a little nervous. 'How long are you staying in Nautilus Cove? I mean, is this just a holiday to help out your sister or do you think it might extend into next year?'

Of all the opening lines Harry could have conjured, Marnie was surprised by this one. She didn't know how much to say. 'No, it's just to help out Libby. I have a lot of other commitments back home.'

As Harry eased forward, elbows on his knees, his shirt stretched across his broad back, one side of the collar disappearing into his hair. He was a hair's breadth away from her. She could have easily straightened his collar just by leaning …

'Do you have a job to return to? I'm sorry, this is sounding like Twenty Questions, isn't it?' Harry grimaced, running a hand back through his hair. He dropped his head and glanced sideways at her. 'The thing is, I have an idea and once I have something on my mind, I have to keep going over and over it until I can find my way through.'

'Well, we have that in common.' Marnie laughed, still unsure where Harry was heading.

'Tick number one then.' He smiled mischievously. 'It's all still forming in my head, but I need some photographs taken. First off, I need some product shots of the works you saw at Pocket the other day, but something really imaginative. Plus, I'm working on other ideas too that are at my workshop. That's probably down the track a little way, but I like to be organised, despite what my brother says.'

'Sorry, your brother?'

'Oh, forget that. It's not important. But it would depend on how you feel about it. I'd pay you, of course.'

Marnie started, unsure if she had heard correctly that Harry wanted to employ her as a photographer. She shooe'd away a seagull that was trying to peck at the banana bread crumbs, took a sip of her tea, and tried to organise her thoughts into some semblance of order. Maybe she'd misunderstood.

Harry obviously wasn't going to elaborate as he looked at her expectantly.

'You've taken me by surprise. Really you have. I mean, you don't even know me.' *Unfortunately.*

Marnie fixed him with a 'please don't lie to me' look and asked the question that was sitting like a stone in her heart. 'Why me Harry? I mean there must be hundreds of professional photographers on the coast that would jump at the chance.' Marnie stilled her fingers, which were tapping against the table, and waited.

Harry seemed to take forever to reply. He fiddled with his

bracelets, then shuffled his chair closer to Marnie, his presence all the more powerful because of the diminishing space between them. He looked directly at her, challenging.

'I knew you were the one when I saw your shots on the beach that day. The details gal, remember? But not only that. I could see right away how you connected with your subject. You know, without sounding all airy-fairy, you seemed to feel something.'

He placed his hand over his heart to emphasise the point, then quickly dropped it. She could tell, despite a hovering reticence, he was very excited about his idea.

'Anyone can use their phone to take a photo, but to get the soul of an image? Well that isn't something you can be taught. It's instinct. You've got it. Trust me.'

Marnie stared at him. She held her hands tightly together in her lap. She had never thought of her photography as Harry had described it; she only knew how good it felt when she was in her zone.

'You're frowning.'

'Am I? I'm thinking. I mean, I'm very flattered. Thank you.'

'But? I can draw up a contract or something if you want.'

Marnie bristled. 'No, that's not what I'm thinking at all. I'm just surprised.'

'Look, I don't know how the timing of all this would work, to capture the works at Pocket and a few at my workshop. Or when you're heading back to Melbourne.'

Marnie thought she saw something resembling hesitation flicker across his eyes, but he continued, 'It wouldn't hold you up. Not really.'

Marnie's heart slipped a few levels.

Perhaps sensing her unease, Harry pressed on. 'I'll tell you what. Meet me at the marina tomorrow about midday and

I'll show you what I'm talking about.' He stood up, placing a warm hand on her shoulder. 'I'd love to work with you, Marnie. I'll see you tomorrow, and be sure to bring your camera too.' He faltered for a moment, then was gone.

Marnie turned and watched his confident stride and realised this was a man who gets what he wants. He had presumed she would come, that she had nothing better to do. But then he had waited a nano-second for her to refuse and she hadn't. What did she have to lose?

CHAPTER FIFTEEN

THE MARINA WAS CROWDED with lunching families and couples, dogs being walked and visitors waiting for takeaway fish and chips or the ferry. Marnie wandered through the crowd towards Harry's boat where she presumed he meant them to meet.

'Good, you're here.'

Harry was right behind her, two takeaway coffees in hand. 'Hold these and we'll get going.' He flashed a delicious smile as he helped her onto *Starlight*.

'Here you go, Harry.' Marnie turned to see a fellow on the deck holding a cooler.

'Thanks, mate. Would you mind just putting it down in the corner there?' Harry pointed, and then turned his attention back to Marnie.

'Where are we going?' Marnie asked.

'I offered to show you my etchings. Ah, I mean my works in progress!' Harry replied. 'So, unless you tend to get fatally seasick, we are to set off on the high seas to my workplace. Not really. It's only about fifteen minutes around the bend. Take a seat.'

Marnie settled into the rear of the cute little boat while Harry cast off. As he steered, she passed him one of the coffees, enjoying watching his confident yet gentle, manner, his focus on what was at hand. His profile was casual, his leg muscles rippling with each change in position. Marnie was relieved she had dressed casually – it was a meeting of sorts, but she was confident her linen shorts, T-shirt and chunky jewellery were more than suitable. Harry's style obviously always ran to Ray-Bans, islander shorts and loose shirts with the sleeves rolled up.

He seemed to sense her watching him and glanced over his shoulder. 'Everything okay over there?'

'Absolutely. What kind of boat is this?'

'This boat is my baby,' Harry replied proudly. 'Thirty-two-foot Gentleman's Cruiser. Displacement hull. Solid teak cabinetry and floors. The boat is Huon pine…'

Marnie let the details float over her. Literally. She sat comfortably in the shade at the back of the little boat, a brisk breeze keeping the heat at bay. It was so calming, sipping her coffee and watching a range of birds swooping silently over the water. A huge pelican glided past, then did a flyby back again, higher and higher to perch on the top of a pole. She laughed at its efforts to fold its legs underneath and nestle down.

'They're amazing, aren't they,' Harry said.

He seemed to know exactly what she was thinking.

'Some mornings there are over a dozen out here, all jostling for position. They can get very territorial.'

'Do you study birds and nature a lot? For your sculptures?' She remembered an earlier comment about using animal characteristics in his creations.

He nodded. 'Of course. I'm into detail like you. Well, to a point – it's part of my architecture background, which is a good and a bad thing. I try to inject a certain artistic licence to proportions to soften things up. But it's still important to really know a species, how it moves and its personality.'

Architecture? That's new.

'There's that frown again. It's true. Bossy, fussy, gentle, dreamy … all the traits humans have can be seen in nature. Except for them it's for survival. Like those turtle sculptures you were looking at. Those little guys have to survive a lot of predators and a long swim, sometimes as far away as Chile. I like to think my versions combine their cuteness with their strengths.'

A comfortable silence accompanied them as they cruised along the river, until Harry announced their arrival.

Marnie hadn't noticed *Starlight* steering towards the bank. A jetty jutted out into the river like a finger beckoning them in. A giant stone pelican sculpture stood proudly at its point. To one side was an open boathouse, painted a dark green and lined with a collection of paddleboards and kayaks. Another riverboat sat inside. Harry idled alongside the jetty and threw up the rope, then turned off the motor and held out his hand for her. The image of him helping her neighbour out of *Starlight*, their laughter as they wandered into her house, flashed into Marnie's mind. She would need to be careful of this man and his charms.

The breeze had abandoned them at the bend, replaced by a steamy silence. The soft nudging of *Starlight*'s fenders against the jetty, a background rustle of pandanus leaves in the wind, and the odd call of a bird as it flew by were the only sounds that drifted over her. Marnie flicked her eyes around, feeling they were quite possibly the only two people on the planet.

'What's this area called? It's magical.'

'Apart from paradise? It's Petrie Island. Named after an explorer, I believe.'

'It's an island?' Marnie was finding it hard to get her bearings. As Harry secured the boat and unloaded the cooler, she turned back towards the river, which she now realised meandered in both directions. Along either side of the jetty appeared to be bush, again stretching for miles then curving away in the distance.

Harry followed her gaze as he wandered to her side. She could feel the whisper of his body near hers, his breath as he turned to speak to her.

'The river flows around both sides of the island, then joins up on the other side before continuing on its way. There are a lot of mangroves and everglades farther along, which are so unbelievable. You should take your camera there on a still day because the reflections across the water surface are really breathtaking. Anyway, walk this way and keep your eye out for snakes on the ground and koalas in the eucalypts.' He gave her a challenging wink as he lifted the cooler and sauntered just ahead of her down a smooth dirt path.

Marnie started as the word snake registered, much preferring to see a koala in the wild. But her eyes were drawn to Harry as he led the way. The sight of his broad back, tanned muscular legs, taut arms effortlessly carrying supplies, and hair blowing in the wind wasn't bad scenery at all.

As they meandered farther from the river the spindly undergrowth started to thin, replaced by lush foliage. Large frangipani trees, poinsettias and poinciana trees formed a green avenue. Lizards and geckoes scuttled away underneath them into the grasses. Along with the promise of a breeze came the unexpected deep chiming of bells. Marnie was delighted to see elongated bamboo and metal wind chimes, interspersed with unlit lanterns, start to appear. They were hanging from tall iron archways on either side of the walkway, like a secret tunnel leading who knew where. The taller trees eased back, unveiling smaller palms and lush bromeliad gardens. At the sound of water splashing she peered ahead beyond Harry, her curiosity answered as she turned a corner.

Marnie stopped in her tracks. 'Wow! Who needs to go farther upriver when you have everything right here?'

The lagoon was a melting pot of every green toning that had ever been mixed and stirred by painters around the world. Overhanging branches kissed the surface, sending gentle ripples to the sandy edge. As Marnie walked farther she found the source of the splashing – a waterfall cascading between ferns down the side of a glistening rock face and into the lagoon. A small water dragon languished on one of the warm rocks, a soft spray from the waterfall drifting across his body, catching her eye. She reached for her camera.

'Come on,' Harry urged. 'I'm getting hungry. There'll be time for some shots later. I'm presuming there's no swimsuit in that satchel of yours.'

'Very funny! Did you bring a picnic? You should have told me, and I could have picked up something from Nest.' Marnie turned back to him, her gaze following the path up a slight incline to where it circled a huge turquoise swimming pool. The sense of tropical luxury, of peace and tranquillity, was overwhelming. A deep veranda browed an L-shaped Balinese-style villa, which towered over a smaller but no less exotic building off to one side. Hardwood walkways interspersed with frangipani trees gave them connection.

Marnie, aware her mouth was probably gaping in awe, dragged her mind back to Harry. 'Sorry, what was that?'

'Take a seat. I'll rustle up something to eat and drink and then you can check out my studio. Okay?' It was fleeting, but she had seen in Harry's expression acceptance of the impact such a beautiful location must always have on a visitor. But there had been a quick searching of her face, the need for Marnie to like it too.

With long strides he set off towards the villa. She sauntered over to the crystal-clear pool, trailing her fingers through the cool water. Butterflies flitted above the surface, then darted into the surrounding trees. She shaded her eyes, doing a complete circle. Crisp muslin curtains billowed softly from several of the villa's windows. They wouldn't be misplaced in an article on India Hicks.

An oversized market umbrella drew Marnie into its shade. She plopped into one of the deep wicker chairs that surrounded a huge dining table, grateful for the opportunity to gather her thoughts. *So Harry uses Pocket, a beautiful studio amidst bushland, to showcase his works, and he has the opportunity to create his pieces in this lush paradise.* It certainly would inspire anyone.

Her eye flicked in and out of potential camera angles; the edge of a marble sculpture against bright blue water, droplets hanging from huge banana leaves, the slow blink of a lizard's eyelid.

'Penny for your thoughts.' Harry stood above her clutching a metal bucket stuffed with ice. He withdrew two frosty glasses containing lemon slices and clear liquid, then a bottle of chilled tonic. 'I hope G&T is okay. It's a bit warm for wine but I have some if you prefer.'

'Thank you, this is perfect.' Marnie sighed, instantly drawn into his aura. 'I was just thinking how inspirational, and distracting, actually, it must be to work here. It's so quiet and you have nature at your doorstep. You can just holler up a gecko as a model. Cheers.' She took a long soothing sip of her drink. 'Who else is here?'

'Cheers. I'm the first to admit it's pretty special. Most of the time it's just me, but there are gardeners and a cook sometimes.'

Marnie observed his lips touch the glass, the liquid slowly being swallowed. Harry placed his glass beside hers and said, 'You sit there and I'll be back in a minute.'

Marnie wondered if Harry rented the studio from the island's owner and if it was the same owner Samantha had mentioned in Pocket. Or perhaps it was some sort of a resort if it had staff. She saw him step out of the villa, then he turned and headed back in.

'Now we're in business. I left my sunnies inside.' He emerged, carrying a platter piled high with fresh tropical fruit arranged around a whole pineapple, and a loaf of chunky olive bread.

Digging into the icy cooler he added, 'I hope you like seafood. I ordered this at the marina before we left.'

Marnie's stomach grumbled when she saw the spread of freshly cooked king prawns, lobster discs and shucked oysters. Somewhere in there she could smell basil and coriander.

'Cheers again.' They clinked glasses, each holding the other in their smiles a second or so longer than either had planned.

Marnie didn't know what to say. Sensing her surprise and reluctance to hastily dig in, Harry handed her a plate, napkin and fork. 'Through that central entrance you'll find the kitchen and living areas and bathrooms. My area is out the back. In that side wing are the guest rooms. The whole island is about seven hectares.'

'You live here?' Marnie paused, her lobster laden-fork halfway to her mouth. She didn't want to pry any further into his private life but couldn't resist knowing more about this mystery man.

'Sure.' Returning to his gin and tonic, Harry didn't elaborate.

'And are they all made by you?' Marnie nodded at the wooden and stone sculptures scattered around the pool and across the terrace and gardens.

'No, not all of them. Some came with a designer.' His dislike for that part of the island's décor was obvious.

'Indonesian architecture seems to be a big influence up here,' Marnie offered. 'I like the old Queenslanders. You know wood floors and cool verandas, but they all seem to be being pulled down.' Marnie dipped a prawn into the aioli and popped it into her mouth down to the tail. It was delicious.

'There is a place for development, but I agree with you. The Queenslander houses were built like that for a reason. You know, off the ground for ventilation and to keep the bugs out. Floodwaters flowed underneath too. But for some reason people think that the thatched look means resort-style and is more appealing. Carved timbers, lush gardens, meandering pathways, mosquito nets and sandalwood will always transport you to somewhere else, I reckon.'

'Have you spent time in Asia?'

'Sure.'

Marnie laughed. 'Not me. I wish I had gone backpacking when I was young or lived overseas for a while after uni. All my travel was during my marriage.' She hesitated, then added, 'In fact, my son is off to see the world soon.'

'You have kids?' Harry stared at her over his glass. Condensation dripped off the base onto his shirt like tears.

'Yes. Claire and Oliver. They both live in Melbourne. We, Philippe – their father, that is – and I are divorced. And you?' Marnie held her breath, waiting to be told he was married.

'Yep, divorced. But all good. I get to see my stepson Jake. He's a great young man. And Angie and I still get on really well.' He shrugged, not elaborating further.

Harry settled back in his chair, his full attention lasered at Marnie. 'So, university. Did you do photography or visual arts or something?'

'Heavens no. A traditional old Arts Degree, then Marketing.' Marnie relaxed in the warmth of his eyes, then followed a chunk of pineapple as he guided it to his parted lips.

'If I had my time again, I think I would have loved to have been a photo journalist. You know, combine writing and photography. I would've needed to be loads more adventurous on the travel front than I was, I admit, but I reckon I could have done it.'

'Of course you could have!' Harry nodded and clapped his hands together.

Marnie was taken aback by his show of confidence. Harry hardly knew her – could he possibly see in her the yearning she had buried for so long?

CHAPTER SIXTEEN

'AND WHAT ABOUT YOU, Harry? You said architecture is your background yet here you are a sculptor. Are you on leave or something?'

Harry shook his head. 'No, but sometimes I feel like I am on permanent holiday. Who wouldn't feel like that when you are lucky enough to live and work around here?' He waved his arms wide to encompass the entire island, his love of the area blatantly clear.

He paused, frowning into the distance. 'Now that you've prodded me, I guess I lost my way a bit with architecture. But a lot of things changed – you know, the need to make money, to suit the clients' wishes rather than my own. Also …' Harry's voice dropped and Marnie had to lean forward slightly to hear him. 'Also, a few things happened with the business that I wasn't happy with, so I took a break. I still have a hand in the company's planning and sourcing, but my life is certainly different to how I envisaged my future. Happily so. Well, that was a long answer to a short question, wasn't it?' He turned away, looking apologetic.

She wished she could see his eyes to gauge his comment, but she could only sense that the topic was closed.

Harry refilled their glasses as Marnie turned her attention to the fruit. Rivulets of melting ice trickled to the edge of the plate, their job of keeping the food fresh done. Delicately she spiked chunks of pawpaw, fresh pineapple, and halved kiwi fruit while Harry bit into bright red strawberries.

Marnie picked up a mango, then, too late, realised she didn't know what to do with it. She glanced questioningly across at him.

Harry started to laugh. 'You haven't eaten many mangoes in your life, have you?' He picked up a small knife and another golden 'egg'. 'Slice off the cheek, then cut the flesh in a criss-cross pattern like this. Then gently bend it back. Voila! Tasty little cubes of mango to suck off.'

Sitting on the edge of her seat, Marnie took the mango from Harry, aware of how he had moved his chair closer to hers. She took the mango cheek and tried to prise off a cube between her lips, only to manage a slurping sound. Embarrassed, she scooped them off with a teaspoon onto her plate and then popped the juicy morsels into her mouth one by one. Harry propped his sunglasses on top of his head and watched.

'Of course, that's not the best bit of a mango.'

She loved how his eyes crinkled at the corners when he smiled. 'And what might that be?' she teased.

Harry took up the remains of the cut mango and hacked into it, leaving chunks of flesh clinging to the large seed. He passed it to Marnie.

She pressed the cold, wet seed to her mouth, its juices running freely down her arm. Unable to delicately bite any of the flesh and not wanting to repeat any slurping, she opened her mouth … and sucked.

Harry sat back in his chair, grinning.

She smiled back, immediately regretting it as pieces of mango came away from the seed and dripped onto her chin. Harry picked up one of the paper napkins. Gently he ran it up her arm, catching the yellow rivulets of juice, and then took the seed from her sticky hand. Marnie ran her tongue around her lips. Harry leaned in, his hands firmly on the arms of her chair, his legs spread either side of her exposed knees. He took off her sunglasses, folding them onto the table, his eyes locked on hers.

Harry kissed her mouth. He tasted of cool gin and hot intent. Encouraged, he gently licked her lips until all the juice had gone. The touch of his finger at the base of Marnie's throat as he caught a wayward drop sent a chill up her spine, despite the day's heat.

'I told you that was the best bit.' His husky voice vibrated around her.

Marnie opened her eyes. What was happening here! Her legs were weak, her arms flopping on the arms of the chair. The island seemed to hold its breath, the stillness allowing notions of what could come next to hang in the air.

Marnie cleared her throat. 'I might actually need to find that bathroom, Harry. I feel a little, actually very, sticky.'

'Straight through to the back.' He pointed, a hitch of disappointment in his voice.

Marnie found her satchel and headed inside, feeling Harry's eyes following her every step. Her mind was zigzagging, and she knew it wasn't completely to do with the gin; she was lightheaded, surprised and wary.

Heat radiated from her core out to her fingers and down to her toes. Marnie put it down to a combination of Harry and the sun. She could still feel the sweet tingle his lips had left on her own.

On entering the villa, she stopped short. Not only from the welcome drop in temperature, but because it was like walking into a luxurious Caribbean summerhouse. It was stunning. Huge paddle fans rotated lazily amongst rattan lights which were on, despite it being daylight. A golden glow filtered across the room.

She wound around cushion-strewn daybeds and giant indoor plants, across richly coloured rugs. A double wood and brass door imposed at the end of a corridor. Marnie presumed it was Harry's domain and would have loved that door to have been open a crack so she could peek through, but it was firmly shut. Her mind could well imagine the comfort and style hidden there, and the intimate moments the walls would have witnessed.

With a sigh, Marnie hunted down the bathroom instead. More clean finishes with floral accents on pretty urns and chairs welcomed her. She washed the last of the sticky mango from her face, neck and arms with a soft gardenia-scented lotion.

Her mind raced through what had just happened – did Harry have an angle? Libby's accusing voice forced its way in: *Why do you always have to analyse everything, Marnie?* Because there could be no avoiding the point that his kiss had surprised her, but no more than her instant acceptance of it. It had just seemed right.

Marnie couldn't summon any ground-breaking answers as to what to do next. Harry had said he wanted to show her more of his work. That's what she would do when she returned to him – find out more about the job. She poked around trying to tame her hair, redid a slick of lip gloss and walked out. She could hear activity from across the living area, so she followed the sound into the kitchen where Harry was putting away the leftovers. It seemed the villa caught her out at every turn as kitchen envy tripped her in the doorway.

He turned and leaned on the edge of the marble bench, a tea towel slung over his shoulder. Marnie paused at the spark of wariness in his eyes as he said, 'It's getting a bit overcast outside. I brought your camera in. It's over there on the sideboard.'

He walked towards her and was about to brush past her, but stopped. 'Are you okay? I planned to show you my workshop.'

Marnie couldn't quite read him, the space between their bodies wavering like negative magnets. He seemed eager to move on with business. 'Of course, let's go,' she said, a little too perky even to her ears.

CHAPTER SEVENTEEN

HARRY'S long strides were a challenge to match as they made their way along one of the narrow boardwalks. Her senses were overrun with the peaty smells and contrasting sights of the thick but beautifully maintained gardens. Marnie glanced at the unsettled sky, feeling the humidity building by the minute, a sure sign of an impending downpour. Before too long there would be the wonderful smell of fat raindrops on the hot ground.

Harry's workshop was hardly a crumbling work shed, but rather a pristine open space. It showcased architectural influences, a nod to his background perhaps, so she shouldn't have been surprised. Works in progress stood alongside completed sculptures. Some were in pieces, to be assembled on site at the studio or a client's home, presumably. Shiny steel storks stood guard around one wall, stone plinths waiting to be adorned lined another; a large copper dolphin was propped in a corner next to a shelf of a dozen or so turtles of various sizes. Hundreds of Harry's tools of the trade lay scattered, but Marnie was sure they all had their place.

Her eyes darted across surfaces, around corners and along various creatures' bodies.

She turned to see Harry watching her intently. There was something in his expression she couldn't read. 'Harry?'

He quickly shook it off, his wide smile back in place. 'So, this is where it all happens,' he said, turning in a circle. With a quick glance back at her he tentatively continued. 'Indulge me a moment, but let me tell you I'm excited by how my work is evolving, Marnie. I'm going beyond the expected birds and fish and experimenting with other forms and materials. Unfortunately, people still want birds and fish, but I thought if I could get some of my other ideas out there, I might make a greater impact.'

He paused, seemingly reluctant. 'That's where you come in.'

The wind whipped its way into the room, sending dust ghosts scurrying across the workshop floor. Harry went swiftly to close the door. It was quiet for a moment as the room around them took on a role of cocoon, warm and safe. Slanting rain started to knock at the glass windows. Marnie glanced nervously out at the storm.

'It'll pass soon. I saw it on the radar.' Harry added, 'I wouldn't have brought you here if we couldn't get back safely.'

Marnie nodded, liking his words. 'So, where do I fit into your plan? Your work plans, I mean.' She couldn't allow herself to assume anything after just one mango and a delicious kiss.

'Well, you saw my new little creation. *Under the Milky Way*. I had already created a version of them, a twenty-piece commission for Galaxy Records in the UK. But that's only a tiny part of what I've got planned. I want to do so much more. I have this thing for wings at the moment. Look over here.'

He went behind a wall and brought back a pile of butcher paper. As he unrolled the sheets onto a large concrete table, Marnie could see they were 3D drawings of angels.

For a moment she couldn't speak, just run her hands over the paper. Wings, faces and full angels were drawn in immaculate detail. Some were brooding and dark, others ethereal or cherubic; each one unique, yet all stunning. Marnie couldn't pull her eyes away from them.

'Oh, Harry. They're incredible.' She wasn't sure if she actually meant the angels or Harry – it seemed there was nothing the man couldn't do. *He can sculpt, surf, whip up a great lunch and sketch angels as though he has them sitting on his shoulder whispering in his ear.*

'As I mentioned earlier, I need someone, you, to photograph what I'm doing. I've been approached by a gallery in Brisbane to do an exhibition. There is a sister gallery in New York, so who knows where it could lead.'

Marnie could sense his bubbling excitement. She quietly got out her camera, adjusted her light settings and took a few practice shots as he talked. 'Keep going,' she urged. 'Pretend I'm not here. Lay your hands on the drawings for a moment.'

Harry outlined to her what he needed: detailed but imaginative photographic representations of his drawings and finished pieces that captured his love for his work and passion for its future. They would form a core collection for Samantha's publicity machine – business cards, backstory fliers and media releases.

As Marnie clicked away, Harry dragged out a prototype of his angel wings and set it on the table. He became lost in his own world of creation, outlining what the wings would become, frowning to himself as he suddenly thought of another way of making it better. Marnie lowered her camera and watched him: how his body moved with such strength and speed around the table, how his hands rolled in explanation, how his eyes came alive with such love and commitment for his craft.

Torrential rain hammered the roof and windows, but Marnie couldn't drag herself away from Harry and the force of his vision for the future. She had to admire that.

'So, what do you think? Will you do it?'

Marnie didn't want to sound ungrateful, but she also had to quell any suspicion that lurked in the back of her mind. She looked him in the eye, daring him to be flippant about his request. About his kiss. She was trying to disconnect the two.

'And what about Samantha? I mean I presume she's your assistant or something. Won't she …'

Harry held up his hand. 'Samantha is the sister of a mate of mine and is only visiting from the States. Her life is embedded in the arts world there, but ask her to pick up a camera and she doesn't know a tripod from lens.'

Harry propped himself on the edge of the table. 'I have to admit I don't easily let people into my workspace. Either physically or mentally. These days I prefer to go it alone if you like, without a lot of external judgements.'

Marnie was unsure if that was another reference to his other business life. She was still torn.

'And so you lured me here to see these wonderful pieces so I couldn't possibly say no?'

Marnie had meant to say how drawn she was to his idea, but just being around this man seemed to set her nerves on edge. They had got the better of her, and her words had come out harsh and critical. She wished she could take the comment back when she saw his eyes darken.

Marnie started to speak when Harry's cell phone interrupted, and he excused himself.

Cursing her use of words, Marnie strolled around the workshop. It had stopped raining in true tropical fashion – as suddenly as it had started. Marnie turned on her camera and lost herself in catching just the right aspect; the powdery dust that had settled on the sculptures, the sharp edges of Harry's tools, the mix of new and well-used. She felt enlivened, as if his creativity and the studio were sparking her own passions like a lit match igniting another. Butterflies in her stomach told her she was on the right track. From the corner of her eye she caught the tip of a wing peeking from under a cover sheet. She had just lifted the corner for a closer look when a gust of wind through the door made her slap it back down. She knew guilt was her aura as she spun around.

'I hope that means yes,' Harry remarked. He was leaning in the doorway, arms crossed, observing her. He looked sexy, assured, and had obviously moved past her earlier comment.

'You tell me. They're only trial shots, remember, and I'll need a tripod, but you get the idea of the direction we could take. Plus, we will need a few profile shots of you for any exhibition programs. Professional, you know?'

'You mean all sweaty and serious?'

Harry strolled over. Gently he took her camera and laid it on a clear corner of the bench. He stepped up to Marnie, so close she could almost hear his heart beating. His eyes scanned her face as though looking for a welcoming word, a sentence, to be written there. Her mind raced with possibilities, her body only a step behind.

Marnie jokingly dusted his shoulders. 'I'll have to think about the dust. You can't look too "country". But then, maybe a bit around the biceps wouldn't hurt.'

Harry eased her back against the table.

'Or in your hair to give you that "little boy" appeal.' She smiled, splaying her fingers through his hair. What had happened to her earlier warning – to go slow with this fellow?

His arms shot around her waist, pulling her against him. Marnie gasped at his strength as he kissed her, hard and direct. It would seem that licking mango juice had been only teasing.

He broke away. 'It's raining again. Pouring, in fact.' His voice was low and quiet.

'We'd better stay in here then.' Marnie nodded seriously. Her heart was tumbling over itself in her chest.

'Only if you want to,' Harry replied, searching her eyes. 'I could fetch an umbrella or a giant banana leaf, and we could make a break for it.'

'I'd rather keep dry with the angels,' Marnie said, glancing around. It seemed heavenly to her. She cleared her throat. 'You haven't looked at my photos.'

'Oh, I know they're what I'm looking for,' he replied abruptly.

Marnie tried not to read too much into his words, tried not to judge his intentions. She gave his lips a light kiss, needing to be cautious. 'You know, Harry, I admire your confidence, but I hope you can take on others' input and bend a little when needed.'

'Do you think I'm arrogant?' He frowned, taking a small step away from her.

Harry's phone gave an unusual ping. He dug the phone out of his back pocket as he held Marnie's gaze, then quickly scanned the screen.

'Well, it might have to be the banana leaf after all. That's my weather alert telling me there's a larger storm on the way. It's down the coast.' He had moved on from his question.

'I'd better get home to the dog. She doesn't like storms.' Marnie frowned.

'I love storms,' said Harry, unperturbed. 'Nature at her best. It's not a bad one, but I'm always cautious on the water.'

He stood in front of her and kissed her lightly, smoothing her hair off her face with both his hands. 'We'd better go. There will be a good lightning show later, particularly if you face south.'

Was this his way of asking where she was living? It might be an opening for her to find out about his night-time sailing partner. The memory brought her back to reality. As Harry rolled up his 'etchings', Marnie assembled her bag and camera gear. Casually, she said, 'Actually I think Libby's house faces south. It's in Cypress Lane, down on the river.'

'Oh, yeah. I know. A friend lives down that way.' He squinted out into the garden, which was glistening and sodden with rain. 'Are you happy to make a run for it? I'm sure the rain will stop for a moment before the next shower comes through.'

Marnie nodded. She was none the wiser about his friend, but she did know she was sorry to be leaving the studio and his arms.

Sensing her hesitation, Harry turned and smiled. 'Thanks for coming. I had a great time.' He cocked his head endearingly, as a child would to a party host.

The tension that had threatened to come between them had gone, but Marnie wasn't sure what exactly it had been replaced with. Companionship? The promise of a future? They stood in the doorway watching the slants of rain shoot off the ground, waiting for the onslaught to ease. Beside them, rainwater gushed from the roof down a thick chain and into a drain, leaving no splash. Marnie draped her satchel around the camera case, her shoes in her hand, ready to make the dash when the break came. Harry took her hand, guiding her across the slippery boardwalk and through the gardens. They ducked under laden branches, the soaked leaves funnelling the overflow of the downpour into the lagoon and onto the path. Their shirts were sodden within minutes, sticking to their bodies in all the right places. The air was warm and thick with the arousing tropical smells of the bush as the humidity settled.

The approaching storm tugged and tossed the palms in all directions, but Marnie knew she was in no danger. She let the unaccustomed wildness of the moment take hold of her. They turned each corner as one and ran to the dock – sometimes side by side but then with Harry leading when the path narrowed. The wind chime rods whipped to and fro, tolling their escape.

Marnie grinned to herself. She felt so alive. Her senses seemed heightened to everything being thrown at her, and it wasn't all to do with handsome Harry. Firstly, she had relished the artistic floodgates that had opened for her in the studio, and now the exhilaration of being at the mercy of nature. She had pushed such experiences, such abandonment of responsibility and appearances, to the back of her life for too long.

As they stumbled to the river, they could see menacing basalt-tinged clouds looming on the horizon. The warning calls of crows echoed across the river while the waiting boat bobbed around on the dark water like a cork at sea. Harry leapt into *Starlight* then held his hand out for Marnie. She tried to jump as he had but slipped on the wet step. He caught her easily, gathering her into his strong, wet arms.

'You'll need better sea legs than that, Marnie Fawkner,' he joked. The rumble of distant thunder distracted them both.

'Oi, Harry. Can I hitch a ride back to the marina with you?' A young fellow was running along the dock.

'Sure, Richard. Grab the rope and hop in. Where's your boat?' Harry asked, looking concerned.

'Katie dropped me off this morning and was going to return later, but I think I'd better head back early.' He turned to Marnie. 'Too lonely on the island on my own in this weather.' Marnie couldn't help but wonder if he had seen them through the windows. She glanced at Harry.

'Richard, this is Marnie. Marnie, this is Richard. Richard is an all-round maintenance miracle worker. Did you manage to get that fence repaired on the other side of the island, mate?' Marnie picked up on Harry's emphasis on 'the other side' and relaxed.

They chatted on, *Starlight* making quick work of their return trip. Marnie immersed herself in the changes on the river – the mauve/grey light was taking on the ominous hues of heaviness from the storm. Darker greens and muddy coffee browns contrasted with the occasional white jetty. Along the banks the uppermost tips of tall silver eucalypts swayed in the building gusts, and she recalled Harry's comment about the koalas. Where did they go in such conditions? She decided to watch Discovery Channel a little more.

In the distance the sky now seamlessly meshed with the river in a misleading blur of silver and pale blue, as if it was a watercolour painting. Harry continued to chat to their passenger whilst keeping his focus on the river and meteorology alerts. Marnie flicked windblown branches overboard as they landed around her – she had never felt in safer hands. She presumed the waves would be pounding the shore at Lantana Bay and half wished she could venture down to witness it first-hand. She also hoped Whimsy was watertight, although presumably this was nothing compared with the annual cyclone season. The marina came into view behind a grey veil of rain. They weren't alone as they headed for shelter, with the waterway a hive of activity as boats returned from their pleasure and fishing trips along the river.

The wind whipped around them, and Marnie could see a wall of heavier rain approaching. 'Harry, I'll head home straight away.' She knew she must look a wreck, hot and sweaty with hair like a shaggy mop, but she didn't care.

He secured his boat then quietly took her hand and gave it a squeeze. 'I appreciate you coming, Marnie, and for your feedback. It means a lot to me. Chat soon?'

Chat soon? Marnie couldn't be sure if she had heard correctly, with the wind stealing away his words. But still, 'chat soon' didn't seem the way to end their time together, not after the passion of his kisses.

'Maybe a coffee at Nest?'

'Sounds good. I'd better secure these boats.' He turned to *Starlight* just as the heavens opened.

Marnie made a dash to her car. It was only as the door slammed shut that she remembered the angel wings, still hidden under their cover.

CHAPTER EIGHTEEN

THE SOFTNESS of a perfect sunrise poked its way through the angled shutters as if saying, 'Come on, be a part of the morning. It's glorious'. How special it was that slices of both sunrise and sunset could be experienced just by looking out of her window. The air was crystal clear as though yesterday's storm had never happened or had at least swept the world clean of all its problems.

Marnie stretched, her nakedness finding cool patches between the sheets. A delicious heaviness remained from another deep sleep that she seemed to manage since being in Nautilus Cove. Her drowsy thoughts turned to Harry.

It had been exhilarating to be held within a man's embrace again; to have strong protective arms around her. Being with Harry had stirred a sexual need she had long suppressed. Her girlfriends had laughingly presented her with a neon-pink vibrator when she and Philippe had split. Of course she had used it to fuel her fantasies, but nothing replaced the real thing. Nothing. She stroked her bare stomach, rapidly needing to revisit those yearnings.

Beebs's persistent scratching at the door convinced her to

rise. Marnie tied her new silk robe around her body, enjoying the way it slipped around her curves. A stretch of the river glistened through the bedroom shutters. It was like an unrolled canvas, reminding her of an artwork in Whimsy called *A New Day* – a large watercolour of metallic greys and blues muted toward pink, from a sky bathed in morning light.

No matter how warm the day, Marnie had never been able to endure a cold shower. She suspected she had got a touch of sunburn as her upturned face tingled under the warm water, but it felt good. Her body warmed further as she recalled her conversation with Harry, her emotions and her mind so conflicted by what had happened. The natural thing for her to do was to mentally draw up her list: Had he kissed her as a way of persuading her to take the job – possibly, but then he'd have to follow through, wouldn't he? Could she fit it around her Melbourne life or was this a wakeup call to live a little? Who knew. If she took the job, she'd need to trust him one hundred percent and not second-guess anything. Here was someone who wanted to hug her, kiss her and believe in her talents. Even hold her close when she was sweaty. Surely Harry didn't have another agenda. *Damn it.* Her family had always accused her of overthinking everything, and now she reluctantly realised they'd probably been right.

Her cell phone flashed blue from the vanity, alerting her of an unread message. Marnie turned off the taps and wrapped her towel around her sarong-style and opened it:

Hi Marnie. Thanks again for yesterday. H. xx

The towel unravelled and she gazed in the mirror. At one point she had asked Harry if he did sculptures of nudes and if so, did the client sit as his muse? He had leaned back, a questioning look on his face. 'Are you offering?' She had scoffed and assured him it was professional interest. 'Not interested,' he had said firmly. 'I did do a piece for a local client, but no posing was involved; the curves were very generic.'

Marnie smiled cheekily at her reflection. Bad luck, Caroline.

As Marnie opened her tub of yoghurt, the photos on the fridge door brought her back to reality and the fact that she could no longer put off calling her sister.

Libby's communication from Hong Kong had become more infrequent, with many of Marnie's email questions about the house and Whimsy earning only hurried one-sentence replies. They had had a couple of conversations about the business's website and social media platforms. Marnie had run her eye over them, realising they needed major work to be effective. Libby had quickly agreed to her tweaks, but then why wouldn't she? And then it had been back to silence.

Marnie wasn't concerned for her sister's safety; that was just Libby. After all, wasn't Whimsy's logo a dandelion – blow and see where life takes you. The realisation frustrated Marnie no end, particularly when ongoing decisions were being left to her to make. But she had made a Big One, which she had to see through, Harry or no Harry.

Her call to Libby went to voicemail, so Marnie left a clipped message for her to call back as soon as possible, tossed the remaining yoghurt in the bin and gave Beebs a treat.

Before confronting Whimsy, Marnie enjoyed a coffee at Nest, avoiding eye contact with the delicious-looking Portuguese custard tarts. Eleanor was busy in the kitchen, so Marnie just waved as she grabbed a takeaway coffee for Nathalie. Ten past nine and Whimsy's doors were shut. She took a deep breath and headed over to Threadz.

'Sorry I didn't make it to yoga.'

'Apology accepted along with that wonderful aroma.' Nathalie reached for the coffee. 'Well you're glowing. What have you been up to?'

'I wish! I'm about to take on Laila. If you see fireworks from over there don't hesitate to call the fire brigade.' Marnie wondered if she had bluffed well enough when her phone rang. 'That's the elusive Libby, so I had better go and check in with her first. Bye.'

'Hi, Marnie. The website looks so much better. You obviously have lots of spare time to work on it.'

Marnie could only admire Libby's perennial naivety. 'Libby …'

'Sorry. You called me. What's up?'

'I know it's none of my business. Well, it kind of is because I care. I care about Whimsy and I care that it's your business that you've worked so hard for. Libby, you have to let Laila go,' she said emphatically.

'Marnie. I'm overseas, remember? How can I let Laila go when …'

'I'll do it,' Marnie interrupted. She had to get it out before she changed her mind. 'I'll work in Whimsy and look after it until you get back. Which is soon, right?' Silence. 'Libby, I don't trust Laila. She borrows stock and returns it dirty. She opens late and closes early. She's rude to customers and has Rachel – your competitor, Libby – into the shop for chats.'

The continued silence wormed its way down the line.

'Really? Are you sure? I mean are you sure you're just not being super critical? It's hard running a business …'

For a moment Marnie reflected on her own reasons for being so defensive, for needing to set things right. She knew that at first it had been a reaction to having worked her butt off for a company herself, only to be let go without so much as a backward glance. Was she just jealous that someone as slack as Laila was able to keep a position and get paid for it? Maybe. But deep down she was trying desperately to inch closer to a more level, caring relationship with both Libby and Claire. She just had to give it a go.

'Marnie?'

Now Marnie heard a tremor in her sister's voice, and she wasn't about to stand by for her to be cheated and deceived. Hearing that unusual waver of fear confirmed her decision was the right thing to do.

'Yes, I am sure. I am offering to do this for you although I know very little about retail. But I do know about customer service and attention to detail. It's your choice.' Silence again. 'It's twenty past nine here, Libby, and Whimsy is still not open. This actually makes me rather annoyed. Why don't I go across, open up and see what happens? If and when Laila does arrive, I'll put her on to you. You just have to make sure you pick up the phone. Okay?'

'Yes. I guess.'

Libby certainly didn't sound convinced. Marnie could picture her chewing her bottom lip, a family trait.

Whimsy was open, lights blazing and jazz playing when Laila burst through the doors. 'What are you doing, Marnie? I couldn't get a carpark, but I'm here now.' She threw her satchel onto the counter, scrunching the layers of tissue paper.

Marnie didn't respond; instead she dialled Libby and handed the phone to an irritated Laila, then escaped to the deck. Marnie could see Laila throwing her arms into the air, then general pointing in Marnie's direction told her that Libby had taken action and she braced for the outcome. She didn't have to wait long. Laila slammed the phone down onto a display table.

'Don't bother calling me to bail you out, Marnie,' she shouted as she snatched up her bag and left.

Marnie was grateful there weren't any customers to witness the outburst, but she suspected it wouldn't have worried Laila in the least. With shaking fingers she quickly texted Libby that all was well, and Laila had left the building like a mad hornet. A quick reply of xxx and a plea to keep her updated came back.

She had gone from having no job to running a store and possibly being the go-to photographer for a hot artist. How had that happened? She could always take Harry's photographs after she closed the store, when the light wouldn't be so piercing – that was a positive. And there would be time after Libby returned. Maybe she hadn't properly thought through the timing of everything, which was totally out of character.

HER MORNING SPED past like a whirlwind. Between an endless stream of customers and gift wrapping, she managed to restock the shelves. She checked customer orders for items that could be in the boxes that still sat, unpacked, in the storeroom. To her, they were like ticking time bombs. Only a couple of mishaps on the register had flustered her, but customers had been patient. She was grateful to one lovely regular who ran across to Nathalie for a replacement EFTPOS roll when Whimsy's had run out mid sale. Marnie had no idea where the spares were kept, if there were any. She made endless notes for the end-of-day totals in case it didn't all tally for some reason.

A coffee delivery from Nest arrived mid-afternoon with a heart inked on the lid. Nathalie had obviously told Eleanor that Marnie might be in need of caffeine rather than lemongrass. She felt touched by her new friends' understanding, as if trickles of companionship were filling a space she hadn't realised was empty.

Thoughts of Harry came and lingered sweetly around the edges. So when she looked up to see him propped in the shop's doorway, she thought it must be wishful thinking. His sexy voice proved he was there in body and soul.

'Business must be booming if you're still here at six o'clock.' He sauntered into Whimsy and glanced around the space. 'It's cute. I like it. Mind you, this is a great location in Figtree.'

'Hi, Harry.' She couldn't believe how pleased she was to see him. She quickly flicked wayward wisps of hair behind her ears. 'Haven't you been in before?'

'No. I probably should have,' he replied.

Marnie was about to ask why he should have been in before but Harry got in first. He turned to her, a questioning look on his face. His hands were deep inside his pockets.

'I just wanted to make sure we had a raincheck for that, um, coffee.'

'Of course.' Marnie put on her Happy Face, but deep down she was tossing around the how and when of being able to see Harry as well as following through on his appealing offer, as well as taking on Whimsy.

'And then there are the photographs. Are you still interested?'

'Of course,' Marnie repeated. She suddenly realised he wasn't dressed in his usual casual gear. His light wheat-coloured trousers and loose ice-blue shirt looked more Long Island chic than beachcomber. As he reached for her hand, she noted he still sported his silver and leather bracelets but the overall look was so sophisticated. Where was he off to? She smiled up into his eyes but quickly looked away. Harry had a knack of looking at her as though her whole life was laid bare.

He dropped her hand. ‘Okay, well I’ll be off then.’

‘G’bye. Have a good night.’ Marnie smiled and waved as he left. She half-heartedly shuffled the candle range into presentable rows, unable to ignore the sudden emptiness where he had stood.

Whimsy’s door flew open and Harry strode across the floor. He swung his arm around her waist and drew her into him, frowning down into her surprised face. His lips balanced a hair’s breadth from her own.

‘I need to go down to Brisbane for a few days to see Jake, which will be really nice. He called me for a man-to-man chat. But Marnie, what would be even nicer would be for us to get together as soon as I return. I won’t take no for an answer, despite Whimsy or anything else that may distract you.’

He kissed her hard, running his hand up and down her spine. Marnie closed her eyes, melting into his warm body. He let her go and once again swept out of Whimsy.

CHAPTER NINETEEN

WITH HARRY away for a few days, Marnie was anxious to fulfil her promise to Libby to keep her sister's business on an even keel until her return. Constant ideas for its presentation and possible stock items buzzed around in her mind like a favourite song you can't get out of your head. She was beginning to feel a personal attachment to the little shop.

She was also mindful that it wasn't all fluff and wrapping. It was a small business that her sister had started and nurtured. It deserved attention and care and needed a good return. The bottom line was income and she was determined, when she had a moment, to draw up a summary for Libby. She liked to think there was a business plan spreadsheet somewhere on the computer but wouldn't bet on it. She also wondered where Libby's marketing dollar was spent, if at all. Christmas was looming – how soon did shops turn their attention to that? She knew the larger stores had started their Deck the Halls message weeks ago, which she always found ridiculous as though the next thing would be mistletoe and hot cross buns in the same window. She dismissed the problem – how hard could Christmas trading be anyway?

Whimsy wasn't the only thing on Marnie's mind. She recognised a change in her whole mindset, as though the tropical lifestyle was determined to make her chill out. She was working hard on clearing her thoughts of all negative vibes, which was immeasurably easier now Laila was gone. Without even trying, she had lost a few kilos from all the walking and fresh foods, in spite of her daily dose of chilled wine. Yoga was a habit she was no longer willing to abandon, so each morning she would do her Salute to the Sun, then head to the beach for more. Then it was home for a quick shower, change, a treat for Beebs and back to open Whimsy for the day.

She had purpose again. She had a drive for something that inspired and challenged her outside of the corporate world. And if that wasn't the real her, then what was?

When Nathalie suggested the trio meet over a glass of wine to welcome Marnie to Figtree, Marnie agreed wholeheartedly, intending to treat her friends as a thank you.

'Sorry I'm late, but I've been prepping for tomorrow,' Eleanor said as she rushed into Pork Bun to join them. Don't you both look fabulous! Nathalie, those little scissors are so adorable – you must have an endless supply of earrings.'

The casual little bar had only recently opened, but by the time the sun set there was a queue for a seat. The trio sat at a high-top table overlooking the river and ordered a glass of Chandon bubbly each and the first rounds of tapas: seared scallops with chilli plus salt and pepper calamari. A colony of bats flew overhead, silhouetted against the fading sky as they headed to night-time hangouts. Marnie had been shaken the first time she had seen the creatures. One evening the sky had been nearly blacked out over the cottage as huge numbers flapped past like a silent black cloud.

Nathalie, Eleanor and Marnie clinked glasses. 'Cheers!

Are you enjoying your break from Melbourne, Marnie, or anxious to get back to your friends and family?' Nathalie asked.

Marnie laughed. 'Well, I can't say I will ever get used to this humidity, but at least my skin doesn't feel like a dried-up leaf for once. I'm sure it looks as shiny as a washed plate the whole time.' She paused. 'I'm loving it, which surprises me, actually. Oh, sorry, no offence.'

Marnie realised she didn't have to be on guard when the two women waved aside her comment as if it was a pesky fly.

'I have a lot of wonderful friends down there.' She nodded. 'When Philippe and I split, it was obviously difficult for our friends. Whose side would they take? I presumed they'd remain friends with both of us – separately, you know. I actually lost a couple of girlfriends who I thought were close. It's weird to look back on.' Marnie shivered at the memory of when realisation had set in – she had been unprepared, questioning, embarrassed, then ultimately hurt and disappointed.

'I read once that friends could be for a season, a reason or a lifetime, if that helps,' Eleanor said.

Marnie thought about it. 'Actually, it does! If only to excuse them, but then maybe I'm naïve. It certainly made me appreciate my core group of girlfriends. And I do so value the lovely welcome you've both given me. Thank you.'

She took a welcome sip of bubbly. 'I'm looking forward to seeing my children. My daughter and I have been on shaky ground so I need to work on that. Gosh, I am sharing my past, aren't I!'

'How is Whimsy going? Have you killed any customers yet?' Nathalie smiled. 'Oh, I shouldn't say that. Most of my customers are lovely but you can get the odd one that is a challenge.'

'Really?' Marnie said. 'So far so good. Although I did have an episode with a broken teacup the other day.'

'Oh, the school holidays haven't even started yet.' Nathalie laughed. 'I have to have a No Food or Drink sign on the door now. I don't want a repeat of a strawberry slushy that was spilt all over my wools last Easter.'

Marnie's eyes widened. 'You're kidding me. Gosh. I'd better pay more attention. Today I had the most divine little boy. I was sweeping the deck and he had found a feather in the park next door and started to help me sweep with it. So sweet.'

Ginger duck spring rolls with sweet potato crisps arrived. The handsome, heavily tattooed waiter lingered, making sure their water glasses were filled, hovering over Nathalie's.

Eleanor smirked and raised her eyebrows. 'Right. I'm never coming here again!'

Nathalie laughed, watching the waiter's retreating backside. 'I might have to get a tattoo or three. I'm definitely giving this place a good review.' She sighed. 'That's another thing, isn't it. Well, probably more in hospitality than retail, I guess. But social media is so powerful. You don't dare call out a customer or you get a one-star review with scathing comments. I'm sure it's happened to all of us.'

'It's so disappointing when you've tried hard or the criticism is unwarranted. I had to deal with demanding parents all the time in my old job,' Marnie said. 'I treat Whimsy as if it's my home so if somebody damages it or steals from it, then it would be like having an intruder.'

'You just have to stay polite and firm if a problem crops up,' Nathalie added.

'Yes, polite and firm,' Eleanor said. 'Like with aging parents.' Marnie glanced at Nathalie, who was smiling too, so she presumed Eleanor must know Nathalie's family story.

'My folks are travelling around Australia at the moment,' Marnie said.

'How marvellous. As are these spring rolls – yum.' Eleanor crunched another bite, then continued. 'I don't know if you've noticed an elderly fellow, very neatly dressed, who often sits in Nest with a coffee and cake. Claude is his name. He has early dementia and half the time his daughter barges in to take him back to the nursing home. He told me he just calls a taxi when he gets hungry and comes into the café. He used to go to the fish and chip shop for potato scallops until Nest opened and he discovered carrot cake, so I feel honoured. He's such a cheeky man, still trying to live life to the fullest.'

Marnie's thoughts drifted to her parents and wondered how long it would be before they would need specific care. 'I should be grateful they are still active and on the road, literally. It's called the Sandwich Years, isn't it? When we're caught between caring for parents and being part of children's and grandchildren's lives.'

Another glass of chilled bubbly accompanied by little servings of hot samosas and lemon-scented whitebait arrived.

'Getting back to our shop chat, I won't be here at Christmas.' Marnie nodded. 'Although it might be nice now that I think about it. To escape the family madness that seems to erupt every year with or without Mum and Dad.'

She had a sudden thought. 'Oh, should I be doing something yet at Whimsy for Christmas? Libby hasn't really said anything.'

Nathalie looked horrified; her samosa paused en route to her open mouth.

'You do know that many retailers order the previous February for Christmas trading? I'm sure Libby would have it all in hand though,' Nathalie said, her tone cautious, not wanting to cause alarm.

'How could they possibly know what they need?' Marnie started to panic. Surely Nathalie was right and Libby had ordered well ahead for what was the busiest trading time of the year? Her sister had been in retail long enough to know, but then the meaning behind Whimsy's dandelion crept back into Marnie's mind.

'Well, everyone is different. Most buyers go to the various Australian gift fairs in February and June and order up then for ongoing months, plus Christmas. From what I've seen at Whimsy, it seems that Libby goes more for the unique, locally made items, so she probably orders direct from the maker here. You'll have to ask her. She might keep aside stock for the December/January trade when some suppliers close, or she might just put everything out and hope for the best.'

Marnie put her head in her hands with a sigh.

Nathalie continued. 'I think it's good to wait. Um, you know, in case one of the discount stores brings out copies of what you've paid good money for. It happens.' She flicked her hand in the air as if trying to wave away Marnie's concerns.

'Really? Would you wait?'

'Heavens no.' Nathalie shrugged sheepishly. 'I'm doing my Christmas windows next week.'

'I had no idea!' Marnie whispered. 'There's more to this than I thought. I suppose all the Christmas wrappings and cards must be somewhere in the storeroom or on the way. God, I hope so.' Marnie slumped in her seat, tingles of anxiety starting to spread through her body.

'Apparently Libby co-ordinates some kind of huge raffle for the local women's shelter every year. She asked if I'd donate some puddings, and also coffee vouchers for the women,' Eleanor said.

'Yes, I've donated some kits and vouchers too. Libby organised it before she left,' Nathalie added.

Marnie was stunned. 'Libby does that?'

'Well, like you said. You won't be here,' Eleanor pointed out. 'So it's not your worry, really.'

Nathalie stood to leave. 'I must love you and leave you. If I eat another thing I will pop out of my yoga pants, that's for sure.'

Eleanor joined her. 'I'll be off too. I have an early start in the kitchen tomorrow.'

'It was so lovely to catch up with you both. Thanks for all the retail advice. It's even more reason to buy this round. Who knows what further help I'll need,' Marnie said as they exchanged hugs.

She knew she was going to need mountains of it if Libby didn't return soon. Marnie buried the sudden sense of responsibility of having suggested Laila be let go.

CHAPTER TWENTY

'YOU'RE LOOKING a bit sad and wilted,' Marnie told the flowers outside Whimsy. Why had Libby even persevered with fresh flowers? It was true, they looked divine propped in tubs along the deck when they were first put out, but the endless work involved to keep them that way just didn't seem worth effort-for-return. Or as Ollie would say, 'Is the juice worth the squeeze.'

At least florists had refrigeration for their wares, but Marnie still had a new respect for their expertise. Libby had mostly stocked hardy varieties of greenery but even the eucalypts, sunflowers and glossy sprays wilted in the heat in a couple of days. There was no time to spray, change the water and keep the flowers trimmed, then drag the tubs inside each night. Marnie had despaired as customers dripped their chosen bunch through the store, in spite there being cellophane cones on offer beside the tubs.

Ongoing orders were delivered in changeover containers every week from the Brisbane markets, which in itself seemed expensive. She knew her sister wouldn't be happy, but the flowers had to go.

Full of enthusiasm, Marnie arrived early to tackle the flower issue. She tossed out all remaining stems, rinsed out the tubs and stacked them at the rear of the shop. She would ask if Petal Pushers around the corner could use the leftover tubes and wrapping sheets.

A horn tooted behind her. Turning, she saw Will from the bakery making his deliveries. He tooted again and gave her a wave as he drove past in his restored old Bedford van. He had stopped earlier to help her lift some display stands and introduced himself. 'Will by name, unwilling by nature according to my wife,' he had quipped.

Marnie grinned. It thrilled her more than she could explain to have someone wave to her. She knew it was ridiculous to feel so pleased, but someone had recognised her and tossed her a greeting. A fine dust of belonging settled happily over her as she waved back.

She was also buoyant after her call to Claire the night before. It had been pleasant with her daughter even enquiring if she had spoken with Libby much. Maybe the light was beginning to squeeze into the tunnel.

'Good morning, Whimsy,' Marnie said to the walls as she opened the doors, ready for the day. The message on Libby's fridge, 'What do you pack to pursue a dream and what do you leave behind' flitted across her mind and was gone.

A constant flow of buyers, browsers, questions and orders buzzed around her. Marnie made eye contact, or tried to, and offered a quick hello to every person who came in the door. Her cheeks hurt with the constant smiling. She soon learnt that she seemed to be the perfect sounding board about family rifts and gift decisions. They weren't monumental corporate exchanges, but she found it somewhat satisfying. Perhaps it had something to do with the gentle hum of expectation for Harry's return which seemed to follow her.

Marnie kept her eye on the many children that raced around the tables and realised that if she said hello and made it clear she was watching, they were careful in the store. It seemed that Nathalie was right about not all having such respect, but she tried not to judge; who knew what had happened recently in their lives? Most customers were lovely though and very complimentary about Whimsy and its products. 'Full of soul' was how she overheard one lady describe the store to her friend, and who could wish for a more wonderful compliment?

Sales were steady throughout the day and Marnie was feeling satisfied with her efforts. In a quiet spell she gave more thought to Christmas decorations and added Christmas CD to her seemingly endless to-do list. She had seen some boxes stacked and labelled HO HO HO at the back of the storeroom – she just had to drag them out after hours to see what treasures were inside. Then everything would be in place for Libby when she returned.

It had become too long to wait for a reply from her sister to every query she had, and Marnie liked to take action quickly, so decisions were made. She was sure Libby wouldn't mind the fifty-dollar gift certificate she had donated to the local Surf Lifesaving raffle, or the candle tins that were to go into the Vinnie's Christmas hamper. She knew the gestures would bring little marketing exposure for Whimsy, but sometimes you just had to pay things forward without expecting a return. What had Eleanor said about Libby's community efforts with a raffle? She couldn't quite recall.

It was difficult for Marnie not to keep thinking about Harry, who was due back from Brisbane. She hoped his catch-up with Jake had gone well. No doubt being a step-parent, let alone an ex-step-parent, came with many hurdles, but he had admitted to enjoying a good relationship with his ex-wife and Jake.

Towards the end of the day, Marnie looked up to see two familiar faces peering at her. They approached the counter.

'Marnie Fawkner, isn't it?' one of the smartly dressed women enquired.

'Yes. You look familiar too. Melbourne?'

They both nodded enthusiastically. 'Paula Roberts and Julia Connelly. We did the Italian cooking classes with you at Raquela's restaurant.'

'Yes, of course. How are you?' Marnie now remembered the duo. They had all had a raucous time learning Raquela's secrets of Italian families, artichokes and fabulous pasta sauces. There had been subsequent catch-ups over Chianti, but then life had got in the way and they had parted company.

Silence.

'So, are you on holiday in Nautilus Cove?' Marnie enquired.

'Oh, yes. We come up every year. I have an apartment around at Sunnyside Beach. Julia is keeping me company this trip.'

'Well, that's the best of both worlds, isn't it,' Marnie said.

'And you're no longer at Manning College, are you.'

It took Marnie a moment to register that it was a statement rather than a question. Was Paula fishing for something?

'No, not for a long while now. My sister lives here in Nautilus Cove. She's on business in Hong Kong so I'm helping her out with Whimsy.' Marnie wondered why she was justifying herself. 'It's only for a short time, then I'll be back in the Big Smoke.' She couldn't stop.

'Oh, well. I guess that's a bit of fun.' Julia glanced through the doorway onto Figtree Street, then lasered back onto Marnie. 'You wouldn't want to live here full time though, would you. Where are all the theatres and concert halls? You'd miss the culture surely.'

Marnie reluctantly accepted that it was perhaps a comment she would have made herself not so long ago. She assembled what her children used to call her 'I'm being very patient' smile.

'I do love a performance as much as the next person, but I can't think of the last time I went to, say, a lecture at the National Gallery. I mean, it's all at your fingertips and marvellous but when can you actually get there?'

Paula and Julia cocked their heads on the side like two shocked budgies as Marnie continued. 'There are so many fabulous festivals on here. You must come up for the Culinary and Wine Festival next year. I intend to, as apparently the country's top chefs hold dinners and conduct workshops. You wouldn't believe the buzz of the Cove Triathlon too; it attracts thirty thousand visitors.' Not that Marnie could give two hoots about a triathlon; she wasn't even sure what sports were involved.

With a few more warnings on regional towns and telling Marnie about 'not being able to buy back into the Melbourne residential market', the women pecked her on both cheeks and left for their spa appointment.

Marnie turned to help a young woman choose some jewellery, all the while smiling to herself. Up until then she hadn't been sure if she could actually take the girl out of the city, even for a brief conversation.

'I DON'T THINK I'll call Marnie for a day or so,' Libby said to Rob over cocktails. 'I'd better give her some space, otherwise she'll think I'm interfering and trust me, you don't want to interfere with my sister. I'm sure she is plotting her Libby's To-Do List as we speak.'

Rob smiled adoringly across at her. 'Well, I think it's pretty amazing that she has stepped in for you over the whole Laila thing.'

The other reason Libby hadn't called was that she had only noticed that afternoon that she had omitted to press Send on the email advising Marnie of a large delivery of stationery. She winced at the thought of all the boxes to unpack and price but just hadn't had the nerve to call her. So for that reason alone, she wholeheartedly agreed with Rob and kept the mistake to herself.

'Yes, but I hope she wasn't too abrupt with Laila. I seriously doubt that she'll stay around, which is a bit of a shame because the figures through the bank are really good. And our social media is amazing with so many more followers and comments. She must be doing something right. I should have mentioned she needs to bank the cash more often. I hope she's on top of the flower deliveries. She reckons she's done visual merchandising so hopefully she knows to do the Christmas window too. I'll have to let her know where the Christmas lights are – I packed them away so carefully last year.'

Libby started to giggle. 'Good lord, Rob. I've started my own Libby's To-Do List. What next!'

As Rob took a call, Libby twirled her cocktail with the little umbrella and thought about Marnie being in Nautilus Cove. She felt a brief twinge of guilt at purposely not rushing back to Nautilus Cove. Libby now realised Marnie actually *was* new to retail, and secretly hoped that her sister could now appreciate how difficult it had been to set up and run a small business. Maybe the 'flaky Libby' tag might get thrown out the window.

She had never seen herself as flaky, although her older sister obviously held that opinion. At times Libby just hadn't been bothered to explain her actions, so what had been quite calculated in her own mind had appeared to have no basis of common sense to anyone else. Her practice had always been, 'Why attract others' input when your own was perfectly satisfactory.'

Her immersion in Claire's life was a case in point. It had seemed totally reasonable when Claire had asked her not to include Marnie in their lovely auntie/niece conversations, to keep news of the baby a secret. Libby was good at secrets. From pretending she'd never kissed Marnie's boyfriend when she was sixteen to when she had squirreled away thousands of dollars during the height of Drew's gambling habit, and all the cases in-between.

She didn't lie, she just wasn't forthcoming with details. Particularly with an older sister who was too quick to judge or offer patronising advice. Then when, or more likely if, she was caught out, she could walk away, excusing herself with having learnt a life lesson. She would tell herself that all would be well on the morrow, knowing that others just considered flaky Libby had struck again.

Libby had to admit it was very tiring, though, to live in such a way. Perhaps she needed to make some changes on her return to Nautilus Cove, to offer a couple of olive branches.

CHAPTER TWENTY-ONE

IT HAD BEEN A SUN-DRENCHED AFTERNOON, although Marnie had only glimpsed it through Whimsy's front windows. She decided to stretch out a walk along the beach after locking up for the night. Memories of seeing Laila's mess through Whimsy's doors were hard to erase. She now knew it was a ritual for visitors to do the circuit of Figtree Street before and after dinner, and she wanted them to be greeted by an enticing display when they peered in. Hopefully it would convert to good sales the following day.

The air hung with humidity and the scents of surrounding restaurants doing their prep for evening service: garlic, curry, onion and seafoods mingled with frangipani and coconut sunscreen. It was all strangely tropical and enticing.

Mums and dads with tired children shuffled past her, heading back to their hotels. Marnie used to love that time of day when Claire and Oliver were wrapped up in beach towels after a big beach day. They'd shuffle back for a bath, fish and chips and bed, then she and Philippe would enjoy a cocktail in peace.

Seagulls swooped along the shimmering shoreline as the

sun started to dip over the far mountains. It was like being on permanent holiday. Marnie sighed, recalling Harry saying the same thing.

The curve of Lantana Bay unrolled ahead. She turned and took in the breathtaking view along the beach and stood for a moment, shoes in hand, and wished she had brought her camera. There was only a small swell in the bay leading to quiet splashes as the water rippled and darkened the sand. Several deep breaths later and she felt her whole body relax as it shed the dust of her day.

Shells were scattered like stars along the stretch of sand. Marnie collected a few as she walked, choosing carefully rather than taking handfuls. Wet and sandy, they weighed down her pocket.

She dug her toes deep into the wave-drenched sand, relishing the coolness. The water curled around her ankles. She stepped up onto the firmer sand, then walking backwards she made big arcs from side to side with her feet, like the edge of a doily. She beamed looking at the pattern, realising with regret that she hadn't done it for a long time. Perhaps she could give in to temptation and try a couple of cartwheels.

'Next thing, you'll be doing cartwheels. Or knocking over sandcastles,' an amused voice said behind her.

'Harry!' Marnie laughed at the possibility that he'd read her mind. 'I didn't know you were back. I mean, there's no reason for me to but…'

Harry patted the large rock next to him, beckoning for her to sit down. He was back to his Caribbean-meets-the-tropics look of pineapple-patterned board shorts and loose T-shirt.

'So, how did the boys' get-together go?' The rock was still warm from the day's sun.

Harry shuffled a few inches closer. When she turned towards him, she could feel his breath, gentle on her face.

'Oh, Marnie, Jake's such a great kid. So motivated about life. I love him to bits. He's tossing up what to do with his future but has all these great plans. I'm so honoured that he asks my advice.'

Marnie smiled at him, not wanting to interrupt or to reveal the unexpected hitch of jealousy she had just felt of their close relationship.

'But you know, I'm feeling guilty. I want the world for him, but I want it to happen here, in Australia. Which is wrong and selfish on my part. I'd miss him so much if he headed off overseas.' Harry stopped, frowning. 'Oh, sorry – you mentioned your boy is going overseas, didn't you?' He reached out, placing his hand onto Marnie's knee.

She shrugged. 'Yes, but it seems his mind is made up without my input. Which hurts a bit, I do admit, but hey, I'm sure he's had advice from his father and other friends. I'm happy for him too, of course. New experiences are the best thing ever, don't you think?'

'Heavens, yes. So long as it's not an AWOL sister, eh?' He nudged against her shoulder, leaving his hand where it lay. Marnie felt awkward leaving hers loose between her legs, so she placed one over Harry's. It was warm, sandy and firm. He widened his fingers so hers could fit neatly in-between.

'Have you reworked Whimsy since I've been gone?'

Marnie put on a mock insulted face. 'And what makes you think I like to control things, may I ask?'

Harry's eyes crinkled with amusement. 'Oh, just a feeling. No, really. Are you enjoying it?'

Marnie gazed out across the inky water, feeling a deep calm creep throughout her body. She nodded. 'I am, and I'm not sure why. It's much more exhausting than I'd ever have imagined, but fun in a way. I've met some truly wonderful customers. Do you know I saw a little boy weeing on the mat and all the mother said was "His nappy is full of saltwater – it must have gone straight through"!'

Harry roared with laughter. 'Retail is a very dangerous business.'

Marnie could see the funny side of it now and threw back her head and laughed. She glanced sideways to see Harry's smiling face, obviously enjoying her release of happiness.

She wondered if he would kiss her again. There, as they sat on the shores of Lantana Bay.

A moment of comfortable silence passed as they both watched a bush turkey hop up the branches of a nearby tree for the night. Several more were scratching around in the undergrowth. It seemed a kiss wasn't coming with the next wave.

'So, what are Whimsy's plans?' Harry asked instead.

'What do you mean?' Marnie wasn't at all sure where he was heading. Maybe he was pressing for a commitment to his offer, but she couldn't help but be disappointed at the missed opportunity to explore a seaside kiss.

'I've offered my services to Libby while she's away, but hopefully she'll be back soon. Christmas is fast approaching, and I've got no idea what to do for that in the store. And I want to get back to Melbourne at some stage.' She nearly bit her tongue at how flippant that had sounded. She tried to make up for the remark. 'I mean, it's been wonderful here. But …'

'But?' Harry was looking directly at her, his eyes unwavering.

'I'm a bit in limbo. I have to sell my house and move. And find another job.' Harry was unnerving her with his direct stare, as though he could see straight through her.

'Yeah, you said as much,' he said offhandedly. 'Even if Whimsy isn't available, I'm sure there are other places that would love a woman of your talents.'

'Why wouldn't Whimsy be available? You mean when Libby finally comes back?'

Harry seemed to skim past her comment. 'And of course there's the great offer of a photographic gig with a local sculptor.' He dipped his head, looking up at her suggestively. 'I promise it won't take much of your time.'

'Yes. There is that.' She smiled back.

'Well. I don't know about you but my backside is numb from sitting on this rock,' he said. 'Damned nice view, but nothing we can't see from the studio. I do believe there is chilled wine in the fridge. Shall we?'

He stood and held out his hand. His board shorts sat low on his hips, his salty T-shirt pinned to his flat stomach. He certainly looked fit for his age. She took his hand, not saying a word. The scent of the sea was layered with anticipation and the promise of something she could only hope for.

'Don't forget your sunnies this time,' she said as Harry stood to one side to let her lead the way. The climb didn't seem as arduous as previously, perhaps because she didn't pay any attention to the number of steps; perhaps because her mind was on their destination.

They both stopped briefly at the top, smiling into each other's eyes. The surrounding bush was still and quiet as if whispering, 'Go ahead'. Marnie could barely hear the soft waves below, just her own racing heart.

CHAPTER TWENTY-TWO

HARRY SEARCHED each pocket for the key and sauntered to the studio. Marnie tried to fluff her hair, to tidy herself back into being presentable. Sexy was a long shot. She quickly dabbed her face with a tissue. By the time she ventured inside Harry had switched on a few lights. Soft and low, they bathed the studio in a gentle golden hue. Moments later the funky sounds of Vintage Trouble's 'Nobody Told Me' filled the space.

The hiss of a fridge door closing caught her attention. Harry emerged from behind the front counter and sauntered across the studio.

Marnie accepted one of the extended glasses. 'This is so beautiful. I mean, it's stunning during the day, but at this hour. Wow, I can't quite find the words, actually.'

Harry nodded as he poured the wine into chilled glasses. 'I'm not often here in the evening. Only if there's a drinks opening or something. Hold on a second, I've left the olives behind.'

On his return they clinked glasses, their eyes dancing

across the rims. 'What shall we drink to? The future, the past? Change?' Harry's toast sounded challenging.

'Mmm.' Marnie sighed as the fruity flavour hit her tongue. 'Can you drink to uncertainty? No, absolutely not. It's not positive enough, is it? Even the past is a bit unimaginative to drink to.'

'Really?' Harry's eyebrows shot up in surprise. 'I think the past is a wonderful thing to reflect on. It's the foundation of the future, really, whether it's good or bad. If it was all positive, which is doubtful, then that's great; if not, then hopefully it could lead to change.'

'Ah, that word again.' Marnie laughed.

'Change is good. I've had a lot of change in my life. Some of my choosing and some not.'

Marnie heard a slight catch in Harry's tone, like a sad memory had surfaced. She was about to ask more but hesitated, unsure.

Harry was quick to continue. 'Dreams! Here's to dreams.'

They raised their glasses again and sipped. The wine tasted so refreshing as it trickled down Marnie's throat. She pushed her sensible thoughts of not drinking enough water firmly aside and turned all her attention to Harry.

'After all, dreams are how Pocket got its name.'

'How so? Who named it?' Marnie wondered if this was leading back to his earlier tentative comment.

Harry looked surprised. 'Well, I did, of course. It's my studio.'

'Oh, of course.' Marnie stuttered, embarrassed. 'I guess. I mean I wasn't sure if you owned the studio or rented the space for your exhibitions.'

'Really?' For a moment he seemed reluctant to go on. 'Do you want to sit over on the couch?'

Marnie shook her head. 'If you don't mind, I think this

view is way too amazing to waste, although I think we're losing it now. There's no twilight in Queensland, is there?' Her fingers tapped her side. 'I'm happy here.'

Harry gave a quick smile as though it was the perfect thing to say. He flicked on a switch next to the window and instantly rods of light shot up the gumtrees. Their own reflections were replaced by a panorama of green and silver treetops, the branches and leaves bathed in a soft light. He grabbed a couple of oversize soot-black cushions from the couch and flicked them onto the wood floor. Marnie slid onto one and propped against a pillar as Harry lowered his body close to hers.

Outside a startled little possum scampered across a branch and away into the night. Harry quietly watched it, immersed in his own thoughts. It was as if they were in a treehouse, just the two of them, and anything was possible; Marnie sat quietly, not wanting to spoil the moment.

As though he had come to a decision, Harry sighed. He flicked his eyes sideways to Marnie, took a sip of wine, then began. 'When I was in my early twenties my parents, Todd and Jean, were tragically killed in a light plane crash. They were checking out a possible property to buy in rural New South Wales. My brother – I have an older brother Lewis – and I were brought up on a cattle property; well, when we weren't at boarding school in Sydney. Anyway, suddenly we were on our own.'

Marnie reached out, her hand resting on his bare knee. He paused, running his hand through his hair before continuing. 'Neither of us wanted to go on the land, so Dad's brother, Stuart, bought out our shares of Mitchelton's Run – that was the property's name. Stu and I always got on really well, much better than he did with Lewis. Stu made sure I was able to keep some special pieces from the homestead, which I've always appreciated.'

Marnie was touched by Harry's sense of nostalgia and respect of his family's history and effects. The old club chair sitting in Pocket's office presumably was near the top of that list.

Harry went to take a sip of wine, but lowered his glass. 'When all the business side of things was done and I was heading off to uni again, my uncle gave me a small copper box. In it was a collection of things from the property. A few photos of Mum and Dad and one of a calf I'd claimed as my own when I was young, a bottle of dirt taken from one of the paddocks and a few river pebbles.'

Harry's concentration wavered as he seemed to transport himself back to that time and place. 'There is an amazing river that runs through the property, and when the water was high Mum and Dad would spend the whole day with us swimming and skimming pebbles there. Stu suggested I keep them as a reminder of my past and as a stepping stone, literally, for my dreams. Mum would have approved.'

It had all come out in a rush, as if Harry was relieved to verbalise it. Marnie sensed his lingering pain, despite the time that had passed.

'Well, I like the sound of your Uncle Stu. Do you ever go back?'

'As often as I can, but I would never leave the coast permanently,' Harry said firmly, twisting his bracelets. His thumb stroked the tattoo Marnie had noticed earlier. She could now see the initials 'MR' – Mitchelton's Run.

'Where is Lewis now?'

Harry hesitated. 'Oh, around. Trying to make his millions.'

There appeared to still be some kind of friction between the brothers, but Harry didn't expand further.

Marnie nodded. 'Every family has its challenges, doesn't it. My sister challenges me constantly, despite appearances.'

She saw a quick flash of something cross his eyes, then his expression softened as he glanced down, then back up at her boyishly. 'Anyway, Pocket got its name from the saying A Pocketful of Dreams. It keeps that memory alive for me.'

'That's incredible, Harry,' Marnie murmured. 'Without going all Oprah on you – mind you, I really admire her – she said you should lean into your dreams.'

Harry's focus seemed to turn inward, the silence stretching like a cloudless sky. Finally, he replied, 'Actually, I like that.'

Marnie leant across, never taking her eyes from Harry's, and kissed him. Her lips tingled with the taste of wine and the green olives. She eased back slightly, placing her hand on the floor, the other holding her wine glass to the side.

Harry blinked, his eyes searching hers, all of his attention now on the woman in front of him. He placed both their glasses gently behind him and cupped Marnie's face. His mouth grew harder as it returned her advances. While his thumb toyed with the corner of her lips, his other hand moved behind her shoulders, pulling her even closer.

As their kiss broke, Harry's chest leant into Marnie's, gently easing her back onto the cushions. He kissed her again, on her parted lips, then her forehead and eyelids. She raised her arms above her head, her trembling hands finding relief either side of the cool concrete pillar behind her.

As Harry's kisses explored her neck and collarbone, she sighed quietly with pleasure. She almost purred at the touch of Harry's hand running lightly down the outline of her body. He gently brushed the side of her breast, then continued down her waist and onto her hip as though he was tracing a map. His hand paused. Marnie feared he was having second thoughts, but as she glanced down she saw his lips spread into a smile. His fingers explored her pocket, rubbing her sandy shells. Then he abandoned them, concentrating on the rest of her.

Marnie could hear his deepening breath, cut off as he kissed her again. He gathered her body against his own. Instantly she felt him harden and thought she would die with pleasure. His broad hand stayed against her back, holding her close.

'Hi,' he said.

'Hi,' she replied.

Harry brought his hand around to Marnie's chest, and ran his finger under her chin, down her neck. She tilted her face up to him, waiting for his next move. Someone had told her once that what the eyes see, the heart feels. She knew in that moment how true the words were.

Then several things happened at once. The cushions slid on the smooth floor, knocking over their wine glasses; the breaking glass mingling with the sound of tyres crunching in the driveway. Marnie jumped, her foot sending the bowl of olives skidding across the studio floor. A beam of light lasered across the bottom of the front door. Was it a torch or headlights? She sprang to her feet.

Harry was already standing. 'It's okay, it's probably only the security guy. They do the rounds about this time. Be careful of the broken glass.' He helped to steady her, pulling her to him. 'Ha, you look so guilty.'

Marnie looked into his laughing eyes, wishing she could be so carefree.

He released her. 'I'll go and let him know I'm here and everything is okay.'

Marnie took the opportunity to regroup, embarrassed for reacting as if she had been sprung in the back of a car like a teenager.

She replaced the cushions and went in search of a dustpan and cloth. When she came back into the studio Harry was bent over like a bush turkey, moving around the floor. The sight of him rounding up wayward olives, together with the return of her sizzling joy was too much. Her laughter erupted with abandon, Harry's deep chuckling soon joining her. They came together in the centre of the studio and embraced.

His broad hands pressed her to him. Marnie tingled all the way down to her sandy toes, splinters of glass glistening like scattered diamonds around them. Their moment was broken like the wine glasses.

Harry sighed. 'I'll clean this up, then I have to head out to check on the island after being away. This was an unexpected detour, but what a delightful one it was.'

Marnie smiled and lightly kissed his lips. Where were the on-site staff when you needed them?

Harry stopped by the front desk and passed her a book. 'You must have left this in the bag by mistake with my sculpture.'

Marnie had forgotten about the dusty baby journal she had found in Whimsy.

As they headed out the door Marnie cast a last look at their secluded haven. She realised with some pleasure they had had silent witnesses to their time there as bronze cranes hovered above, and tiny turtles peered across the floor.

CHAPTER TWENTY-THREE

UNFORTUNATELY, Harry was true to his word and drove her straight back to her car. He had asked her about the journal.

'So, have I been kissing a grandma?' he asked cheekily.

'No, no. It's a leftover copy that I found in Whimsy. I don't really know why I kept it except to remind Libby to order more.'

She paused before continuing. Her emotions were all over the place, thanks to him, but she still felt safe sharing the details of her life with Harry.

'I guess I will be in time. Mind you, things can change in an instant, can't they? Just as they did for you when your parents tragically died. My daughter and I were in a car accident. It was actually pretty minor but enough for Claire to have ongoing back problems. We were so lucky.'

Harry stretched his hand across to rest it on her arm.

'The worst thing is, I think she blames me, as I was driving. Since the accident we seem to be constantly tiptoeing around each other. I don't know why, and as a mum I always thought I'd somehow know about things, that I would pick up some cosmic signal. But I can't, and I don't know how to fix it.'

'Don't be too hard on yourself, Marnie. You can't be expected to know every twist and turn of another person, even if she is your daughter. Some things just take time.'

Marnie glanced across at him and placed her hand over his. 'Thanks.'

Harry gave a silent nod, and they sat comfortably with their own thoughts for the rest of the drive to the cottage. As the car idled, Harry leant across and gently smoothed Marnie's hair off her face. He kissed her, wished her good night, then headed off to the island.

EVEN THE NEXT day Marnie's body had been yearning for more. She redirected her energy to a yoga class in the fresh morning air. Nathalie gave her a welcoming smile as they quickly positioned their mats on the hard sand and focused within.

Yoga, the walks with Beebs most evenings, plus always being on the go in Whimsy, had helped Marnie's fitness no end. She actually welcomed the satisfying ache of muscles she had forgotten existed. With every roundabout she encountered whilst driving, she would work on her pelvic floor exercises with gusto. It had been Dee's advice years before: strengthen those pelvics at every corner 'cos you don't know what or, more importantly, who is around the next corner.

Harry.

A large group of surfers were taking advantage of the swell at The Point, some skidding along the tops of the curl whilst others chose to bob on their boards and wait for the next big one. The waves raced to the shore, breaking and running up the sand. Marnie closed her eyes as Paulo led the poses, absorbing the salty air and crashing sounds of the Nautilus Cove surf.

At the end of the session Nathalie and Marnie headed to Nest.

'I have so much to do, so I'll have to be quick today,' Marnie said. They waved to Eleanor in the kitchen and ordered ginger tea and croissants. Marnie added a salad wrap to go. She knew Eleanor would drop a coffee into Whimsy for her at some time during the day.

Nathalie layered her croissant with butter and jam. 'Oh dear, I guess this is really bad after our session.' She took a big bite. 'Do you know there's a Christmas parade along Figtree tomorrow? Around five o'clock, I think. They close the street and you can't get out until they re-open it at six. Which is fine if you want to hang around but if you need to go, I'd suggest you close early.'

'I did see a flyer but didn't think it would be a big deal.'

'It's not if you know about it; there was a very irate bridal party that got caught up in it all last year, the poor things. I'm going to head off early,' Nathalie said. 'How are things at Whimsy anyway? I noticed you wrangling the Christmas decorations.'

Marnie laughed. 'Was it that obvious? It's all done now and I must say I think it looks pretty good. Oh, doesn't it?' She suddenly had second thoughts.

'It does, it does!' Nathalie protested. 'I only meant that it was very entertaining watching you unravelling the bud lights. If only I could lip-read.'

'Mm. I must tell Libby to put them away with more care. Mind you, it's always more fun putting up decorations than taking them down, so I can't blame her. I'm sure she thinks she was being careful but they were just tossed in a box.'

Marnie looked around Nest, which sparkled with Christmas cheer. It was obvious that Eleanor had a Masters in Bud Lights and Sundry Christmas Décor Arranging. The café had miniature Christmas trees in each corner, each laden with green and silver balls. Hundreds of little glass baubles hung from the ceiling on looped strings of forest-green ivy. Nest's window showcased Eleanor's home-baked treats, like a Christmas version of the Easter window from the movie *Chocolat*. Mini fruitcakes, ornate gingerbread houses and shortbreads – in fact, everything for a foodie to give as a gift or indulge in was beautifully arranged. Complimentary tiny iced gingerbread men, like Tiny Teddies, came with every drink within the café.

'When did she manage to do all this?' Nathalie asked as she took in the display.

'I can't imagine, but your window looks so pretty too, Nathalie. The felt bush animals and the embroidered Christmas stockings are all so gorgeous. Don't tell me you did them yourself?'

Nathalie shook her head. 'I have a few local makers who oblige with that. They're not cheap but so much work goes into each piece that I think they're worth every cent. I usually sell out, thank heavens.'

'And not a snowflake in sight. I was so relieved when I unpacked Whimsy's Christmas boxes that Libby doesn't stock anything with snow featured. Not in this little Aussie store! Libby's candle maker asked if we wanted to personalise the labels for the season so I quickly took a few photographs of bright baubles in the sand for her to mock up and voila! Christmas Candles à la Nautilus Cove. I hope

Libby doesn't mind. Gosh, look at the time; I have to dash if I'm to open on time.'

When she hadn't heard from Harry by early afternoon, Marnie was unsure what to do. What was the protocol these days? Perhaps Nathalie would have the answers if she's in the loop of dating. Were they dating? No. Marnie sighed. She didn't want to appear like another desperate middle-aged, suddenly single female. Well, it wasn't all that sudden, but it had been a while.

There seemed to be so much involved in dating; in fact, there were times she felt like she was in a Diane Keaton movie. She had ventured out for a Thai dinner and movie with a fellow she'd met at a gallery party, but she knew by the time the fish cakes had arrived that it wasn't going anywhere. And then there was Ever Hopeful Evan the plumber, so called because he kept 'running into her' since fixing her shower tap. She had no idea how to tell him he didn't stand a chance.

Since leaving Pettigrew's her social life had ground to a halt. Invitations to armchair travel evenings and charity golf days filled her with dread, particularly if they were in the vicinity of Philippe's mother's golf club. Tales of disastrous online dating episodes were fun to laugh at over a glass of wine, but she was sure the actual experience must be awful. Her cousin Jennie had sat through an entrée at a Dinner for Six event before realising it was for those interested in gardening. As she had always been more of a gold-digger than a digger of any agricultural nature, Jennie had spent the time getting sloshed on organic wine.

Harry didn't seem like the kiss-and-run type to her. Marnie had to admit she had kept a sly eye out for any visits by *Starlight* to her neighbour but hadn't spied the little boat. Anyway, what was to stop her having a secret sub-tropic fling to get back in the saddle, so to speak. She had a gorgeous, funny, talented man at her fingertips who didn't seem to find her too dull, so hallelujah. It certainly trounced Tinder or dodgy dinner parties.

As Marnie totalled the day's figures, her phone pinged with a message:

Hope you are free tomorrow evening. Will call you soon. Harry x

There you go – ask and you will receive. Marnie did a little jig on the spot, experiencing one of Libby's Magic Happens moments. She happily plopped her bag back onto the counter and slid to the floor. Leaning against more boxes of unpacked Christmas decorations, she took a deep breath and called Harry back.

'Hey, Marnie. All finished for the day?'

'Yes, thank heavens. I need to be twenty years younger to keep up the pace.'

'I don't know. I think you're pretty damn fine for, um, however old you are.'

'Very diplomatic, Harry.' Marnie grinned. 'How are you anyway? Did you get some of my *Milky Ways* made today?'

'Whoa, cracking the whip, are we?'

Marnie could hear the chuckle in his voice.

'I've become quite the bossy shop manager, I'll have you know. It would seem that Rachel from Posh Pit is telling everyone so, and that I fired Laila.'

'Well you did, didn't you, with good reason?'

'There is that. I just don't like playing politics, you know. And I'm a bit thin-skinned when I'm the subject of the gossip.'

'Well you know what my uncle told me once? If you don't respect a person, then why seek their approval.'

'Ah, wise words.' Marnie agreed wholeheartedly and promised herself to remember the advice.

'I hope you're around tomorrow night. There is a Christmas parade thingo on,' Harry said.

'So I heard. It's the lighting of the huge tree farther along Figtree as well. Nathalie said I should close early and leave before they block the road. But I thought there may be extra customers.' Marnie was thinking aloud.

'I'm with Nathalie, as I have plans for us. And a parade isn't part of it.'

'And what might those plans be?' Marnie relished Harry's habit of hinting and teasing his way through a conversation.

'I figured I would pick you up around six and we could float out on the river in *Starlight* and watch the fireworks. It's supposed to be a warm, calm evening. Then dinner somewhere.'

His plan sounded heavenly.

'Well I am a bit of a sucker for good fireworks. Thank you, that really sounds perfect.'

After reminding him of her address, Marnie sat awhile on Whimsy's floor. The shop looked so pretty with the little pops of lights tracing around the walls like a row of fireflies. As a gecko ran across the wall, Marnie couldn't help but share her joy: Guess what Gordon Gecko? I have a date tomorrow night. With a sexy sculptor called Harry.

CHAPTER TWENTY-FOUR

MARNIE'S PHONE rang when she was half-way home. It was Valerie, one of her girlfriends in Melbourne.

'Hey, Marnie. How are things up north?'

'Val, so good to hear from you. I'm great, thanks. How are you, Steve and the kids?'

'Oh, normal pre-Christmas mayhem. We're going to Steve's family in Perth just after the girls' lunch. You'll be back for it, won't you?'

Marnie had actually forgotten about the get-together but assured her friend she'd be there.

'I can't chat long, but I wanted to run something past you. You did a marketing contract with Pettigrew's, didn't you, after Manning College?'

'Yes, I really enjoyed it.' Marnie chewed her bottom lip.

'As you know my brother has a vineyard down that way too and he mentioned that they're doing some promotional something or other, and they're looking for someone to help. I don't know the details, but give him a call. I'll text you his number if you like.'

Marnie was taken by surprise by the suggestion. She thanked Valerie but remained deep in thought after the call ended. Without a timeline she was unsure how to feel about the possibility, but an offer could prove to be what she needed to earn an income in the new year. She heard the ping of the text as she pulled into the drive.

Before Marnie had a chance to follow up the lead, Valerie's brother made contact that same evening.

'Barry Murphy here, Val's brother. Look, I know this is all a bit rushed, but I believe she has filled you in on a job opportunity. We, that is, my business, Port William Estate, and a couple of other wineries are putting a team together. Val said you've worked in marketing and public relations before and that's the expertise we're after.'

'I have, Barry, but it's been a few months …'

'That's okay. I've spoken with Hilary and John at Pettigrew's, and they've given you the thumbs up. Look, I'm in Melbourne tomorrow. Can we do a coffee about nine in Chapel Street?'

'Oh, I'm in Queensland at the moment. I would love to meet with you but I won't be able to until my sister returns from Hong Kong. Hopefully in less than a week.' Marnie silently cursed her absent sister. 'I'm more than happy to do a Zoom meeting,' she suggested.

Barry said it would be too difficult to peg him into a time, so before Marnie knew it, she had instructions to call Barry as soon as she arrived back in Melbourne. Her head was spinning as he had pretty well guaranteed the job was hers but, for the sake of appearances, she insisted on emailing her resume through.

That night Marnie dreamt of her mother. She was standing, hands on hips in the caravan park, wagging a finger as though Marnie was a naughty toddler. Although she couldn't hear a word, Marnie was able to lip-read oddly enough, as her mother shouted, "The in-love-in-the-sun life will have to wait. You need to get serious and take the job, Marnie!"

As the tinges of sunrise crept through the bedroom shutters, Marnie lay staring at the fan as it idled around and around.

MARNIE ARRIVED at the shop earlier than usual. She regretted missing yoga but knew she wouldn't have had a hope of concentrating. The call from Barry Murphy, together with a due delivery of who-knew-what, wouldn't have allowed any navel gazing no matter how much she needed it. Her impatience with Libby was growing by the minute. She should just ring and recall Laila and let the two of them work it out, but deep in her heart she knew she couldn't and wouldn't.

On the edges of Marnie's thoughts was the approaching evening with Harry. She had to pin him down on a day to fulfil his photography needs but was hesitant in mixing business with pleasure. Is that what it was? If she could have wiggled her nose, à la *Bewitched*, and just skipped to six o'clock, she would have.

It was obvious Libby had a fair amount of product on backorder with various suppliers as boxes and boxes arrived at Whimsy's door. Marnie had only just received an email outlining it all, together with payment schedules. She strongly suspected her sister either forgot to inform her or didn't want to scare her off.

Whilst it was hard physical work to unpack, price and redistribute the items – to say nothing of her ruined nails – Marnie was working on adrenalin and set a steady pace through bubble wrap and spaghetti foam. It had been very tempting to stop and flick through the interior design books as they emerged from the depth of the boxes, but she forged ahead. She had made a good go of it by the time Whimsy needed to open its doors for another busy day.

When railings started to be erected to stop traffic driving up Figtree, Marnie finalised the last sales and closed the doors. Nathalie gave her a wave and thumbs up as she headed to her car as well. Nest was still open, a busker dressed as a reindeer setting up in front of the windows. Marnie couldn't help but be caught up in the village's festive atmosphere as she snaked along the street. Parents in Santa hats and children dressed as elves and fairies chatted and played like they were a part of a department store Christmas window. The expectant expressions on the children's faces as they waited for the parade was so precious.

It seemed every man and his dog, literally, was in town. Marnie was definitely becoming a local if she considered a barricaded street full of families busy and was eager to escape early. What did beckon was Harry's plan to indulge in a quiet evening on the water in *Starlight*. Perfect.

After a refreshing shower that used up a large percentage of Libby's delectable lotions and potions, Marnie took her time applying her makeup, yet kept it minimal. It had been another hot day with the humidity promising to continue into the evening, so she pinned up her curls into a loose 'do' with Libby's little diamante clips. She was becoming more determined to go all out and get it cut short. A new woman for a new year, perhaps.

As she stood in the spacious closet looking at her dress options, the Lab lay on her back in the doorway.

'That's all I need, Beebs,' Marnie teased as she scratched the black tummy with her toe. 'To trip over you and be sprawled across the floor when Harry arrives.' Suddenly, Marnie realised that she didn't know if Harry was to pick her up in his car and drive to the marina or from the jetty in *Starlight*. For a moment she almost texted him to ask, but tried out her new resolution to be more laid-back, and let it go.

The flattering cornflower blue and white silk dress felt refreshingly cool as she slipped it over her head and let it skim over her curves to kick out at her knees. Marnie smiled down at her pedicure – Dee would be proud of her for swapping her usual Burgundy Baroness for Fuchsia Fantasy. Matt silver sandals, a clutter of sterling silver bracelets and understated diamond studs completed her attempt to look attractive and not too 'mumsy'. She hoped she'd be able to get on and off the boat gracefully, then ignored her habit of overthinking. A good long look in the mirror, a light squirt of her favourite Jo Malone Pear & Freesia cologne, a nervous sigh and she was ready. Early as usual.

She checked along the river, then paced through to peek onto the street. It didn't matter where Harry picked her up, so long as he did. She had read that the fireworks weren't due to start until eight, which would give them plenty of time for a drink first. She had never considered whether you can drink and drive a boat. She supposed the limit was .05, the same as in a car. But would he arrive in the boat or car?

Marnie had stocked the fridge with a few recommended boutique beers, bubbly and a crisp Pinot Grigio. She left a Shiraz and a Chianti on the bar. She didn't think he seemed like a cocktail kind of guy. Maybe she should have got some vodka anyway.

Pretending to deadhead a shrub whilst peering up the river, she heard the ring of the front doorbell. Beebs leapt to her feet and ran, tail wagging, to meet and greet. Marnie threw the twig into the garden and raced inside.

CHAPTER TWENTY-FIVE

THE DOOR swung open and there he was. All squeaky clean, pressed and smiling. Marnie beamed. 'Beebs, Beebs! Stop sniffing. Sorry, Harry, she loves visitors. I'm afraid I've been a bit neglectful of her lately.'

Satisfied with Harry's scratch behind her ears, the Lab strutted back inside the house as if to lead the way.

'Marnie, you look wonderful. All ready for a night on the waves?'

'Thank you,' Marnie replied, hoping the waves reference was a joke. 'Oh, sorry. Come in, come in.'

Harry paused in the entrance, with eyes for her alone. Gently he cupped her elbow, leant in and briefly kissed her welcoming smile before strolling past, leaving a soft scent of bergamot in his wake. It was such a signature fragrance that could have been blended just for him; Marnie vowed to find out what brand it was. Despite the early evening humidity, he wore linen trousers, honey-coloured loafers and a lightweight shirt. He had added a couple of Pig & Hen bracelets which sat easily along his wrist over the tattoo; the other wrist was highlighted by a vintage Tag Heuer watch. Marnie wondered if it was another treasured piece from his past.

As he sauntered through to the back deck, he nodded. 'What a great spot.'

'And this is coming from someone with an island workshop and an eyrie studio?' It had come out wrong and Marnie could have kicked herself with the slight pause in his stride. 'I mean ...'

'They are amazing, I'm the first to admit. But I admire all sizes and styles of architecture and homes,' he said, not turning to her. 'Could this have been part of a larger estate?'

Not waiting for a reply, Harry slid easily into the Adirondack chair, crossed his legs lazily and gazed along the river. Marnie moved to him, standing just within reach. She smiled down at him, reached out and placed her hand on his shoulder.

'We could have a drink, if you like?'

'Wonderful. Shall I get it for you?' He flashed one of his trademark grins, half rising out of the seat.

'No problem, what would you like? I have everything; well, except for cocktails, that is.'

'Beer? Whatever you have. Anything cold would be great.'

'Done. Sit there and soak up the view.' She realised he had seen the view when he had dropped her neighbour home but didn't bring it up. In fact, she needed to toss that image firmly into the river. 'Hopefully the mozzies aren't too bad.'

A moment later Marnie wandered back out to the deck with a Peroni, her Pinot and a bowl of pistachios. She placed the drinks and nuts on a small table, a sandalwood incense stick in its holder, and slid into the other chair. Tossing a dog biscuit to Beebs, she explained, 'It's a ritual now. I have an end-of-day drink and nibble and so does the dog. Word must have spread around the animal world because ducks and pelicans are often waiting for me and the bread now. Although someone told me bread is bad for them and it should be grapes.' Hearing herself ramble, she feebly added, 'I even saw two black swans last week.'

'She's great,' Harry said, rubbing Beebs's head. 'I had a Ridgeback until last year and I miss her every day. She got old and arthritic and in the end it was too much for her. It broke my heart to finally have to take her to the vet. Her name was Velcro because even as a puppy she stuck to my side. I still think I see her out of the corner of my eye sometimes. I'm tossing up whether to get a rescue dog.'

Marnie had always had the opinion that someone who loves animals must be a good human being. They had had a small terrier called Minx when the children had been young. Marnie had become chief carer of Minx and had mourned the deepest with the dog's passing, but little Minx had never been replaced. Another example of life becoming too busy.

'It's so hard to lose a pet, isn't it.' Her mind wandered to farm animals and the country life. 'Do you ever regret not going onto the land, Harry?'

Harry laughed. 'No. I was okay with how the sale of the property to Stu panned out after the sheer trauma of losing Mum and Dad. They were such a wonderful couple who loved each other and us kids to bits. But I wouldn't have been able to live the life I do or be in Nautilus Cove with such freedom if I'd stayed. Where there's a will there's a wave.' He raised his glass in a toast.

Marnie couldn't help but feel Harry was being a bit flippant. She wondered if he meant a 'surf wave' or a 'goodbye wave'; if the latter, then what family secrets was he wrestling with?

Harry eased back, his beer propped casually on the arm of

the chair. He stretched and closed his eyes. 'Well, this is relaxing. It's a wonder you ever make it into Whimsy.' He cheekily opened one eye. 'Sorry, Marnie. It's just so nice to chill. It's been a rather full-on week. Physically and mentally. Lots of decisions to make.'

'Oh, that sounds serious. Maybe you should come to beach yoga one morning.'

'Would it fix my pain in the neck?' He winced, reaching around to press his thumbs into the base of his neck. Marnie watched him roll his head from side to side.

'It absolutely would,' she replied, moving across behind him. 'Sit up straight please, Mr Mitchelton, and drop those shoulders.'

Harry straightened obligingly. Marnie placed her hands over his shoulders, feeling the sinewy muscles tight beneath her palms. Her thumbs massaged Harry's neck as her fingers crept along his collar-bone. Gently increasing the pressure, she concentrated on the knots that sat like nubs of concrete under her hands. As she rotated, pressed and massaged, Harry rolled his torso against the chair.

Bergamot mixed with the sandalwood candles and incense floated heavily in the air as the evening became thick with its own promises.

A low groan arose from Harry, encouraging her to be a little reckless for once.

'Is that pleasure or pain?'

A party boat passed, sounds of laughter echoing across the water. As Marnie paused to watch it go by, she felt Harry's hand enclose her wrist. He drew her around in front of him, holding her as he rose in one smooth movement. His lips brushed against hers.

As he cupped her face and looked deeply into her eyes, he murmured, 'How keen are you on fireworks again?'

'Oh, I can take them or leave them.' She had her own Catherine Wheel whizzing in her stomach.

He gave her one of his wide smiles and nodded. 'Me too.'

Marnie felt glued to the deck. She chewed her bottom lip, unable to drag her eyes away from his. Her whole body was alive with a trembling knot of anticipation. Harry waited.

'Have you seen the rest of the house? I suppose not. Would you like to?' She gathered Harry's hand, leading him into the cottage, his other palm giving the glass hearts a nudge on the way past. Marnie eased the door closed behind them. As they stopped at her bedroom door, Harry stepped around her, pulled her gently across the doorway and into his arms. His kiss was hungry, his embrace deliciously firm.

Soft light caressed its way through the plantation shutters into the bedroom. A small part of Marnie's brain registered it was from the large pillar candles left burning in their glass holders; the rest was lost to Harry. Her palms, flat against his back, could feel his strength rippling with desire. Her pounding heart must surely be sending tremors across the river, alerting the universe to her arousal.

Harry's lips took their time in finding their way down her neckline, as his hands gently cupped her buttocks. She heard him whisper her name into the curve of her shoulder. He straightened, breathing hard as he searched her face. Marnie kissed his lips, answering him.

Harry's fingers quickly slid her straps over her shoulders. In her dream world the silk would have eased down over her body and floated to her ankles. But it wasn't that kind of dress and Marnie suddenly visualised it getting stuck on her hips. The corners of her mouth twitched with delight and she lifted her arms above her head, remembering to hold her tummy tight. It had been a long time since she had been with someone and it seemed there were so many things to remember. Harry eased her dress up and over her fingers, then tossed it onto the bedside chair.

Self-conscious, Marnie stepped closer to him. She faltered when Harry took a step backward and shook his head. One of his hands gathered hers together to his lips, then raised them over her head, gently rotating her in a circle. Marnie projected heartfelt appreciation to Libby for having dimmer switches, and to the lady in the lingerie store for suggesting the silver satin and lace underwear. Marnie only hoped that no one was facing their way from the river.

It was a silent, sensual dance that left Marnie in no doubt of Harry's sincere delight in her. Doubts and inhibitions cracked and slid away like an iceberg, leaving only an appetite for more.

Marnie hooked her fingertips under his waistband. Slowly she brought them to the front of his trousers and undid the button. She slid the zipper down. They fell to his ankles as he kicked off his shoes and easily stepped to the side. As they slowly embraced and kissed, Marnie could feel the hardness and heat from inside his Hugo Boss boxers.

Harry took his own sweet time unclipping her bra, sliding it down and away. She arched back with another silent thank you, this time to Paulo for beach yoga pose #6 whatever that was called. Harry's lips circled her nipples. Marnie, from the comments Philippe had made, had always worried her breasts were too small, but Harry was handling them like they were precious jewels. He bent forward, one warm hand cupping a breast into his mouth, as his other hand moved down the front of her panties. Marnie heard his breath quicken as though she had arced his dial up a notch. She probably had. She rolled his boxers down, releasing his length. It stood, rigid against her stomach.

As Harry guided her to the bed with purpose, Marnie

glanced at the shutters, trying to gauge what could be seen from outside.

Harry sighed with impatience. 'Are you going to be this coy when we make love on the beach one summer night soon?'

The thought of them both rolling around in the sand in a secluded cove, hot and sweaty, was too much to wish for. She shut the door on all rational thought and let her body take her forward. She stepped out of her remaining underwear and sandals, swept back the bed cover and lay on the cool sheets. Harry slipped over her, Libby's salt lamp bathing him in an orange glow. He was her own sweet angel.

Harry's lovemaking was strong and determined. He moved his body slowly around Marnie's as if he already knew every centimetre, every crevice. He anticipated the rise and fall of her breathing and her hips, and welcomed both with care and attention. At times she watched him, then closed her eyes in pleasure; but all the while she knew he was gazing into her eyes, gauging her reaction, prolonging her pleasure. Finally, as he towered above her, Marnie took him in, the thrusts of his body tipping her over the edge.

He whispered something soft and low, but Marnie didn't catch his words. She was too busy catching his rhythm of perfect peaks and gentle slides inside her. She lost herself in their lovemaking, relishing every tingling touch, every unexpected move. Harry shuddered as Marnie caressed the line of his back, both of them damp with pleasure.

Exhaustion, exhilaration and something else flooded through her. Marnie realised it was relief. Relief that she could still be aroused by the flavours of sex, that she hadn't closed the door on sensuality after all. A tear rolled down the side of her face, to be quickly rubbed away on the pillow before Harry saw it.

The cracking of fireworks broke the intimate silence. Over Harry's shoulder Marnie could see white lights shooting into the distant summer sky, exploding and sprinkling the horizon. The irony wasn't lost as a smile crept over her.

'What on earth.' Harry gave a muffled sigh.

'Sorry, Harry. Look.' Marnie pointed out the window. 'They're playing our song!'

More fireworks shot up and burst into joyful waterfalls. Harry slowly moved alongside her at the same time a pattering of feet approached down the hall. Next moment Beebs leapt onto the bed, shivering at their feet.

'Great!' Harry said. 'What's next?'

'Oh, she doesn't like fireworks,' Marnie tried to explain.

'Neither do I at this moment in time,' Harry said as he pulled Marnie to him.

They lay together watching the vivid display through the shutters, both too lazy to venture out onto the deck. A gentle breeze curled its way through the slats and across their glistening bodies. Marnie nestled under Harry's shoulder, reliving the exquisite passion she had possessed from his body during their lovemaking. She teased his knotted bracelets, running her finger around the intricately inked MR. He gently stroked her skin, his finger circling each freckle and dip that her body offered him.

After the fireworks were over, Harry rose from her side. She watched him casually pull on his pants, hugging herself at the memory of him being inside her. He deposited the dog outside with a treat and disappeared to the kitchen. Marnie stretched, dimly aware of Adele singing her heart out about something being a million years ago. She briefly closed her eyes, enjoying the floating sensation of post-sex that her body had all but forgotten.

She wasn't quick enough in turning as icy drops fell onto

her exposed back. Harry stood naked and tousled beside the bed with two frosty glasses of champagne and a dripping bottle of Veuve. She hadn't heard him bring in a couple of lit candles, which now added a sensuous flicker to the bedroom and a golden reflection off his body.

The candlelight caressed their bodies as their lovemaking resumed in earnest, shadows falling amongst their curves and along skin slick with perspiration. Neither cared that the champagne sat warming on the floor.

Marnie's body felt heavy, exhausted yet lit from within. She nestled against Harry's length, dozing lightly like a cat in a ray of sunlight, until she sensed a shift in the space beside her. Her eyes flickered, then opened to find him silently scanning her face.

'How's your neck?' Marnie whispered, tracing her finger across his broad, tanned chest.

'I think, Marnie Fawkner,' he replied, looking deep into her eyes. 'What my neck needs is a nice warm shower with a lot of soap massaged in. Then I'm going to raid your pantry and see what I can rustle up because it would seem we've missed dinner.'

'I'll get the soap,' is what Marnie said. *Perfect* is what she thought.

THE FOLLOWING MORNING, they caressed and rediscovered each other's bodies before leaving the crumpled bed for a well-earned coffee. Marnie's legs ached, and she blushed inwardly remembering why.

Harry flashed her a knowing grin across the rim of his mug. 'Not bad for a couple of oldies.'

She rolled her eyes. 'Speak for yourself.'

Harry wanted to take her out on *Starlight*, then to the island but, reluctantly, she knew she had to be at Whimsy. Laila was hardly going to come to her rescue. As her front door clicked closed behind him, Marnie ran her hand down the wood, missing him already.

CHAPTER TWENTY-SIX

IT WAS a hectic day with all the early Christmas shoppers collecting gifts, making orders, leaving purchases for gift wrapping and fretting about their long not-so-festive lists. It was at the back of Marnie's mind to check any emails from Libby; she really needed her sister to come home for so many reasons.

Firstly, although Marnie was becoming more confident in Whimsy, she was still uncertain about the whole supply and demand thing.

Secondly, she needed to head home soon, back to reality, the interview and her future. The fact that this didn't excite or inspire her was unexpected – it would seem that Nautilus Cove, or more specifically Harry, had wound their tropical roots around her more than she realised.

And that was the third thing – or rather the primary thing, if she was honest with herself. What about Harry? How could she spare even a day to take the photos he wanted, let alone spend more time with him, when she was committed to Whimsy? Any possibility that their physical relationship was linked to her taking the job had been pushed firmly into cyberspace. She couldn't deny that her body called out for more, but she trusted him. He not only helped her relax and made her laugh, but he unknowingly encouraged her to appreciate life and herself again. And it felt good. Marnie heard her phone go through to voicemail, hoping it was Harry with their dinner details.

She glanced up to see Nathalie moving through the door, two takeaway coffees in hand.

'Hello, stranger,' she said handing one of the cups to Marnie. 'Caffeine hit!'

'You're a lifesaver, Nathalie. Thank you.' Marnie took a deep sip. She flicked her eyes across to Threadz where a Back in 10 Minutes sign swung on the door.

'Just a tick,' Marnie said as she turned to serve a customer laden with notebooks.

Nathalie wandered between the displays, collecting a few items along the way before making her way back to the counter.

'You're looking very chirpy. What have you been up to?' Nathalie asked.

Marnie couldn't make eye contact as she handed over Nathalie's purchases. 'With street discount for coffees owed, and I've popped a little giveaway bookmark in there too. I'd love to do dinner again soon.' She had no idea when that could be. 'Oh, you have a lady waiting at your shop, Nathalie. It's Mrs Tuttle. She comes in here and buys a card every second day. Such a sweetie.'

'Gloria Tuttle. And it's one ball of wool from me every week but always in a different colour. She's threatening to yarn bomb the street in about ten years! She is such a lovely lady, as you said. Have a good one,' Nathalie said as she wiggled her fingers goodbye.

Marnie headed over to tidy up the gift cards, adjust the

jewellery and give a warning smile to a boy who was flicking the Christmas lights with his plastic beach spade. It was some time before she got to her phone: a missed call from Harry and a voicemail.

'Marnie. Damn. I wanted to talk to you. Sorry, but I can't do dinner. I have to drive down to Brisbane; in fact I'm on the road already. The traffic is horrendous but I have to attend a last-minute dinner meeting. I may even stay overnight down there. Give me a call in the next hour if you can while I'm in the car, but after that I might not be able to pick up.' There was a slight pause before he continued with a cheeky tone in his voice. 'Last night was wonderful, by the way.'

Marnie's return call went to voicemail. 'Harry, hi. I got your message. Sorry you won't be around though. Let me know when you're back. Oh, and yes. Last night *was* wonderful for me too.'

It seemed her evening would be spent with Beebs at the cottage.

A FAMILY OF DUCKS PADDLED, the giant Vs left in their wake catching the reflected mix of coral and pink as if the river was liquid fire. An occasional bat flew overhead and tiny birds flitted across the lawn catching the early evening's insects. Somewhere a dog barked. She could hear the odd car in the distance, and a laugh farther along the river but it was generally quiet in her little world on the deck. She had quickly adopted Libby's habit of setting out thick sandalwood incense sticks to ward off the mozzies whilst enjoying her time outside. She was becoming more like her sister each day.

She would turn on some mellow music inside the cottage

and hum along when a song she recognised drifted outside. Music had always had such an influence on her: Sting's 'Brand New Day' as a balm after hectic days at work, or Florence and the Machine backed up with Pearl Jam to kick-start a marathon cooking session before a dinner party. Music could make her cry – Green Day's 'Time of Your Life', after it had been played at a friend's funeral; or it could make her dance – The Stones' Blue & Lonesome tracks. Steve Perry's 'Open Arms' had been their wedding waltz. Elvis's 'Let's Pretend' described their marriage towards the end, except that Philippe hadn't returned to her. She decided to seek out some new tunes to bring her up to date; to make new memories.

A gentle breeze had broken the day's heat and it tenderly caressed Marnie's bare limbs.

When she had bumped into Harry at the beach, he had asked her which of the local beaches she had swum at.

"I haven't actually been swimming, in fact I didn't bring a swimsuit. Not that I've had time anyway,' she had mumbled.

'Why on earth not?' He had taken a step back, a look of disbelief on his handsome face. 'There's nothing quite like the feel of powerful waves beneath your legs or a gentle swell at your back.'

Marnie had explained she hadn't planned on staying in Nautilus Cove for long, which had sounded totally lame when he pointed out it didn't take long for a dip in beautiful clear water. She smiled at the memory of him waving his arms around as though she hadn't noticed Lantana Bay's beauty at all. She hadn't shared her dread of wearing any sort of swimsuit in public, but then he hadn't been able to keep his hands off her body last night. A warmth spread through the pit of her stomach at the memory.

She was happy with her own distractions: her photography and the routine of setting up her laptop in comfort on the outside table. She worked on building Whimsy's social media sites or called Ollie or Claire in the hope of a long chat. Even repetitive emails and eBills didn't seem so onerous when she could have the calm blue river peeking over her screen. She had even thought of starting a blog, but the exact subject eluded her: 'Fabulous Fifties', 'Parties and Other Non-events', 'How to Get Staff Offside in Five Easy Lessons'. That idea was soon abandoned. She was constantly reviewing her photographs, hoping some were worth enlarging as prints or onto canvases. She tended to cull her shots as she went, finding it frustrating to wade through hundreds of useless images later. Would Libby like one for the cottage? No. Marnie wasn't sure what wavelength her sister was on these days.

When a party boat drifted by with groups of friends chatting and drinking together, she was still glad of her own company. If needed, she knew that Dee would always be at the end of the phone with advice, whether requested or not, if her children were unavailable. In her marketing position at Manning College, she'd been good at working a room, introducing herself and promoting whoever it was she was representing at the time. But deep down inside she had never really enjoyed it. Like a duck – calm on the surface and paddling like crazy underneath. She had put on her confident face and did her job but always with an anxiousness that would rear its ugly head when she least expected it. Her Pettigrew contract had helped enormously – working with positive, inclusive people had made all the difference.

It dawned on her that Nautilus Cove was having a similar effect. It hadn't bothered her to turn up at the yoga class not knowing a soul, plus she had welcomed her time with Nathalie that day. Even the mess with Laila hadn't tipped her over the edge.

The river shimmered a silvery triangle from the light on a neighbouring jetty. Marnie glanced in both directions, chewing her bottom lip. Her pulse quickened, urging her on. With firm instructions for the Lab to stay, she tiptoed down to the waiting water as if her footsteps could be heard throughout the coastal town. All was silent and dark, the moon her only witness as she slid out of her sundress. The cool shallows welcomed her as she eased in, then crept deeper until only the tips of her toes caressed the sandy bottom. She chose to think the flicker against her legs were tiny fish. Libby hadn't mentioned river sharks, although a fleeting memory about a bull shark being found somewhere nearly sent her scurrying back to shore.

Marnie had never been a strong swimmer, once again the cautious one in any group. She made her own attempt at breaststroke for a few metres then trod water. The jetty lamp popped off just as the moon emerged from behind a thin cloud, sending a thin javelin of light across the ripples. She ran her hand across the surface, making it disconnect and quiver.

The hush of the river coaxed Marnie backwards to float upon its deep jade surface as it caressed her body. Her wild hair spread like gossamer. The cool water had decided not to take her away from the cottage but rather it allowed her to drift quietly, her hand lazily directing her near-naked body into circles. It felt glorious, liberating; like being a piece of rice paper caught in a gentle whirlybird. She closed her eyes for a time, enjoying the bobbing waterbed sensation as the river held her in its palm. Marnie blinked at the wide, star-scattered sky and continued to float, picking out the saucepan and the evening star. The Milky Way.

All her anxieties of doing enough in her life and of the need to be totally organised all the time evaporated. She gave them to the moon and closed her eyes. Imagining herself as a little pinprick bobbing gracefully on a giant ocean, her fingers flicked her worries away like pebbles leapfrogging across the water. She couldn't say how long she was in the river, nor did she care, but when distant voices forced her back into the moment she reluctantly drifted to shore. Rising out of the moss-green river, the water swooshed down her body, leaving behind fine grasses over her bra and panties.

Beebs stuck her wet nose under Marnie's hand, eager for a reassuring pat. 'Ah, Beebs. I can't tell you how enjoyable that was. I'm no mermaid, but I do feel just a little reborn.'

A relaxing soak in Libby's spa bath beckoned. Despite her swim, she felt a little deflated that Harry wasn't there with her.

CHAPTER TWENTY-SEVEN

AS THE SUMPTUOUS bath slowly filled, Marnie added drops of chamomile and lavender, then pulled an oversize, fluffy bath sheet from the linen cupboard. The fragrances from the soy candles that sat around the bath's edge intensified the illusion that she was somewhere else – Mauritius or Petrie Island, perhaps. With an old Sade album crooning through the speakers, she headed to the kitchen and poured a chilled glass of wine and wandered back into her haven. Beebs flopped in the doorway, watching her, ever hopeful of a change of mind and a biscuit.

Stripping off, Marnie lowered her body into the warm water. It enveloped her, soothing every inch like a soft glove.

It was heaven, almost better than yoga. She took a sip that verged on a gulp of wine and let a delighted sigh escape her lips. A thick cotton towel cupped the back of her head. *Someone should design the perfect head-rest*, she thought vaguely. A designer somewhere probably already had, although she didn't own one. Her thought threads led to Ollie, concern about his decision to drop out of his design course still hovering. Little worry beads threatened to stick to her thoughts, so she shooed them away for another time.

The wind had come up, scraping the palms against the windows. It was mesmerising listening to the swish of the foxtails. She could just see the other side of the river through the shutters, where a jetty light had just blinked on. Marnie closed her eyes and sank a little lower into her liquid cocoon.

Meditation had often helped to clear her head of her rotating mental checklist. Some efforts were more successful than others; this seemed to be the ‘others’ option. She hoped she hadn’t made any mistakes in Libby’s store, under or overpriced items or misled customers. Marnie tried again to regroup her thoughts, to let her thoughts float away like a dandelion. *A dandelion. Whimsy!*

Deep down she knew she was trying to refocus her every thought away from Harry. More specifically sex with Harry. *S. W. H.* It had been fun and deliciously unexpected. Sexy and liberating. Harry had gazed adoringly at her in their most intimate moments as though she was the most beautiful woman on the planet. Marnie had to admit it had been breathtaking to, once again, experience a tender touch in the dark of night. She gave another deep sigh, her chest breaking the still surface. Where was all this leading though?

Images of Harry drifted in and out of her mind; his lean body, cheeky smile and welcoming eyes. He had not held back in showing his pleasure at their lovemaking and she had had no second thoughts in returning the joy. Her body tingled as it recalled his caresses, his heavy breathing, the weight of him on her open body.

When a distant ringing wormed its way between the images, Marnie cursed at not having put her phone on silent. Harry had hinted he would be unavailable so she doubted he was calling, despite her message. She draped a warm cloth over her face and told whoever it was to go away. Another ten minutes went by before the buzzing started again, then stopped. But her sense of calm had been broken, and what if it is was Harry returning her call? She stepped out of the bath, wrapped herself in a bath sheet and padded out to find her phone.

Two calls. She was disappointed to see they were from Libby and Libby. No voicemail, so presumably nothing was urgent. Marnie threw it onto the bed. The ringing started again.

'Libby. I was …'

'Marnie, I need you to check something on the computer for me. Right away.'

'Okay, but it's not on. Can I get back to you? I'm all wet. What do you need to know?'

'I've just checked the Whimsy emails from here and there's a message that's just come through from the solicitors for the owners of Sandypoint. You know, the apartments that Whimsy is attached to. I can't really make head or tail of it. I need you to double-check that any earlier emails haven't come through from them. I might have missed them or sent them to Trash.'

Libby's agitated voice started to ring alarm bells in Marnie. 'Sure. I'm turning the computer on now. Just wait a second.' Marnie hurriedly threw on a robe and sat in front of the computer. 'Who are the solicitors?'

'Cartier's. Ironic, I know. Probably worth about as much too.'

Marnie opened the inbox and found the email. She checked the Trash file, and then clicked on Correspondents to see if any earlier Cartier messages were sitting there unread.

'No, there aren't any other emails. What's up? You sound worried.'

'That's just it. It's all legal gobbledegook. Something about the Sandypoint building having been sold and the new owners want to develop the site. And Whimsy is part of it.'

'But what about your lease? They can't kick you out if you have a lease. I remember something like this with Barb's shop in The Village. Her building was sold but she still had two years on her lease. She …'

'Marnie. This is different. Rob has had a quick look at the email and it might be that there is a clause in my lease, that I never knew about mind you, that says they can develop the site when there's a change of title. With me, or without me or around me or ... I just don't know.'

'But you must know what's in your lease, surely.' Marnie regretted her patronising comment as soon as it was out of her mouth. There was only silence from Hong Kong. 'I'm sorry, Libby. I didn't mean that. I realise it can be confusing.'

'It damn well can be. What I'm going to do is forward Cartier's email to my solicitors asking them what it all means.' Libby sighed at the other end of the phone before continuing. 'And the thing is, this all costs me money. I may have to come back earlier than planned.'

Marnie could hear her sister was thinking aloud, no doubt chewing her lip. As she wandered back into the bedroom, she took the opportunity anyway. 'Libby, you really do need to come back.' When her sister didn't reply, a pang of remorse made Marnie ask if there was anything she could do in the meantime.

'Just keep Whimsy's doors open and the customers happy to spend. This might end up costing me a small fortune. Philippe crunched some numbers for me and my solicitors checked the lease before I signed, so it might be nothing.'

Marnie gasped. 'Philippe crunched some numbers? When? I didn't know Philippe knew anything about

Whimsy's business.' Marnie slumped onto the bed, nearly sliding off the edge in her now damp bathrobe.

'Well I guess he didn't tell you because of professional privacy or whatever it's called. Anyway, it was ages ago and has nothing to do with you and Philippe. This may all be nothing, as I'm hoping. Maybe they're just flexing their muscles. Anyway, we'll give Starlight Enterprises a run for their money if that's the case.'

'Sorry? Did you say Starlight Enterprises? They are the developers?' Suddenly there seemed to be no end to her sister's revelations.

'Something like that. But keep all this under your hat for the moment, Marnie. I've got to be careful. I'm going to have a very long G'n'T now. We'll talk later.'

Having dropped her bombshell, Libby ended the call. Marnie gazed at her phone in disbelief. It was so typical of Libby to cause havoc, then leave everyone panicking in her wake. It had always been the same.

Marnie scrambled back to the computer and opened the Cartier email. She scrolled quickly through the preliminary paragraphs. Blah blah – draw your attention to – acting on behalf of new owners – been instructed by Starlight Enterprises. There it was.

Marnie stared at the screen, fingers tapping rapidly on the desktop. Starlight Enterprises. Harry. *Surely not.* Her mind darted back through their conversations. Architect. Knows about planning and development. Pocket. The luxury of Petrie Island. Whimsy being a great location. Whimsy not being available. *Surely not.*

Her head spinning, she minimized the email and brought up Google and searched for Starlight Enterprises. Blank. She cursed under her breath, wishing she knew exactly what she was looking for.

Her earlier twinge of alarm started to escalate to paranoia; her heart beat wildly in her throat as she desperately took deep breaths. Still pinched by doubt, she tried to think of all the possible scenarios but knew deep down that she just wanted someone to tell her that her fears were unfounded. That there had been a mistake, a coincidence. Starlight was a common word. It can mean a million things. Harry himself had said so.

CHAPTER TWENTY-EIGHT

AFTER A RESTLESS NIGHT, her thoughts zigzagging between Harry and Starlight and crazy dreams floating around Whimsy, Marnie kicked off the sheet. There was no point lying in bed worrying and wondering. She pulled on walking gear and heard Beebs yipping. At least one of them was enthusiastic for a new day.

Sweat built up on Marnie's skin like condensation on a kettle. She had come to realise that in Queensland the day started with a punch and stayed that way, rather than the heat building throughout the day. Tradesmen were already hauling tools out of their vans as she passed, no doubt to finish early for a well-earned beer. Unless the surf was good, and then good luck waiting for your plumber to arrive, according to Libby. For many it was a life choice, and Marnie couldn't blame them.

She considered that wonderful phrase 'life choice'. It certainly hadn't worked for her most of the time, and now on the brink of her own life choice – or was it a love choice – she was bloody stuck.

Pounding along the river, jaw clenched, she reviewed her short list: Had she been on the verge of rejecting the Melbourne job offer outright to stay with Harry in Nautilus Cove? Libby's phone call had changed all that, so what did it matter? Maybe her mother was right, even in a dream; she couldn't put her life on hold for a summer romance.

And yet, was she so blind to any deviousness on Harry's part? He had given no indication at all that Marnie should be worried about Whimsy.

In contrast to the voices fighting for space in her mind, the silvery river was serene. Marnie turned her focus to its calm surface, the stillness interrupted only by an occasional dinghy humming by and the odd plop of a fish. She paced out along the track, her body settling into a comforting rhythm. She headed back for a shower, Beebs trotting by her side. Marnie managed a smile at the thought of the poor dog never having had so much exercise.

She needed the yoga class that morning too, for an extra shot of Om, but no amount of deep breathing could outweigh her growing concern. Despite herself and Nathalie's puzzled expression, she was distracted. She couldn't hold poses and her attempts to meditate at the end of session were a waste of time. She couldn't wait to check her phone.

Marnie had left another voice message for Harry but he hadn't returned her calls. Nothing. There was the possibility that it was all an over-reaction by Libby; more drama from the drama queen. But she wanted – no, needed – to speak with Harry about it.

Although Whimsy was busy and a welcome distraction, when she finally heard the ping of a message, she snapped up her phone. Dismayed, she saw it was a text from Libby:

Lucky to get a flight out of HK tonight. Landing Brisbane around 7 tmw am, then bus home. CU then

Marnie's fingers tapped furiously on the counter. It wasn't a good sign that Libby was rushing back. Starlight Enterprises must be a real issue. However, she couldn't help but feel total relief that her sister was heading home at last. It would take a lot of pressure off coping with Whimsy, as well as shedding some light on what was going on. She surprised herself at how sad she felt at the thought that the little shop might have to close.

And, of course, it would clear some headspace for Marnie to concentrate on her feelings for Harry and where their relationship was heading. Was it a relationship or a huge mistake? She had let her defences down; she had slept with him for heaven's sake. Marnie blinked away tears as she remembered how good it had been.

Her thoughts of Harry must have carried across cyberspace, as only a moment later her phone buzzed. *Harry.* Marnie took a deep breath and picked up. She tried not to project her agitation down the line.

'Marnie, hi. Sorry. I've only just got your messages.'

Marnie wasn't too sure what to say. She was so conflicted over him and Starlight Enterprises' intentions, but at the same time she desperately wanted to believe he'd done nothing wrong.

Harry continued, oblivious to her silence. 'I must be becoming a real country hick because this traffic is too much. Anyway, I'm well on the way and should be back in Nautilus Cove soon. How have you been? I'm looking forward to seeing you.'

'Oh, I'm fine. What were you doing in Brisbane, Harry?'

He paused before replying. 'Well, I used the time for a quick catch-up with Jake ...'

'I thought you had meetings.' She dug her nails into the palms of her hands; a warning that she sounded like a shrew.

'I was about to add,' Harry continued in a paced voice, 'I was in meetings. Long and tedious ones.'

'What about? I mean, I thought you'd left all that corporate life behind. What corporations are you still involved with?' She tried to lighten up, but Harry had picked up on her tone.

'What's up? You don't sound too happy.' He sounded concerned, his voice softening.

She could picture him, frowning over the steering wheel, running a hand through his hair. A thought suddenly struck her – what steering wheel? She had no idea what car Harry drove. Did he drive the van all the way to Brisbane or was there another car? Where was it kept? Not that she cared what the make was, but it was another thing she didn't know about him. She couldn't help but overthink everything.

'Hey, are you still there?' he said impatiently.

'I'm actually in the shop, and I have customers.' She was about to break off the conversation but couldn't. Her heart pounded against her ribs. 'Harry, I have to see you. There's something we need to discuss.'

'You're worrying me, Marnie. Is everything okay?'

'I've got to go. Can we meet for a drink, about 5:30? Leo's Lounge?'

'Sure. I can drop by and …'

'No,' she replied quickly. 'Let's meet there.' Marnie knew she would need the walk down Figtree to sort out her thoughts and gain some composure before confronting Harry. But confronting him with what? Libby had been firm in wanting her suspicions kept under wraps, and it all may be nothing. But Marnie had to clear the air before pursuing anything more with Harry. She would keep the conversation general and see what cropped up.

He was waiting for her when she entered. Leo's Lounge

was described as casual Nautilus Cove with a shot of sophisticated New York. Subdued lighting, leather booths, a long, brightly lit bar, with no insulated glass holders in sight. With Christmas around the corner they had added a single large black ceramic reindeer to the counter. The gold wreath around its neck reflected the hundreds of candles and lights that dappled the large room. Slick waiters hovered and skated around the tables.

Harry stood as she reached their table, reaching for her. It was so good to see him, to feel his hand on her waist. She blinked away the tears that threatened to swell, smiled and slipped onto the seat opposite him.

'I've ordered some arancini balls and spiced nuts. Oh, and olives. To make up for those that are probably still rolling around the floor at Pocket.'

When Marnie didn't smile at the memory, she sensed him studying her face, looking for a clue to her behaviour. She pulled herself together with a reminder that she needed to find out information.

'What would you like to drink?' Harry asked cautiously.

She should have a simple mineral water. 'Just a glass of white wine. Whatever you think.' She added quickly, 'Thanks.'

Harry's scrutiny didn't leave her as she sat, fidgeting, looking around at the chatty crowd. She was relieved when their drinks arrived promptly.

'So how is Whimsy?' Harry asked, leaning back into the leather.

'Why?' asked Marnie, taking a long sip of her wine. 'I mean, it's good, great in fact. Whimsy means so much to Libby, you know. And to me too. I realise I've really enjoyed being there.'

Harry leant forward, his hands reaching for her across the

table. He had to ease back as the waiter arrived just at that moment.

'Why do I get the feeling you're leading up to something?' he said, a deep frown creasing his forehead.

Marnie had melted under Harry's direct gaze when they had made love, but now it was different. Her fears had constructed a wall, and she knew from past experience that she was very good at building those. His gaze threatened to laser straight through it to read her every thought, caress every hardened emotion.

She needed to keep on track, not to prolong any stilted conversation.

'I wasn't supposed to stay in Nautilus Cove this long, and I need to get back for Christmas, um, to the kids, you know.' She flinched when Harry didn't indicate whether he 'knew' or not. 'And I've been offered a job.' It just tumbled out.

Harry started, his leg jiggling under the table. 'When? How long have you known about this?'

She looked down into her lap to avoid his hurt expression.

'And what about us working together; what about the angels?'

'Harry, you know how much I love your angels.'

'Not enough, obviously.' Harry took a long sip of his wine.

Marnie slumped further into her seat. 'Anyway, Libby's coming back.'

'That's news. You've obviously moved on from us working together and whatever else we had, or what I thought we had. So, let's talk about Libby. When is she back?'

The conversation wasn't going quite according to Marnie's plan. 'Within the next day or so. She has some business things to work out before the New Year.'

'Her lease isn't up until mid next year, is it?' Harry popped an arancini ball in his mouth. Marnie couldn't take her eyes off his lips, the tiny smudge of oil left behind.

Suddenly she realised what he had said. 'How do you know that? When her lease is up, I mean.'

'Whoa, Marnie. What does it matter if I know about her lease?' Harry threw down his napkin. His blue eyes darkened, his arms straightened, his hands clutching either side of their table.

'I don't remember telling you,' Marnie replied. Was she prepared to upset Harry for Libby? She had to find out the truth. 'Harry, what part do you play in the Starlight organisation?'

Surely it was Marnie's imagination that the room fell silent as her words were thrown across their drinks, unable to be taken back.

She willed him to say *none*. Marnie was so ill at ease but still expected that to be his reply.

It took a moment for what he actually said to penetrate. 'You mean you are a decision maker?' she gasped.

'Sure. But there are a lot of different divisions within Starlight. I don't have an active role with all of them. What happens is …'

She flicked away his words, impatience on the rise. She had always felt at a disadvantage when discussing business with Philippe and his patronising attitude. She was perfectly capable of discussing projections, budgets and corporate structures; in fact, she had been a victim of one.

'What about their developments, their properties?' she probed.

Harry stiffened. 'Ah, okay. Now I see where this is heading. You want to know, actually you are accusing me …'

'I'm not accusing you of anything.' The tip of her finger poked a wayward nut around the table.

'What then?' His brooding eyes bore into her.

'Does Starlight Enterprises own the property that Whimsy is a part of?' She didn't mean it to sound so accusing, but it did.

'Yes,' Harry replied shortly, returning to his wine. 'Is that a crime?'

'Harry, please. I'm only trying to understand what's going on. So you knew Whimsy has become a part of Starlight.'

'It's not a part of Starlight. How can it be?' Harry ran a hand through his hair, then leaned towards Marnie.

That hadn't been what she meant, but she was getting caught up. She looked at Harry, so conflicted with her feelings for him. She noted the rugged stubble on his chin, the flecks of steel reflecting in his eyes, that his nose was ever so slightly crooked – probably from some macho football match in his teen years – why hadn't she noticed it before? But she also expected total honesty and she couldn't get rid of a nasty little niggle about what he hadn't told her. She had to be careful not to divulge Libby's suspicions.

'But you knew the lease was coming up next year. Is Starlight going to renew it?'

Harry frowned. 'It's not as easy as that. It totally depends on the lease, the options. Tenants have the option usually, you know like a three-by-three. But that's not my …'

Marnie's heart clicked sideways. 'Why didn't you tell me, then, about Starlight being the new landlord? I would have thought it would have come up in conversation at some point, unless you purposely didn't mention it.' Marnie could hear the desperation in her voice.

'Actually, may I mention here the matter of you accepting another job when I had presumed my offer had appealed to you.' His words were slow and deliberate, his eyes never leaving Marnie's face. 'When I'm with you, business is the farthest thing from my mind. I still don't really see why you are getting so enmeshed with Whimsy. You said yourself you didn't know why you were stressing over a shop you knew very little about. Marnie, what have I done to make you so mad?'

At that moment they were interrupted by a couple eager to greet Harry. He stood to shake hands and do the double air kiss. He introduced Marnie, a look of surprise on his face when she could hardly raise a smile. She was starting to regret the conversation, particularly in such a public place. The couple left, nodding at Marnie. Harry breathed out a deep sigh and remained standing, his hands shoved into his pockets.

A moment passed, but it felt like a solid hour to Marnie.

'Marnie. I'm not going to argue with you here.' His voice had a determined, no-nonsense edge to it that she had never heard before.

She pushed herself up. Her anger and panic had gone and she was left feeling confused and empty as if all the air had been sucked out of her. She knew in her heart it wasn't all about Whimsy. Deep inside she wanted to trust someone, to not second-guess their reasons or her feelings. She'd been blindsided again and hadn't known how to react.

Harry put his hand on her arm, seeming to sense her upheaval.

She shook it off. 'I'm not sure what to think just at the moment. But I guess I'm going back to Melbourne. There doesn't seem to be anything to keep me here anymore.'

She looked into his face hoping for an answer, but all she saw was exasperation. He frowned, his voice dangerously low. 'It would seem that when you're wrong you are, in your mind, still right.'

He strode past her to the bar, slapping down notes but not waiting for change. When Marnie turned only the barman was looking at her.

CHAPTER TWENTY-NINE

'BUT WHY ARE you leaving so soon?' Libby had arrived back from Hong Kong and had breezed into Whimsy.

She told Marnie how impressed she was with how the store looked for Christmas, but Marnie had no time for Libby's casual chatter. Her new-found drive and excitement for the future had disappeared; the hurt at having lost Harry overwhelming. She'd decided she would finish the job she started and leave without looking back. Between customers Marnie shot out instructions, filling Libby in on what had arrived and where she'd stored spare and unpacked items.

Libby frowned when Marnie told her of the demise of the flowers but admitted the Christmas theme along the deck looked fabulous and was a great draw. They continued to dance around each other.

'I've grouped all the festive cards and decorations for sale on this table. We've already sold a lot of the Australiana decorations for people to send overseas, so you might want to quickly order more. All the delivery dockets are in this folder. I cross-checked items against the order and everything is okay. I presume you kept track of payments while you were away, but I've highlighted amounts still to be paid according to the paperwork here.'

'Whoa, Marnie. Slow down. I was hoping Whimsy would help you chill out, but you sound totally stressed.' Libby was almost laughing as she held up her hands to ward off more of Marnie's instructions.

'Well you stayed away too long, Libby. I've had to deal with a lot.' Marnie knew she was running on overdrive and saying things she would no doubt regret later, but she couldn't help it. She accepted she was reverting to her old blinkered self, unable to let anyone in.

'Hang on. I'm the one with the business on the line,' Libby protested. It was becoming difficult to continue the conversation in any privacy as more and more customers filled the store.

Libby wandered away from the counter, and was nowhere in the store when Marnie glanced around a moment later. Her prodigal sister had probably escaped through the back door. Typical.

At least the customers looked happy. Several young mums were having a lovely time, chatting as they popped stocking fillers and decorations into red Whimsy carry baskets.

'The lady in Nest seems nice.'

Marnie looked up to see Libby offering her a cup and doughnut. She quickly slipped the doughnut under the counter before taking a step around its corner.

Marnie relented as Libby smiled at her over the rim. 'Thanks. You go home and unpack, Libby, and come back later. It's good to see you.' The sisters hugged cautiously.

Marnie couldn't help but hope that Harry would materialise or she would see his van drive down the street. She wasn't sure how she would handle it if he did walk through the door, but it wasn't to be anyway. He was nowhere to be seen.

Closing time came with no sign of Libby returning, so Marnie completed her day and headed back to the cottage. Her problems with Harry weren't her sister's fault, but disappointment weighed her down, with Harry's non-appearance only adding to it. She tried to practice a few calming yoga breaths in the car, the pelvic floor squeezes having been forgotten.

Libby was sitting on the back deck, her laptop open on the table, a glass of wine in her hand.

Marnie poured one for herself and went out to join her sister. She only realised she had flicked the heart mobile after soft rainbow prisms started to shoot around the deck.

'I have to admit it's so good to be back in clean air, at my little cottage with my favourite dog … and sister.' After registering the significant pause that followed that comment, Libby tiptoed on. 'You never answered me, Marnie. What is wrong and why do you have to leave as soon as I get home? It's pretty inconsiderate.'

Here we go, Marnie thought, sinking into a chair. The river vista suddenly didn't seem so tranquil; a flock of cockatoos screeched as they flew overhead. 'Libby, I've outstayed my welcome. I am tired and I need to get back to Melbourne. I've so much to do down there with the house, and the kids and, and …'

Libby stared at her. Her cell phone vibrated on the table, but for once she let it go. 'Well. We both know that is such a load of rubbish. For one thing, you were tired when you got here and I would have thought that Nautilus Cove would have been the perfect panacea. Something's happened. You're cross with me because I don't understand the whole lease thing. Is that it? Is it another case of Libby the flake?' She paused, then softly added, 'Or are you just jealous of the little business that I've built here?'

'Don't be ridiculous, of course not. I have a terrific life in Melbourne and I want to get back to it in time for Christmas. Plus, it looks like I have a job.' Marnie took a mouthful of wine, not wanting to have a discussion about her working plans. Seeming to sense her unease, Beebs pushed her nose under Marnie's elbow, hinting at a pat. The dog had become a good companion, and Marnie knew she would miss her nightly welcome and wet nose. She tried to concentrate on the stunning view, the stars that were beginning to pop through the evening sky. *The Milky Way.*

She couldn't ignore the scowl that was being thrown at her across the table.

'Sister-to-sister chat here ...'

Marnie sighed. That sentence brought back so many memories of their teenage years – it was usually followed by a criticism of something or other.

'You know you never could stick at anything that you didn't want to.'

Marnie gasped at the accusation.

Libby's crossed leg started to swing and Marnie's short nails drummed the table, but Libby wasn't finished. 'Philippe always used to say …'

'What did Philippe always used to say, Libby, and why should I give a shit? And why would he have said them to you anyway? Was this an earlier affair I didn't know about? Did he look after your books in exchange for a dinner or two?' Marnie regretted her spiteful words as soon as they were out of her mouth. The horrified look on Libby's face answered her questions.

Libby faltered. 'Well, let's face it, Marnie. You are an overachiever at things of your choosing. But with anything else, or should I say, anyone else, you put up a wall.' Libby sniffed. 'You always have. But if other people's needs come into the picture …'

'Like when?' She didn't expect Libby to be ready with a reply.

But, scratching at a piece of flaking paint, Libby was ready. 'Well, now that you ask. Why do you think Claire always rang me? She would be crying down the phone, not understanding her own mother's actions, or lack of them.'

A sledgehammer fell on Marnie's chest, alarm bells ringing.

'How dare you presume to know my daughter more than me. You don't have children, you wouldn't understand.'

Libby flicked her hair. 'Well, it's not rocket science. We've all been young once. All I know is that Claire was a teenager feeling abandoned by a father having affairs and a mother more interested in her career.' She held up her hand at Marnie's protests. 'Then later, the divorce was the sickly icing on the cake. At least Philippe kept the lines of communication open with her. Your mother-daughter bonding attempts came too late.'

Beebs had retreated under the table, not even game to beg for a biscuit.

Simmering, Marnie quelled the urge to yell. 'Oh please, Libby. I can assure you I was constantly there for her. You've never grown up so I'm sure you were just enjoying some girlie time. You've always been the attention seeker and Claire was the prime candidate to satisfy that for a while.'

'Well, at least she had me, and I am proud that I could help her smooth away the sharp edges of her life.' Libby turned her face to the river, biting her bottom lip.

Marnie stalked inside, all too aware that Libby was close behind her. She refilled her glass, then slid the bottle across the bench; she wasn't quick enough to catch the carry bag as the bottle pushed it to the edge of the counter. The baby journal slid to the floor, landing open at the front page.

Libby's swearing at the near-broken bottle receded into the background as Marnie reached for the journal. Her hand gently smoothed the bent page as she read aloud, "Claire bear. Congratulations – what wonderful days are ahead for you and your little one. Love always, Libby. Kiss kiss."

Marnie slowly turned to Libby, registering but not caring about the look of devastation on her sister's face. Clearly she was never meant to read the message.

'What does this mean? Claire's pregnant?' Marnie whispered.

'Marnie, she …' Libby stuttered. She reached for the journal.

'You knew, and you didn't think to mention it to me? Claire hasn't said a word.' Marnie went cold. Disappointment rolled like a tumbleweed through her heart.

Libby straightened her back and prised the journal from Marnie's hands. 'Well, have you ever bothered to wonder why Claire doesn't communicate with you?'

'That's none of your business. Unless you've had that discussion with her as well, and had a chuckle about it at my expense.'

Silence fell thick and heavy on the sisters.

'For heaven's sake, stop being so melodramatic,' Libby said. 'I'm sure Claire wasn't chuckling about anything. Really, you seem to be totally lacking in the compassion department lately.'

'That's a really unfair thing to say, and stop trying to change the subject. We sat together while you went behind my back and chatted with Claire. I stepped in when I saw you were being kept in the dark by Laila and others. Where would you have been if I hadn't come up and filled in your responsibilities whilst you were fluffing around Hong Kong?'

Marnie tried desperately to blink back the tears of frustration and hurt that now threatened to spill. *Heavens, do you ever really know family?*

Around them the breeze had dropped to a tentative stillness, as if nature was holding her breath, unsure if the argument would continue or all had been resolved.

Libby took a nervous breath. 'She's not pregnant. Now. She asked me not to …'

Marnie held up her hand. 'Either she is or she isn't, Libby. Which is it?'

'You should speak with Claire. I'll call her.' Libby shuffled on the spot, as if reaching for her phone was the last thing she wanted to do.

Tendrils of anxiety were winding their prickly way around Marnie's heart, squeezing the tears up her choked throat. But they wouldn't fall. Libby's words started to filter through her racing thoughts.

'Now?' Marnie paused as the cold spikes of reality hit. 'The accident? Are you saying that Claire was pregnant then? She lost the baby because of the car accident?'

Libby blinked back tears. 'Call your daughter, Marnie.'

STILL UNABLE TO SLEEP AT 2 a.m., Marnie fumbled her last items into her suitcase. She stood, hugging her tired body, and gazed at the moon's beautiful touch on the river. Her mind was sluggish and sad as she went over and over Libby's words. Had there been any truth lurking there? Had she really been a bad mother? In all honesty she couldn't accept that –

she had loved Claire with all her heart every day. She had shown it, hadn't she?

How comforting it would have been to discuss Claire and the baby with Harry, to ask his advice on what to do.

MARNIE WAS thankful she had pre-ordered an early cab – she couldn't have faced another sister-to-sister outburst in the car. She ached enough from the deterioration of her relationships with both sister and daughter. Marnie gave Beebs a big hug at the door, the only one to see her leave.

The driver's endless chatter washed over her. She quickly sent text messages to Nathalie and Eleanor, saying she had to return unexpectedly to Melbourne and to apologise for not saying goodbye in person. She would call them both later. The bush flashed past the window in a blur, as if her life was suddenly on fast forward. She wondered if it would be the last time she saw this beautiful part of Queensland – the realisation released a hard little stone into the pit of her stomach.

CHAPTER THIRTY

LIBBY THREW HERSELF INTO WHIMSY, discarding her ghastly conversation with Marnie into the "too hard" basket. She mentally smothered it with a tea towel.

She had expected to spend a good part of the morning catching up on deliveries and paperwork, but when she saw the colour-coded list that Marnie left for her, she knew everything was in perfect order. It made their parting even more poignant. Libby was pleased to be back in Nautilus Cove, but she felt flat. She found herself watching the clock until she could head home.

When the workday was finally over, Libby returned to her cottage, poured herself a long gin and tonic, and settled in to relax, on her back deck. A lone kayaker slid by the cottage, leaving only a silent, watery trail. Libby breathed in the tropical air then slowly released it, her lips tilting in delight as Beebs ventured under her hand.

'Hey, Black Betty Bamalam, I did miss you. You're looking pretty trim I must say – I doubt that Auntie Marnie took you for many walkies, so maybe she didn't feed you enough. We'll give you extra tonight. This is so beautiful after the hustle of Hong Kong, and I bet Marnie didn't even dip her toe in the water.'

Libby lost track of time, staring down the river and contemplating how the conversation with Marnie had managed to go bad so quickly. She was a Libran, a lover of peace and balance, and the whole episode had certainly upset her Chi. She shook her head. Why on earth had Marnie thought she and Philippe could have had an affair? That comment had been laughable, but the other accusations had hit home, as if Marnie had forced her to peek into a window she had never opened before.

That damned journal – she had meant to throw it away after Claire miscarried, but she hadn't taken the time.

Libby acknowledged that her secret friendship with Claire had initially instilled a certain sense of achievement; a smugness that she knew something that Marnie obviously was missing about her daughter. Libby had been let in where Super Mum was banned, and she had secretly revelled in it. But now she regretted the words she had cast at Marnie and feared her sister would never believe how her genuine affection for Claire had grown over the years. She would speak with her niece, try to convince her to come clean with Marnie. For all their sakes.

For her whole life Libby had had the urge for freedom, the need to go with the flow. The promise of adventure had tugged her away with Drew and away from the commitment of parenthood, then when times became rocky she had moved on again, no longer prepared to put up with his deceit. She still hadn't reconciled if that had been through courage or cowardice.

A sudden surge of gratitude swelled within her for her coastal home, for Rob and Whimsy. She was going to fight for her business, whatever it took.

The truth was that Libby had seen something in Marnie's eyes, had recognised the haunted look of someone a little at sea. This was her rock of a sister who was always in control, had done wonders with Whimsy, and for a time seemed to be enjoying her break in Nautilus Cove.

But Marnie seemed to be running for cover, so what else had happened in her absence? Libby turned her attention to the Lab. 'If only you could speak and tell me everything that happened whilst I was away.'

Libby raised her glass to the fading sky. 'Due credit to you, Marnie. You juggled children, a career, a rocky marriage and money worries and have come out the other side a pretty top person. Mind you, a bloody annoying and uptight one too, but from past experience there's nothing I can do to change that.'

Despite the little puddle of sadness she still felt, Libby chuckled to herself. She must be tipsy if she was toasting her sister.

CHAPTER THIRTY-ONE

MARNIE CLICKED her front door closed behind her. It sounded so final and her hands started to shake, as they had so many times over the last couple of years. Her keys clattered onto the glass-top entrance table. A sob caught in her throat. She closed her eyes, tears brimming over and falling onto her T-shirt like warm raindrops.

Suddenly it all seemed so hard, as if her future was drifting full circle, around and around her. She was unable to think clearly about which direction to take or to see a break in the endless, thick cloud.

Behind her came the buzz of the doorbell, the call of her name.

Marnie whipped around and threw open the door.

'Oh, Dee,' she whimpered as her friend quickly took her into her arms. 'What am I going to do?'

'Good lord, Marnie. What on earth has happened?' Dee looked shocked. "I expected to find you high on the joys of Nautilus Cove … and Harry. I wanted to hear more about this dashing sculptor of yours and what your next steps would be." She paused, then cautiously asked, 'Is it Harry?'

Marnie sniffed and shrugged. Dee guided her friend into the lounge room, then hustled off to make some strong tea.

Dee and Marnie sat curled at either end of the couch. Marnie hugged a cushion and wet tissue to her chest with one hand and tried to hold a mug of tea steady with the other. It tasted sweet; Marnie knew her friend had added extra 'crisis' sugar. She wished she could pull herself together.

'I just knew, Dee. Something shifted inside my heart and I knew that Harry was The One; that my days had to have him in them. Melbourne and the job didn't seem to matter so much. And then, *bam*! It all came tumbling down. When Libby said Starlight Enterprises were involved with the Sandypoint Development I started to wonder – was Harry interested in me only to find out about Whimsy? I thought I knew him. But maybe I didn't. But maybe I did and I should have given him more time to explain. Oh, I just don't know.'

'Well, I think he sounds lovely and I believe there are always two sides to every story. Let's do a Marnie and overthink this together, shall we? The sculptor offered you a wonderful job which instantly appealed to you, right? The artist shared the most creative part of his professional life, and the man let you into his personal history and heart. Right? I just can't see where the problem is.'

'I feel so stupid.' Marnie shrugged, fresh tears welling. 'Like some silly teenager. Who did I think I was? Some desperate woman, thinking I could find someone amazing again who would appreciate me for who I am and take me on …'

'Whoa, back the truck up!' Dee said firmly, her palm stopping Marnie's desperate words. 'Take you on? What the hell does that mean? You will work this out, Marnie, but I do not want to hear words like that. Good lord, you sound like your parents! And we know how that would pan out.'

Marnie sniffed, then smiled. 'How come you're here anyway?'

'Complete serendipity. I was driving home and saw you sitting in a cab at the traffic lights, so I did a U-turn. I thought I'd say welcome back etcetera, etcetera. I obviously missed the huge black cloud of remorse hovering over the cab.'

'And instead you were greeted by a crying lump.' Marnie reached across and gave her friend's arm a squeeze. 'Thanks for coming.'

'So,' said Dee, grinning, 'if you were Julia Roberts, island boy would be?'

Marnie laughed through her tears. 'Mm. Harry would be a cross between Matthew McConaughey and that mature guy on the health fund ad.'

'The one with the dentures?' Dee prodded innocently.

Marnie grimaced. 'No. The gorgeous one with the grey-flecked hair, dazzling smile and warm eyes.' She waved her hand in the air as if that would take away all memories of Harry. Marnie gave a big sniff. 'That's not all. I had a huge blow-up with Libby.'

Dee shrugged. 'What's new there? It's probably about time you two stopped tiptoeing around each other.'

'This one was terrible, but that's not the worst part. She told me that Claire was pregnant when we had the car accident. I didn't know. Claire didn't tell me then or since. My own daughter had confided in Libby about everything, and not me. Why would she do that, as if it had been a choice between the two of us – am I that much of a terrible person? What did she think I'd do – disown her or something?'

'Oh, my friend. I can't imagine why she would have done that. Maybe it just slipped out to Libby, maybe she was scared and …' Dee stopped short, then appeared to change direction. 'Look, why not ask her? Not over the phone. Invite her over, tell her what happened with Libby and, well, just ask her. Libby has probably already warned her that you now know. I'm sorry about the baby, Marnie, but you've got to clear the air with Claire.'

Marnie nodded. 'Of course.'

They sat for a moment in silence. Dee redirected the energy.

'Are you planning on renting for a while once you've sold? You know, until you're sure you are going to stay in Melbourne. Then if you stay you can hunt around a bit more until you see something you love,' Dee suggested. 'It's just my opinion, but I don't think you should rush into buying something just for the sake of it. Where's this job based that you told me about?'

'I have to meet the guy this week. I presume it's around here.'

Shelving all thoughts of starting a new job and the challenges associated with that for the moment, Marnie turned her exhausted thoughts back to the house. She knew what Dee was saying made sense. But renting first would mean two moves, expensive moves, and renting would dig into her capital if it went on too long. Thoughts of Julia and Paula's comments about Melbourne's rising house prices wormed their way in.

'I'm staying in Melbourne. Whatever I had with Harry is over.' Marnie nodded to back up her words.

'Well, um, you know I wouldn't make a comment without you asking …' Dee continued, raising her eyebrows.

'Ha, yeah right!' Marnie managed a smile.

'But I was glad when you didn't sell up so quickly and kept this as your home. This house is gorgeous. But why have you done a turnaround? Because the kids have left?'

Marnie forgot she hadn't filled Dee in completely on all

her plans. Or maybe she hadn't on purpose; she couldn't remember. It was still a blur in so many ways as she had tried to keep some privacy about the ongoing dramas of her marriage breakdown.

'It was Philippe's mother's fault really. She gossiped around the golf club that Philippe was, quote "letting me and the children stay in the house out of pity", unquote. Of course she didn't mention that I'm paying the mortgage. Catherine Salter told me. Then the kids did move out and I knew it was decision time. I need a clean slate on all the finances, if nothing else.'

'What! The cow! Well, I totally understand your reaction,' Dee exclaimed. 'I never liked golf anyway. "A good walk ruined", as they say. Despite the red eyes and puffy cheeks, I happen to think you look great. According to my hotness rating, you (a) look fit and trim, and (b) have a bit of a tan happening. The former could be due to extended sessions in bed with the before-mentioned Harry and the second could be due to long walks on the beach with the same Harry.'

'He certainly has taught me a few things.' Marnie waved away Dee's raised eyebrows. 'What I mean is …' She paused, searching for the right words. 'He showed me how not to sweat the small stuff, that it's okay to chill and not panic about things, to not have to instantly tick all the boxes.' Marnie sighed. 'Despite how I appear now. But I said some really mean things. There's a loss of trust and too much space between Harry and me now.'

'Oh please.' Dee sighed. 'Have you heard of planes that can fly interstate?'

'Thanks for coming, Dee. Really. But I'm okay.' As if to herself rather than to Dee, she continued, 'I'm going to have a clean slate. Get back on track. I can't, won't, let myself spiral down.' She nodded in double reinforcement, but deep inside, Marnie's heart was breaking.

'You won't spiral anywhere,' Dee said seriously, giving her friend's arm a squeeze. 'You are a different person now. Stronger. Probably still as stubborn as all get out, but stronger. I know it.'

'Thank you. You're better than those affirmation sites. But what's the point? I'm stronger for what, and for whom?'

'For yourself, silly. No-one else.' The friends hugged across the couch.

AFTER DEE LEFT, Marnie unpacked and, like a robot, walked from room to room. She wanted to be overcome with joy to be home, to accept that Harry had just been a sizzling holiday romance that was now over. So be it. But all she could think about was how inspiring, fun and heart-warming her time with him had been. She had welcomed his opinions, admired his values and skills, and of course his way around her body. She had felt different in his company – confident, sensual and happy. When he'd walked out of a room, she couldn't wait for him to reappear. She had believed he had responded the same way to her. Until the mist of desire had cleared and she had seen the possibility of another side.

Although her stomach clenched at the memories, she couldn't help picture him wandering along the sandy foreshore, chiselling a block of stone, laughing in the rain, stretching in the sun. Making gentle love to her, over and over again.

CHAPTER THIRTY-TWO

OVER THE FOLLOWING DAYS, restless torment prodded Marnie to phone Harry on several occasions, just to hear his voice. She figured she could then hang up like a lovelorn teenager. But she never made the call. As usual she searched through their many conversations, trying to find hints of his deception. She had picked up on vulnerabilities and his reticence to talk in detail about his family. He had referred to his brother a couple of times, but in a way that had left Marnie presuming they didn't see eye to eye. Nothing from their time together could have prepared her for the disaster that was crouching, waiting.

She then moved to another instrument of torture – her camera. Flicking through the photos she had taken of Harry brought him into the room. She zoomed in to his face, trying to find a curtain over his eyes, but only saw an openness she had come to adore. His arms, muscles taut as he lifted a sculpture, had firmly encircled her body; his hands, moulding an abandoned nest they had found, had tenderly cupped her breasts.

Sniffing, she dropped her camera on the sofa and headed

in search of a tissue. As she passed the front entrance, she noticed a shadow through the glass just as the doorbell rang. Jumping, she jerked open the door.

'Philippe!' Marnie stumbled backward, knocking her hip against the entrance table.

'Oh, Marnie, are you okay?' Philippe quickly stepped forward and caught her arm. As he continued to hold onto her, she saw him quickly glance around at the open packing boxes that littered the rooms.

'Yes, of course I am. You startled me, that's all.' Marnie regained her composure, removed her arm from Philippe's grip and turned away. 'Take a seat. I'll be back in a moment.'

She quickly tidied herself in the bathroom, adding saline drops to her red-rimmed eyes, and putting on a slick of lipstick. She took a deep, centring breath and wandered back into the lounge room.

Philippe was flicking through the Nautilus Cove gallery on her camera. 'Who is this then?'

Marnie heard a faint snippy tone underlying the question. She didn't need to look at the viewer to know he was checking out her shots of Harry. It was such an intrusion on her privacy that she nearly demanded he leave the house then and there. Calmly, she took the camera out of his hands before sitting along from him.

'Just a job I was working on in Queensland.'

'I thought you were working in Whimsy.'

What was this, an inquisition? How does he know what she was doing, and more importantly, what was it to him?

'Well, there you go. It might surprise you that I was doing both.'

'Jeez, Marnie, I didn't come here for a fight.' Philippe turned on his dazzling smile and held up his hands in mock surrender.

'What are you doing here?' Marnie was simmering with suspicion, her thoughts leaping to all possible scenarios, but her voice was strong.

Philippe's eyes narrowed. 'What *did* you get up to up north?'

Marnie did her best to hide her smirk. If only he knew.

'Marnie?'

Philippe's hand on her arm brought her attention back. She couldn't help but flinch.

'Claire said you were back.'

Claire. Marnie had so many bridges to build there and was impatient for her daughter to return her call. She waited for Philippe to continue with whatever was on his mind.

He shuffled closer. 'I want to talk to you. Don't look so defensive.'

Marnie had stiffened, waiting for the next bombshell. She edged farther away as if they were playing cat and mouse, with her role being the mouse.

'We've had our differences of opinion and our time away from each other, but I was hoping that we could somehow work something out.' He reached for her hand, unable to reach it hidden under her knees.

Of all the things in the universe her ex-husband could have said, that would have been lower than the last item on the list. She was blindsided.

'What type of something are you thinking of? Is this about the house or us, because you are not making sense. We are divorced, remember? Divorced. So, what I'm hearing is that you are panicking about where you are at in your life.'

His patronising expression urged her on. 'If you are asking for a greater percentage than we agreed on from the house sale, you can forget it. And to come here to try and what, stay here or … or … what exactly?'

'Please, Marnie. Relax. All I'm asking is that, for the children's sake …'

'What!' Her voice reached fever pitch, but Marnie had had enough. Something dangerous was bubbling up inside her. She rubbed her temples.

'Don't sell the house. I think you should buy me out and stay here to keep our family memories alive. You could buy me out now.'

Twenty seconds felt like a long time. Sounds of distant music, dogs barking, a rattling skateboard came and went, all amplified in the space between them.

So that was it. He wanted her to stay in the house and pay him out, so it all went his way. She needed to quell any notion of that happening.

'This sounds like your mother has been in your ear again. No. I need to move on – as you did.'

Suddenly all her anger and anxious momentum dropped away. Marnie rose to her feet, confidence flowing like liquid gold through her body. Fleetingly, it felt as it had when she resurfaced in her underwear from the river, water and worries sliding slickly away.

'Claire and Oliver are adults and are fine. Of course, I would never, ever, do anything to undermine their happiness. You should know that, and I'm pretty confident they know it too. Ollie is off overseas and Claire happily does her own thing.' A pang of regret came and went as she wondered if Claire had told her father of the pregnancy, but Marnie had no intention of raising the subject with him.

Philippe's expression hardened. Standing to face Marnie, he said, 'Working in a shop in a regional town is different from the business world back here, Marnie. How exactly do you expect to earn a living?'

'You forget I was very capable with my work, and now I

have a very clear idea of my future, but that's none of your business.' She walked to the front door, holding it open as she added, 'It doesn't include you. I'll email you the real estate details.'

The silence was deafening as he brushed past her and out the front door. Marnie watched him reverse his new 4WD down the driveway. Strains of Gary Moore's 'Still Got The Blues' hung in the air as he accelerated away.

Marnie had no idea what those ideas might be for her wonderfully lucrative future. She could only hope that Barry's job would suffice.

PHILIPPE'S REFERENCE to family experiences lobbed Marnie back in time. Images of happier days kept sliding across her mind like a PowerPoint presentation: dragging home the fresh Christmas tree to find it was too tall for the lounge room; Friday night pies while watching their team play football; curling up and watching *Ice Age* DVDs endlessly with Claire after she broke her arm; enduring school formal after-parties in their backyard; hilarious dinner parties with friends.

It had also reminded her, all too harshly, of what they had lost. But one thing that Philippe's visit had done was to strengthen her resolve to sell the house. Marnie knew with all her heart that it didn't need bricks and mortar to hold treasured memories close – she would never forget, no matter where she was. She was now resilient enough to stand up to his demands, to not give in to his persuasive mumbo-jumbo. The lingering threat of loneliness still remained but it had lost its essence of desperation.

CHAPTER THIRTY-THREE

CHRISTMAS WAS UNFURLING all around her; Marnie couldn't help but wonder how Whimsy was faring. Were the customers appreciating the little bells she had bought to top their gifts? Was Libby playing her mixed carols CD rather than Christmas with Michael Bublé like every other store? Was there a giant Christmas tree nestled in the corner at Pocket?

It hadn't escaped Marnie's attention that Dee was keeping a quiet eye on her, with her friend insisting on catch-up coffees or a cocktail at Ruby's Bar. Dee had flicked off Marnie's tale of Philippe's visit with 'pathetic', 'good on you, Marnie', 'unbelievable', and 'have you heard from the sculptor?'

Marnie tried to turn her attention to the house but ended up just shuffling her belongings from one spot to another. One morning, while she was sitting at the computer, she heard the front door open and in strode Oliver. She had only spoken with him on the phone since her return.

'Ollie!' Marnie jumped up, gathering her lanky son into her arms. 'Oh, I've missed you. How are you?'

'Geez, Mum. It's good to see you too. Want to go for a coffee?'

Marnie pushed him to arm's length, searching his face for signs of trouble. 'Is everything okay?'

'Yeah, of course. I just thought I'd visit. Actually, I wanted to check if you're okay. You didn't sound too flash on the phone the other day.'

Marnie gave him another big mother hug. 'Blow the coffee. Let's just go for a walk.' She knew from experience that it was easier to talk to kids whilst they were contained but moving. She had used that advice from someone or other on many occasions to instigate one-on-one chats with both Claire and Oliver in the car. It had sorted through many problems over the years.

They had gone some distance down the street before either spoke.

'Mum, I'm sorry I dropped the overseas thing on you. Out of the blue like that. But I had been thinking about it for a while.'

'No problem. You and I are the same that way. We have lots of head conversations before letting in anyone else. I'm pleased that you are going.'

Oliver gave her a disbelieving sideways glance.

'Really, I am. It's a great opportunity. I guess …' Marnie paused, trying to find the right words. 'I guess I'm in a place where I just don't know where I'll be next week, let alone next year. You and Claire are a constant and with you off overseas, well, I guess I …'

'Feel left behind?' Oliver offered.

Marnie missed a step as she acknowledged her boy had grown up. 'Well, there was always the danger of empty nest syndrome. You're right – I suppose it felt like I was being left out and that everybody but me knew what was going on.' She left the inference to Philippe hanging in the air. She wasn't sure how much Ollie knew of Claire's situation.

'But that's in the past, and I'm fine. I hope you know that I am always here for you to talk to, Ollie,' she added with a nudge.

'I think Claire is being a bit selfish. I haven't seen much of her lately. I know about the baby though. She told me the other day and said she'd kept you in the dark. She wants to talk to you about it.'

'Really?'

They both laughed, realising this was another example of a lack of communication. A little warm glow was shimmering in Marnie's heart.

'Apparently she's going to a friend's place in Sydney for Christmas. We were supposed to be going out to lunch with Dad, Nanna and Pop for Christmas, but with her gone it will just be me.'

'In the firing line!' Marnie laughed. Ollie would be the golden-haired grandson having to answer endless life questions over a huge Christmas meal. She felt for him.

But at least he had somewhere to go. Marnie batted away her maudlin thoughts. Christmas. She had always recognised that it was the hardest time of the year for those who are alone or not on the family roster that year.

'What are you doing for Christmas, Mum? Grandma and Grandpa are still touring out west somewhere, so I thought you'd probably head back to Auntie Libby's.'

Had Ollie picked up on her thoughts? 'To Nautilus Cove? Why? I mean, I always spend Christmas in Melbourne. I'll probably be starting the new job sometime in January too, but I'll find that out this week.'

'That's a good reason to head to Nautilus Cove then, I guess.' Oliver shrugged simply. 'You made friends up there, didn't you? You sounded pretty happy whenever we spoke on the phone. Happier than you do now, actually.'

Was it that obvious? Marnie glanced at Ollie, but he was looking ahead, oblivious to her reaction.

'Actually, Libby has invited me. I think she feels guilty for being so mean to me when she got back from overseas.' Marnie heaved a sigh. 'But then, I probably need to be a bit more forgiving with her too. So many bridges.'

'So long as you're back to drive me to the airport,' Oliver said, digging her in the ribs.

'Never in doubt,' his mum replied, knowing full well she would be in Melbourne for Christmas, not Nautilus Cove.

DON'T ASK her how she is, don't ask her how she is, was Marnie's mantra as she waited for Claire. The café her daughter had chosen was half-way between their homes, and Marnie only hoped that a need for neutral ground hadn't been Claire's priority. She was relieved that it was busy though, so any raised voices or sudden departures would go unnoticed.

'Shall I order?' Claire's voice interrupted the space.

Marnie hadn't seen Claire come in but here she was, standing by the table. She was pleased to see a smile on her daughter's face that spread to her eyes.

'Hi, Claire. A latte please, darling. Do you want to share a slice of something?'

'No, just coffee for me.' Claire placed the order, gave Marnie a quick peck on the cheek and sat down. She waved away Marnie's offered money.

They chatted about superficial subjects like stones skimming across ice, not wanting to settle on one thing.

'Ollie called in the other day,' Marnie ventured. 'He's so excited about his trip, although not too keen to be spending Christmas with his grandparents. He said you were going to Sydney to see a friend.'

'Yes, you would remember Bronnie? She's working up there now and thinks I need a bit of fun in my life.' She glanced across the lip of her coffee cup, a look of defiance on her face. 'What are you doing?'

'Libby has asked me to Nautilus Cove,' Marnie replied. She had slowed her breathing, determined not to rush her words or gloss over any subject that involved Libby. She had decided to leave the door open for Claire.

'You should go,' Claire said.

A change in her tone caught Marnie's attention. As their eyes met, Claire's cup started to shake as she desperately tried to support her hand and calm her trembling lip. The café absorbed the sound of the clattering crockery as Claire jiggled it onto the saucer, coffee spilling over the sides. Marnie quickly lifted the cup and slid a napkin onto the flooded saucer, then placed a steadying hand over Claire's fingers.

Marnie so desperately wanted to jump up and give her daughter a hug but stayed seated, her words held deep within her heart. For the moment. She could see that Claire was drawing breath. *Here it comes.*

'Mum, let me say that I don't hold you in any way responsible for my miscarriage. The accident wasn't your fault. But I don't think it was my fault if I didn't want to tell you about being pregnant. That was my business.'

It didn't go unnoticed to Marnie that Claire's demeanour had gained strength and a certain bitterness as she had voiced her opinion.

'Well …'

'No, let me finish.' Claire stabbed at the wet table with the soggy napkin. She waved away the waitress, who was approaching with a cloth. 'Marcus and I hadn't worked our way through the situation ourselves and we didn't need anyone else's opinion in the mix.'

'Except your aunt Libby's.' There, it was out.

Claire stared at her mother. 'Is that what has got you so upset? The fact that I spoke to Libby about being pregnant and about Marcus's position? Heavens, I thought you were concerned for me.'

Marnie fixed her daughter with a gaze that she hoped conveyed how heart-wrenching the situation was for her too. 'Claire, your health and wellbeing are the only things I care about. I have to accept the fact that you were under no compunction to tell me at that stage. But why couldn't you include me at a later point?' She frowned. 'What do you mean, Marcus's position?'

'He was never going to stay around. I knew that. It wasn't like we were in love or anything.' Claire shrugged, trying to appear nonchalant. 'That's part of why I didn't tell you. You were going through the shit with Dad, and it was just another example of people who couldn't stay together.' Claire's eyes brimmed with tears. 'Libby seems to be so cut and dried about life, and I thought she'd understand and chat about what I should do. But it didn't matter in the end. I lost the baby and Marcus isn't around anymore.'

'Oh, Claire. Are you okay?' Marnie was relieved when Claire only raised her eyebrows at her. 'I was pretty hurt that Libby knew and I didn't,' Marnie repeated, hoping that her daughter would really understand where she was coming from. 'But I would have supported you no matter what. I still would.'

'I made Libby swear not to tell you, so don't blame her. You should be pleased that she kept my confidence. In fact, she rang to say I should chat to you about the whole mess.'

It was important that Claire had had someone – anyone – to confide in, but Claire's explanation had done nothing to bolster her sense of being a good mother or confidante. She still felt as though she had been left in the backyard while everyone else chatted around the dining room table. She brought the focus back to Claire, away from Libby.

'Did you see anyone about the loss, you know, a psychiatrist? I mean …'

Claire nodded, chewing her lip. 'I thought you would have been relieved I wasn't going to be a single mother. That my life wouldn't be put on hold.' She flicked her eyes to her mother's as if to gauge the reaction.

Marnie was horrified. 'Oh no, why would you think that? I'm so sorry you would think that. I support you, Claire, no matter what position you find yourself in. I only wish I could have been there to help you. The pain of losing a child must be devastating.' Her words shuddered with concern.

'You just seemed, I don't know, indifferent. I guess I shut you out a lot.'

Marnie gave a short nod. 'I just didn't know why you were so angry at me.'

It was Claire's turn to reach across the table. 'I'm fine. I have come to terms with it. Honestly. I want that to be the end of the discussion. I'm moving on.'

Claire couldn't be drawn on any other information about Marcus or how their relationship had come to an end. Marnie was left trying to read between the lines, but their departing hug had held the promise of a truce.

It was a long drive home for Marnie, her thoughts pinging back and forth like the old Windows downtime screen. But she felt a glimmer of hope that just a trickle of progress had been made with Claire, and she was relieved to see her daughter was happy. Libby's fridge magnet came to mind: *What do you pack to pursue a dream and what do you leave behind.* Maybe that was how Claire had managed to move forward.

CHAPTER THIRTY-FOUR

'IT'S SO good to see you back!' Marnie's childhood school friends raised their glasses to welcome her home and wish each other a Merry Christmas. It was the night before Marnie's meeting with Barry, making it the perfect opportunity to thank Valerie for the introduction to her brother.

A booking had been made at a trendy bayside restaurant, recently refurbished in an austere style. The only hint of Christmas was a large metal ball at the entrance which could have passed as a bauble. They all agreed they preferred the previous Art Deco décor and the huge fresh tree that used to adorn the restaurant every year, laden with lavish ornaments.

It was a clear Melbourne day, lazy with a slight breeze off the aquamarine water. The girls asked about Nautilus Cove, discussed the differences between living in a city and regionally and caught up on the dramas of one another's lives. They agreed wholeheartedly that they were all at a challenging 'age and stage' of being caught between children setting out in the world and aging parents.

Their customary Kris Kringle of a wrapped book brought

up strong opinions and light laughter on authors, films and themes. It was always touch-and-go as a couple of the old friends were more inclined towards Margaret Atwood than Cathy Kelly.

'Here is a little something extra from me to hang on your trees,' Marnie announced, handing each of the girls one of the handcrafted ceramic hearts from Whimsy. She was pleased with all the *oohs* and *ahhs* as her friends held up the presents.

'So flush with your experiences in retail, are you going to open a Whimsy II in Melbourne?' Chloe asked.

Marnie laughed. 'No way. I've got a few irons in the fire, so we'll see if anything eventuates.' As the waiter refilled glasses, she mouthed, 'I'm seeing about the job tomorrow' across the table to Valerie.

The afternoon trickled on happily with many more laughs, iPhone photos and stories. Conscious of drink-driving levels, they all finished their lunch with wicked desserts and coffee, serious New Year resolutions and warm hugs. As usual there were more prolonged chats in the carpark before going their separate ways.

It had been a panacea to reconnect with her girlfriends, to feel a part of a long-established group, but something niggled at Marnie. She needed to be somewhere else, to dispel the restlessness within – she couldn't quite put her finger on it.

EARLY AS USUAL, Marnie waited in Barry's chosen café in Prahran. She spotted the man who had to be Barry as soon as he walked through the door. He had the same confident style as Harry, Marnie observed, as he wound his way around tables towards her, checking out who else was sitting at the tables. Her heart gave a skip as she acknowledged Harry wouldn't have done that; he had always made her feel as though she was the only other person in the room. She had put a lot of thought into her interview outfit; after all, it was Melbourne, so no casual linens were suitable for this one.

She couldn't remember Valerie sharing any information on her brother over the years, but after a quick greeting he went straight to the point, and quickly outlined what the winery group was looking for.

Marnie's head was spinning. 'Barry, let me get this right. The group is putting together a team to market the ranges on a more global scale, specifically south-east Asia. Right?'

'You got it. There's a huge opportunity for lesser known wines to be marketed and sold throughout the region. We have the local managers in place overseas so the Australian team just needs to link in with them. We have top-notch sommeliers to lend their weight, but there's a lot of communication work too, particularly in promoting our sustainable methods. That's where you come in.'

'I'm not sure if you received my resume via email, but I brought a hard copy in case you didn't and …' Barry didn't even glance down at it as she pushed the folder across the table.

'You'd be part of a larger team, Marnie. It's possible to pull a communications plan together here to start with, from a distance.' He ticked off a list on his fingers: 'Campaign announcements, event planning for trade and private clients, top quality hard copy materials for tastings, press and invitations. The potential is huge, but we want to keep a firm hand on the reins ourselves.'

Marnie's adrenalin started to spike. Old habits died hard as ideas bubbled to the surface. 'You'll need major social media posts throughout too. Video and visuals for YouTube, Instagram and Facebook.'

Barry nodded, seemingly pleased with the direction her mind was heading. 'Done. We have a social media guru on board.'

Marnie was relieved, then asked, 'Have you got a good production company and photographer?' Somewhere in the back of her mind popped up a hope that she could help with some of the draft photography.

At the thought of Harry and his offer, she faltered. He had given her back her confidence, urged her to follow her love of photography; to dig for the creativity he believed she had. This position was out of her comfort zone but then most of her appointments had been initially. Thanks to Harry she knew she could do this job. So why was she hesitating?

'What's the timeline?' she asked, stalling.

'We'd like you to meet the Victorian team late January so we can all be on the same page. It will probably mean a quick trip, probably to Singapore, to meet the managers and familiarise ourselves with the venues. We'll be rolling out over time in Singapore, Hong Kong, Beijing, Shanghai and Chengdu. So keep that passport current.' He glanced at his watch. 'I have to fly, literally.' Marnie stood up as Barry pushed back his chair.

'I'll get my assistant Simone to shoot you an email with all the employment stuff. Salaries and such. But you come highly recommended, so the job's yours. We hope you'll be on board.'

They shook hands and he left. Marnie chuffed out a deep breath and ordered another coffee. Strong. The first thing she needed to do was get stuck into some research.

CHAPTER THIRTY-FIVE

TRYING TO CATCH HER BREATH, Marnie grabbed the buzzing phone from the entrance table. She had promised herself to, firstly, keep up the exercise routine she had established in Nautilus Cove; secondly, to leave her phone at home while walking; and thirdly, to splurge on new gear. She would have to find time for the third, but two out of three wasn't bad, although she did envy the yummy mummies in their latest fluoro Lycra. She missed Beebs's company too and was seriously considering offering to walk her neighbour's labradoodle.

Libby's contact flashed on the screen. The sisters had had only irregular, stilted conversations and texts about Whimsy since Marnie's rushed departure, so she was surprised to hear unsuppressed excitement in Libby's voice.

'Marnie. It's all okay. After all that worry, there's no problem,' Libby exclaimed.

'Sorry? What are you on about, Libby?'

'I thought you'd want to know about Whimsy's lease. Remember?' Libby now sounded indignant and hurt. 'Or is it out of sight, out of mind since you arrived back in Melbourne?'

'The lease? But I thought the Starlight people were going to force you to move on or something.' Marnie was at a loss to know what to think.

'It turns out that, yes, Starlight Enterprises did buy the complex, but I still have my option. There was a problem with one of the other retailers whose premises were privately owned. A clause in his lease said that the rent can be increased at any time, and if the premises are sold the lease is null and void. Ugh, imagine that. It's so complicated and I'm not great on all that – as you pointed out.' Libby paused for a reaction from Marnie but when none came, she pressed on. 'Anyway …'

But Marnie wasn't listening. Her thoughts were spinning like Alice down the rabbit hole, round and round. She tried to clearly sift through what Libby had revealed: Starlight wasn't pulling a swifty; Harry hadn't been behind anything untoward, hadn't become involved with her to find out information on Libby's plans. She felt sick, wondering what on earth she had done, what conclusions she had stupidly jumped to.

'Marnie, are you there?' Libby asked impatiently.

'Sorry, what was the last bit you said?'

'I was saying that the solicitor's letter had just been an advice letter, to make sure I was aware the new Sandypoint owners were Starlight Enterprises. Their property general manager is a guy called Lewis something who has tried to get around a few rules in the past. But he can't get anything deceptive through without approval from his whole board. My lease is solid.'

Lewis. Harry's brother. 'What about any development though? What if you've got building works around Whimsy?'

'Ah, well I can't do anything about that apparently. But there is someone on the board who is quite adamant nothing will go ahead until my lease is up. By then I'll know whether I want to be a part of what they have planned or not.'

Marnie could imagine the smile spreading across Libby's pretty face. 'How do you know all this?' Marnie asked, trying to sound nonchalant.

'I have influence in Nautilus Cove!' Libby giggled. 'No, actually Rob did some snooping for me.'

Marnie recalled that Rob had been the one who misread it all in the first place.

'I'm so pleased for you and Whimsy.' But where did that leave her with Harry? Farther down that rabbit hole with no way out, that's where.

Marnie clicked off the phone, turned and walked straight out the door again. She needed space to think. She needed to draw up her mental columns. On the positive side, what Libby had divulged proved that Harry had done no wrong. Yes, he had known of the purchase of Sandypoint; he had admitted that. And it sounded as if he had stepped in for Whimsy's interests – he had been an architect and would be their board's primary advisor, presumably. On the negative side, he hadn't shared any of that with her, not even over their disastrous drinks meeting when she had accused him of everything under the sun. Deep down, she knew he was under no obligation to share any details with her; in fact, some privacy agreement probably would have prevented it.

Marnie groaned at the memory of how she'd behaved. She really hadn't given Harry a chance, so why would he bother pursuing her? She hadn't trusted him and had let him down professionally as well. She had kept the job opportunity a secret and hadn't gone through with his project. She sighed at all the probabilities and presumptions that seemed to hover around her head like a swarm of bees but didn't have the least idea about what to do.

She needed to call Harry. She'd call and say she'd just found out about Starlight's involvement and that her silly sister had jumped to conclusions. That she was dreadfully sorry. But it had been her, not Libby who had hurled distrust in Harry's face – she couldn't blame her sister. There was no time like the present. Marnie pulled up his number and called. Voicemail. She tried again with the same result.

She stopped, other joggers having to suddenly veer around her. Embarrassment was outweighing good intentions. Surely he must see her as a strung-out, presumptuous idiot. He would have decided he didn't need such negative, suspicious vibes in his life – unwanted judgements, as he had stated at one stage.

Disappointment that he hadn't contacted her hovered as she sank onto one of the riverside benches. She squinted at a pelican, following its path as it slowly made its way over the water and distant trees. Was it heading to Petrie Island? Marnie's phone rotated between her palms until, decision made, she sent a text:

Harry. I apologise. There, it's so much easier to write than say. You had shaken my little snowdome of a world and I couldn't see through the flakes when doubt crept in. I jumped to hasty conclusions and made a fool of myself before allowing things to settle. Except it wasn't snow. It was palm trees and sand and stars that meant the world to me. I'm sorry. x

CHAPTER THIRTY-SIX

AS OFTEN HAPPENS the universe conspires for or against at various times. At this particular point Marnie Fawkner was hoping the approaching full moon would choose in her favour. There had been no reply from Harry and she needed to make a decision.

It was going to be a busy start to the year if she accepted the winery job. Barry was expecting an answer by New Year, but what choice did she have? Marnie had gone over and over the ins and outs of the offer. The salary was more than she had expected and, of course, there was the prospect of travelling to new countries. The role would be challenging but she needed to sink her teeth into something.

She had resolved several issues if she was to move on with her life. There would be no more tears at midnight, nor wondering where Harry was sailing in his little boat; she would keep active; no more dissecting their every conversation and embrace. She would indulge in her photography whilst overseas. In fact, she secretly thought that sounded more appealing than actually promoting wine.

Marnie gave exclusive agency to local Sails Real Estate to

market the house after Christmas. She was firm that no sign was to go up on the property, preferring to keep Philippe in the dark for as long as possible. Wearily she had shut the door on the sales team when her phone rang.

'Hi, Eleanor. How are you doing?' Marnie sank into the lounge, kicking off her sandals, ready for a chat. The girls had obviously been worried about her hasty departure from Nautilus Cove and had called several times, but Marnie had managed to dispel any concerns. Marnie still wasn't sure how much they knew, but she presumed Eleanor would still be in contact with Harry through Dave and Nest. They had probably nudged Libby for other possible details.

'Great to hear your voice, lovely. This is a quick call. Customers, gingerbread houses, Christmas cakes, you know,' Eleanor said.

'Oh, my mouth is watering just thinking of your delicious shortbread. I'm sorry I missed getting one of your whisky cakes too before I had to rush home.'

'I've popped a party invitation in the mail to you. Libby kindly gave me your address. I can't stand E-invitations; it's snail mail for me. Dave suddenly wants me to have a birthday party so he's pulling something together for Boxing Day evening. He thinks I should have slowed down by then after the Christmas build-up. Hah – don't you love men! Actually, he's being a real sweetie and has organised extra cooks and chefs to cover Nest.'

'Oh, lovely. Is the birthday a big one with a zero on the end?' Marnie asked.

'Yes, it is. I don't usually celebrate my birthday because it falls in the Christmas-New Year holiday season, but he insists.'

Anxiety raised its ugly head, as Marnie's knee-jerk reaction was to think she couldn't possibly go.

Eleanor continued, 'Now please don't feel obligated to come. I know you're busy there and will have exciting things on, but I would so love you to be here.'

'Oh, Eleanor. It sounds wonderful but, um …'

'I know it's an expense to fly up but I put the word on Libby to kick you some frequent flier points from her Hong Kong trip, seeing you saved her bacon.' Eleanor gave a cheeky little chortle.

Marnie laughed at the thought of Libby's reaction to that. She was still surprised at Libby's Christmas invitation considering the air remained thick with so many unresolved issues between them – her sister certainly was hard to work out.

'Eleanor, it sounds wonderful. But I really don't know where I'll be. I've been offered a job that starts in January and I may have to go overseas for it and …' Marnie felt guilty at telling a few little white lies, but she didn't want to commit to returning to Nautilus Cove and all it held for her there. Or didn't hold, to be precise.

'Wow, you jetsetter. Good on you. Well, I'll leave it with you. I have to go but look out for the invitation and we would all adore it if you could possibly come. Nathalie says hi, by the way. Bye, love.'

CHAPTER THIRTY-SEVEN

AFTER SPENDING a delightful early Christmas Eve dinner with her children before Claire departed for Sydney, Marnie had headed home. It had been like old times with lots of laughs as she caught up on their news. It warmed Marnie's heart to be able to chat with Claire again, to enjoy a larger part of her life. She had thought long and hard about Libby's observations and had talked through some of the issues with Claire over several coffees. Who knew Libby would be the one to guide them together again?

There were certainly no black trousers in Marnie's luggage on this trip to Nautilus Cove. She was busy searching for her self-tan moisturiser when Dee arrived to scoop her up for champagne and watch the traditional fireworks and Carols by Candlelight telecast. It would end up a sniffling session as they sang along to each carol – 'When a Child is Born' had always tipped Marnie over the edge into tears.

'It's because you're a mum,' had been Dee's philosophical summary. Her husband and son were on Santa and elf duty at the football club family night, so the two friends could join in the telecast's 'Hallelujah Chorus' without ridicule.

'So, Marnie,' Dee began. 'This Harry fellow. Did you say he owns an island? That's pretty impressive. I mean, I prefer my little life here, but an island!'

'Desiderata! Your hippie mother would be proud of you.'

Dee laughed. 'My boho heritage does break through the Armani from time to time.'

'I'm not exactly sure how Harry came by Petrie Island. It's all a bit cloudy as it's tied up with Starlight somehow. Anyway, it doesn't matter, does it.' Marnie shrugged.

'Well, it seems to me that the stars are aligning if Libby has asked you to stay for Christmas and you're going to a party on Boxing Day. Why did she ask you, do you think?'

It warmed Marnie's heart that her friend knew Libby nearly as well as she did. 'I guess it's to say thanks for my help with Whimsy. Also, something to do with us having the opportunity to clear the air, whatever that means. Rob is arriving at some stage so that's good if it all goes pear shaped.'

More to the point, she couldn't help but imagine what Christmas would have been like in Harry's arms. Like hugging a heart full of colourful bubbles, except now they'll be floating away, leaving emptiness. She had been lucky to clinch a flight Christmas morning, which had suited her plans to arrive in Nautilus Cove as close to Eleanor's party as possible. On one hand she didn't want to run into Harry whilst out walking or catching a coffee somewhere, but then perhaps that would give her the opportunity to follow up on her text.

CHRISTMAS DAY at the cottage began in an amiable, relaxed environment, despite Marnie's misgivings. The sisters were both on their best behaviour, treading carefully around each other's expectations. Libby giggled through lengthy calls to Rob who was still overseas, and Marnie chatted to Ollie and Claire for updates on their festivities.

They took a deep breath, and armed with a margarita each, put the phone on speaker to video call their roaming parents. The older couple's festivities had started early if their grins and lopsided paper hats were anything to go by; their reference to a progressive yuletide drink tradition around the camping ground proved it.

Their father's eyes grew misty as he admitted what a joy it was to see his two daughters enjoying Christmas together. The sisters could hardly control their laughter at being told a couple of Outback Oz fridge magnets were in the mail for their Christmas presents. Eyebrows were raised when Libby admitted to having their lunch catered by Nest, prompting their mother to give endless warnings about not properly refrigerating leftover turkey. All was forgiven when Libby promised to pass on to Eleanor the family's recipe for fried leftover pudding.

Marnie remembered Eleanor's tale of Claude and felt happy for her parents' joy of life.

They nibbled on coconut lime prawns whilst licking the salt from the margarita glasses, then moved on to a chilled Mornington Peninsula Pinot Grigio that Marnie had brought with her.

When they agreed exercise was needed, they wandered the short distance across the grass to the end of the jetty. Marnie took great delight in relaying her story of Beebs taking off around the marina, but stopped short of sharing her own swim under the stars. Wine in hand, they slowly raised their glasses to the odd passing party boat, then meandered back to the deck.

The sisters had given each other novels as gifts, so it was an afternoon of reading about crime in the outback and love in Ireland, in between nanna naps in the warmth of the cottage's back deck. Beebs was in seventh heaven, enjoying the company of two humans, plus a few properly refrigerated leftovers.

The river was enticingly tranquil throughout the hot day but came alive as the sun set on another Christmas. Owners had gone all out decorating their boats and jetties with every imaginable Christmas light that flashed, pulsed and changed colour. Huge Christmas trees could be seen flickering behind glass windows of neighbouring homes, and Marnie could only imagine the lengths Caroline had gone to in swathing her mansion.

'You know, Libby, I like your decorations the best. A stylish green and gold wreath on the front gate, a simple tree with those little copper seed lights, and a nice thick strand of lights along the deck. Simple. And white. And enough.'

Libby laughed, slapping her palm against her chest. 'Well thank you – I'm all overcome.'

Feeling tipsy, Marnie continued, unaware as the ground started to shift under her words. 'Mum and Dad never really go all out, do they? Maybe they don't want to or can't, seeing they have such a limited budget.'

Libby stilled, frowning. 'Who says they're on a limited budget?'

'Oh, don't panic, Libby. They told me all about losing their money when your business went bust. I think it's good we can chat about these things now, don't you?'

'And did they also tell you that, through hell and high

water, I paid them back every single cent? I actually think camping is their choice, not a last-ditch hope at a holiday.'

Marnie glanced across to her sister, finally picking up on her sudden chilliness. 'No, I didn't know that.'

'Well there you go.' Libby turned away.

'I always thought that you'd done really well. You know, to recover and buy this place and have the confidence to set up another business.' She hoped her back-pedalling wasn't as obvious to Libby as it sounded in her own ears. 'I think I need some water.'

When Marnie re-emerged with two long, chilled glasses of water, Libby was waiting, leaning against the table, arms crossed.

'Our business didn't fail, Marnie. We had to let it go to pay our debts. Or more particularly, Drew's gambling debts. By the look on your face that's something else you didn't know before making assumptions about my life. Are you going to give me one of those glasses, or just stand there?'

Marnie was glued to the deck. Even through her foggy head, she questioned how she could have been so blind to her sister's problems.

Libby took her glass and they sank into their respective chairs. The flashing Christmas lights suddenly seemed part of other people's lives, garish and unnecessary. Beebs moved from one sister to the other, obviously unsure of why the happy atmosphere had turned static.

'So …' Marnie began, unsure of where to go.

Libby ran her finger up her glass, collecting the drips before they escaped onto her lap. 'In hindsight I probably should have been more pro-active earlier, asked more questions of Drew and our accountant, but by the time my suspicions were proved to be valid it was too late. We had lost pretty much everything, including trust.'

Trust. Starlight. Harry.

'If it's any consolation, Libby, I've come to realise how tricky trust is. It's something that should exist and not be questioned. It should just be. Don't beat yourself up that you allowed yourself to believe in it with Drew. It's better than living with suspicion and being wrong.'

Libby looked Marnie directly in the eye. 'No more of your snippy comments about me and money or about me and my business decisions. Agreed?'

Marnie smiled in reply. 'Agreed.'

Libby nodded. 'We obviously need a strong coffee! But first our belated dessert.'

Marnie could hear Libby fussing in the fridge. Her sister finally emerged with a platter holding two of Nest's mini champagne and mango pavlovas, a bowl of strawberries, and a little pyramid of rumballs.

Marnie's attention was caught by a large plastic stem of holly stuck in the middle. She tried for an injection of light-hearted humour. 'So much for your exquisite taste in Christmas decorations. But this looks beyond delicious.'

'I didn't see these in the bottom of the hamper. Look what Eleanor put in for us.' Libby waved two large bonbons in the air. She tossed aside the miniature calendar and read her quote – '"Plan today for tomorrow." Good lord, this is obviously not meant for me. What does yours say?'

'"Star light star bright, I wish I may I wish I might, get this wish I wish tonight",' Marnie replied, trying to sound flippant. She reread it, tucking it into her pocket with the little moon that had been inside her bonbon.

FIGTREE STREET TRADING was at its peak from Boxing Day onward, so Libby had headed in to the shop early. Marnie hadn't offered to go with her, preferring to be alone with her thoughts. She had enjoyed Christmas Day with Libby more than she had anticipated and despite their argument. She'd had no idea about Drew's gambling, how hard Libby must have worked to recoup from such a ghastly turn of events. Plus, Libby had paid back their parents, having not once asked Marnie for help.

The day had ended well with a lot of their personal baggage being unpacked and, she hoped, resolved. Marnie was relieved to be able to apologise for her assumptions. It seemed she needed to apologise to several people these days.

The possibility of seeing Harry again brought all her insecurities to the surface. She chewed her lip at the memory of having said so many hurtful, unsubstantiated accusations. Who knew what his opinion was of her?

Her old room had welcomed her with lit candles and fluffy towels, but Marnie was looking at it all through different eyes now. Sitting on the edge of the bed and running her hand gently across the covers, she had taken a moment to waltz down memory lane. She relived the intimacies they had shared, the peaks of pleasure that Harry had brought her to between the sheets. She was sure she could still smell his scent on the pillow, knowing full well it wasn't possible.

Harry had said she was beautiful. She couldn't recall how long it had been since someone had offered her that compliment. How long would it be, if ever, before she heard it again?

LIBBY ARRIVED home later than usual due to Nautilus Cove thriving with shoppers. She propped herself wearily in the guestroom doorway, smirking at the bed strewn with clothes. It appeared Marnie had taken hours deciding what to wear to the party, despite the limited options carry-on luggage had afforded her.

'Usually it's me having trouble in the decision-making department,' Libby teased.

Marnie shot her a friendly 'don't go there' look as only an older sister can.

Libby shrugged, clicked her fingers for Beebs and headed to the deck for a welcome glass of wine. As she put her feet up, she could hear her sister huffing and puffing around the bathroom.

When Eleanor had mentioned inviting Marnie to her party, Libby had waited for her own invitation to be accepted. Marnie had tentatively asked to stay at the cottage which Libby quickly agreed to, throwing in the offer of the plane fare as thanks for looking after Whimsy. After all, in hindsight the waving cat figurine gift she had brought back from Hong Kong hadn't come close to being enough.

She had been surprised that Marnie returned to Nautilus Cove, albeit briefly. She had been convinced her sister would be happy to be back amongst the city life, readying herself for her next corporate role. But she could now see what role Whimsy had played over the previous weeks. The shop had obviously been a major focus for Marnie, as it had been immaculate when she returned, with everything ready for Christmas and New Year trading. Libby had to acknowledge that was no mean effort for someone out of the loop of how retail works – and doesn't work. Extending an olive branch for Christmas had been her way of trying to be more appreciative, as well as smoothing over any niggling issues about Claire.

The fact that Marnie actually had a space in her heart for Nautilus Cove made Libby more chuffed than she cared to admit. Which made her wonder if Marnie's focus had actually been on a sculptor rather than the sculptures. Libby had heard along the grapevine how close her sister and Harry had become. Whilst she considered she should be congratulated for unwittingly staying in Hong Kong so long to allow their friendship to get hotter, Libby also felt guilty for suggesting prematurely that Starlight Enterprises was up to no good. She had no idea about Harry's connection and less idea that Marnie would react so bullishly. But then they hadn't really been sharing their lives with each other at that stage.

Is that what Marnie had been referring to when she spoke about trust? Or the naïve lack of it.

The fact remained that she had been surprised and touched at how Marnie had stood up for her.

The Harry angle was an added bonus to her inquisitive mind. Any hope of a juicy retelling by Marnie of their time spent together hadn't eventuated on Christmas Day, despite the number of margaritas consumed. Libby's attempts to find out more than Eleanor had been willing or able to share had threatened to roughen the still waters of their reunion, so she'd let it be. Even her probing about Marnie's upcoming job hadn't gone well.

'Marnie, you seem "resigned to" rather than "excited by" this wine job,' she'd ventured. When there was no reply she added, 'But hey, the travel sounds fabulous. Lucky you.' Their argument had followed, so that was the end of that.

Libby put down her empty wine glass as Marnie finally emerged. 'You'll arrive in time to clear away the balloons if you don't get a move on. Wow, you look fab. Go get him, sis.'

MARNIE HOPED SHE LOOKED OKAY – more than okay if she was honest – she couldn't gauge anymore but she had made a few changes before leaving Melbourne. Her chestnut hair now shone with copper highlights and had been styled into layers that curved around her face. She had splurged on a Camilla-style sleeveless dress that fell straight to her ankles. The pure cotton shift was cool under the slinky, sheer overlay, its bodice scattered with tiny apricot- and gold-coloured sequins. Simple gold drop earrings, a band of bright tangerine resin bangles and gold sandals completed what she hoped was a sophisticated, but fun, beach party look. The birthday invitation had said to swap stilettos for sandals as the party venue was to be in the gardens of one of the beachfront resorts.

'I'm going to celebrate Eleanor's birthday, Libby, and to catch up with friends. Nothing more.' Marnie tried to sound as though she meant it. Not for the first time, she wondered if any gossip had circulated in her absence, and if Harry's name had been woven in.

'Yeah right. I forgot.' Libby smirked at Beebs. 'Let's get this show on the road. Are you sure you don't want me to pick you up?' Libby bent over, clutching her chest and laughing at her question. 'God, I sound like our mother.'

Marnie laughed with her, relaxing. 'Perish the thought. No, really. You have your own plans for tonight and I might want to come home early. I'll get a cab. Thanks for dropping me off though. Now, where's the present? I bought her a gift voucher for that great Balinese-style spa Issykan. I thought she could use a bit of pampering after being so busy in the café. What have I done with it?'

'Are those your nerves I can feel fizzing across the car seat?' Libby teased as they drove to the party. 'From past experience I know how hard it can be to separate life's remnants from life's possibilities, but you'll be okay. Just have fun.'

'Is that another magnet quote?' Marnie looked sideways at her sister, a hint of a smile on her lips. 'You have fun too, and I look forward to actually meeting this famous Rob.'

CHAPTER THIRTY-EIGHT

MARNIE COULD SENSE Libby's eyes trailing her back as she walked away, suddenly feeling like the younger sister rather than the elder. She could hear music, even over the buzzing in her ears that must be an echo from the butterflies in her stomach. It was a stunning, clear night. A half-moon hung in the sky amidst a million stars. *Under the Milky Way*, Marnie thought sadly.

The party was in full swing, the electric atmosphere welcoming and loud. A couple of tipi marquees were erected on the beach next to the hotel's fence line, offering a magical spot for the band. Coloured lanterns swayed around the dance floor, guests spilling over to jive in the warm sand. The tropical garden was dotted with tables laden with dozens of tiered candles, iced fruit pyramids and giant platters piled with cheeses, olive breads, fruits and terrines. Party lights, punctuated with large clumps of clear balloons filled with sparkly silver and flamingo-pink stars, crisscrossed the summer sky.

Eleanor spotted Marnie and made her way through her guests, instantly pulling her friend into her arms.

'Marnie. It's wonderful to see you. I was sooooo excited to learn you were coming. I feel privileged that you put off Singapore just for me. Thank you, thank you.'

Marnie winced at the reference to Singapore and quickly replied, 'No, thank you for inviting me. Wow, this looks amazing, as do you, birthday girl. When on earth did you have time to pull this together, and please don't tell me you've made all this amazing food.'

Eleanor laughed. 'Dave did it all! Well, with a bit of help from my friends and To Dine For Catering, I presume. I think he was plotting and planning long before he admits. It's fabulous, isn't it? I should step back more often, I've decided. I'm so lucky to have such a generous, thoughtful husband.'

Yes, you are, and you deserve it, Marnie thought as she handed Eleanor the spa envelope. 'Here, happy birthday to you.'

'Oh, thank you, but it's more than enough that you've come all this way. Come on, let's get you a special drink.'

They linked arms and Eleanor organised a dangerous-looking cocktail before she had to meet and greet more guests. Marnie felt a little out of touch and cast her eye around for Nathalie but couldn't see her. She was relieved when a couple recognised her from Whimsy and engaged in conversation. Marnie smiled and nodded at their chat, not sure how she was going to get through the night. Her eyes flicked around the guests looking for a certain tanned sculptor.

Party chat swirled around her as she accepted that Harry may not even be there. He could be in Brisbane seeing Jake or staging an exhibition. How wonderful it would be to be with him, witnessing his success.

The couple was pulled away into another circle, so Marnie wandered towards the tipis. The view was breathtaking, like an advertisement for a luxury resort or premium champagne. Lights from clifftop apartments dotted around the bay sent shimmering reflections onto the water. Floodlights from the beachfront restaurants swept across the sand, highlighting couples embracing or strolling along the boardwalk. She could just make out a lone fellow with his metal detector sweeping the beach for any abandoned treasure.

The gentle whoosh of low waves running to the shore echoed in her mind, her soul. The clear water returned to the bay only to creep up the silvery sand again and again. *As sure as the sun rises in the east and sets in the west.* The evening breeze brought the salty scent of the sea to her, nudging happy memories of her walks and yoga in the sand. Marnie glanced up at the headland. A line of lights, like a string of pearls, led up the stairs to Pocket, the studio hidden in darkness at the peak. She inhaled the gentle scents of salt, summer and loneliness.

The band changed pace to a salsa. Willing herself to let go and enjoy the party, Marnie glanced back. And there he was. Dancing in the sand with a stunning red-haired woman. Her laugh tinkled across the beach as Harry dipped her backward, her loose hair cascading to the sand. She appeared to be supple too. He grinned back at her before scooping her up to twirl amongst other dancers. *We never got to dance*, Marnie realised. She shrugged off her reaction. What had she expected?

Raucous calls for everyone to gather for the birthday cake gave her a welcome excuse to dissolve into the celebrations. Guests' merriment buzzed around her like an annoying bee. She quickly squeezed herself on the other side of the crowd so Harry couldn't see her as he brought his date in from the dance floor. It didn't stop her peering between shoulders, watching them chat intimately. The speeches were funny and the coconut and passionfruit cake 'good enough to have been made by Eleanor' – or so Eleanor's husband boasted. Only a crumb of Marnie's attention was on cake.

She planned to make her escape as soon as the formalities ended, but the sound of her name being called made her turn. Nathalie was waving enthusiastically, telling her to stand still so she could catch up. Marnie waved back, so relieved and pleased to see her friend. Flicking her eyes to the right of Nathalie, they rested on Harry's piercing blue eyes looking back at her. A shiver spiked through her as she held his gaze. It felt like eternity. Then Nathalie was embracing her, spinning her around.

'Eleanor said you were coming. Good on you, Marnie. I thought that after, you know, after …'

Marnie looked at her, surprised. 'After what?'

'Well you left so quickly. And Harry made it clear you were a no-go zone whenever we asked him about you, so we figured there was no love lost there. Eleanor even tried to get Dave to find out but that didn't work either.'

Marnie started to tap her fingers against her leg. Nathalie, picking up on Marnie's silence, looked at her earnestly. 'Sorry, Marnie, I didn't mean to pry.'

Nathalie had been such a good friend when Marnie had arrived in town and she didn't want to seem standoffish. She owed her an explanation, certainly more than a couple of phone calls had permitted, but how could she put it all into words?

'Well, suffice to say I did "a Marnie". I rushed in without thinking. Actually that's not a Marnie thing. Well, it didn't used to be, but I think it's a new, rather annoying habit. The bottom line is … I made a mistake and a bit of a fool of myself. Not all my fault, mind you, but enough. I'm sorry I didn't say goodbye properly before leaving,' she added softly.

The two friends were jostled as guests nudged past to the bar or stopped to say hello. Marnie ended up with her back to where Harry and his girlfriend had been standing. She started to unwind, excited to hear all the news and gossip from Figtree. Nathalie told her about the collection of silver studs she had bought Eleanor for her birthday gift – miniature cupcakes, teacup, saucer and spoons to mix and match. Marnie listened intently, assuming Harry was back on the dance floor or had left the party. It seemed there was always one little slice of her mind where he refused to exit.

'And you'll love this!' Nathalie continued, hooking her fingers to emphasise her words, 'Your "friend" Laila got the boot from Posh Pit. Turns out she was borrowing stock and only remembering to return it sometime later, if at all.' Nathalie suddenly lowered her voice as her eyes glanced over Marnie's shoulder. 'Oh, tall handsome man with name beginning with H approaching at twelve o'clock, or is that six o'clock? Behind you.'

Marnie stiffened as Nathalie's commentary continued. 'Has been stopped by blonde busty guest, but smiles and moves on. Looks nervous, or maybe ate something that didn't agree with him. Only joking. Should be here in five, four, three, two … Harry! Hi! I didn't see you there.'

Marnie shook her head slightly at Nathalie. She missed her, that's for sure. Ripples like little waves spread up and down her spine as she sensed Harry just behind her; she caught his familiar woody scent. She steeled herself to be introduced to the redhead. As she half-turned Harry was bumped by a waiter, pushing his firm body against her. They pressed together, his warm hand quickly around her arm, steadying her. There was no room to ease away.

'Hello, Marnie,' he said, his voice deep and rich. He dipped his lips to her cheek. 'Lovely to see you, Nathalie.' Harry leant across and pecked Nathalie on the cheek as well.

'Hello, Harry,' Marnie and Nathalie chimed.

Marnie flicked her eyes behind him, watching the redhead elegantly swaying through the crowd. Marnie's fingers tapped rapidly against her glass. She missed him so much.

'It's great you could make it up here for Eleanor. She was hoping you could

come,' Harry said.

Marnie's heart felt as if it had tripped down a step. He knew she'd be there, and yet he had still brought a date. So be it; when you cast a stone, you have to accept where it lies. Just at that thought, the redhead materialised. She was more beautiful up close, natural with a huge, beaming smile.

'Oh, hon, come here and I'll introduce you,' Harry beckoned. Marnie shuffled from foot to foot, literally kicking herself for coming.

'Angie, this is Nathalie who owns Threadz on Figtree. And this is Marnie. Marnie is up from Melbourne. But she has been running Whimsy. She's Libby's sister. I don't think you know Libby.'

Marnie smiled back and shook the offered hand. Angie, Harry's wife. Of course. Ex-wife. She would know Eleanor. Or maybe she and Harry are getting back together.

An awkward moment's silence followed before Angie spoke. 'What a stunning night Eleanor has turned on. You can't beat a summer beach party, can you?' She turned as a young fellow joined them. 'There you are, Jake! Where did you get to?'

Jake raised his eyebrows. 'I got caught with the Millers. They're just through there and want you to go say hi.' He pointed through the partygoers at an elderly couple who

Marnie recognised ran the boat hire service. They were waving enthusiastically at Angie and Harry.

'Lovely to meet you both.' Another megawatt smile and Angie wandered away. Jake headed to the tipis.

'Oh, I was going to introduce you to Jake,' Harry apologised, shrugging. The pride in his voice seemed to echo around the bay.

Nathalie glanced between Marnie who was chewing her lip and Harry who was repeatedly running his hand through his hair.

'Did you have a good Christmas?' Harry asked.

'The family were busy, and Eleanor's invitation arrived, so I was able to venture north again. I arrived early yesterday,' Marnie replied, clearing her throat. 'It was, um, lively. I probably shouldn't let Libby hear me say that as she is so busy in the shop and Christmas Day was her only day off.'

Remembering that Whimsy was at the root of her misunderstanding with Harry, she quickly added, 'How about you?'

'Great. Yep, great. Angie and Jake came up from Brisbane, so we had a typical Queensland lunch of seafood and too much pudding and champagne, then a lazy afternoon recovering and fishing.'

It sounded idyllic to Marnie. They both looked at Nathalie, waiting for her input. 'Oh, same old same old for me, but I can't complain,' she said.

'Is everything okay with your daughter?' Harry enquired, a small frown appearing.

'Yes, thank you. All sorted.' How special that he had remembered her issues with Claire.

Another moment of silence, so Nathalie offered to fetch

them cake. Neither accepted. 'So, Marnie, what's this I hear about you going to live in Singapore?' Nathalie asked.

Marnie felt Harry's body stiffen next to her. He turned, his blue eyes searching her face.

'Harry, come and look at this. Hurry!' Jake was calling across the fence, eager for Harry to join him.

Harry hesitated. 'I guess I'll catch you later, Marnie. Bye, Nathalie.'

Nathalie looked alarmed. 'Did I say something wrong?'

Marnie patted her arm, watching Harry shoulder his way through the crowd to meet his step-son. 'No. Don't worry. I'm not actually going to live in Singapore, just to visit on occasion with a new job I have. Gosh, the Nautilus Cove chat network is still alive and well, obviously.' She couldn't drag her eyes away from Harry.

The rock 'n' roll music pulled them down to the tipis. 'We could have a dance if you want. You know, get rid of all those Christmas carbs,' Nathalie suggested.

Marnie had no qualms about hitting a dance floor with another girl, but she wasn't in the mood. Harry had seriously unnerved her.

'I think I'll call a cab and go actually, Nathalie. It was so wonderful to see you and we'll definitely catch up for a chat at Nest before I head back.' She gave her friend a hug.

Marnie found Eleanor on the dance floor and gave her a quick goodbye and thank you hug between songs. She turned to leave just as Harry grasped her by the arm.

CHAPTER THIRTY-NINE

SWIFTLY AND SILENTLY HE pulled her to him, one arm around her waist, the other clutching her hand between them. He searched her eyes with his own. Marnie couldn't trust herself to speak. Her emotions were on edge at seeing him again, not to mention the wondrous spark of his body against hers. She could feel his every muscle through her sheer dress, sense his containment, like a coiled spring ready to let loose. Not for the first time over past weeks, images of them making glorious love replayed in her mind like a sensuous movie. Harry steered them through the crowd and out of the tipi.

Slowly turning and swaying in a silent dance, Harry guided her across the sand. He gently rubbed his chin against Marnie's hair, neither of them speaking, as if to do so would be to break the evening's spell. Thousands of stars watched on from the Milky Way far above them. She looked up at them, then blinked her eyes closed.

'We never got to dance, but they say the stars always dance with possibilities.' Harry's whisper wound through her hair.

'And pockets full of dreams,' she added, opening her

eyes. They were close to the waterline, the sheen of water tugging at the shore inches from their feet.

Harry's expression relaxed as he smiled down at her. 'You remember.'

Could Harry be as nervous as she was? She nodded, not able to drag her gaze away from his lips. 'Of course.'

'And then you left.'

The underlying accusation was tinged with questions. 'Harry. I …'

'You didn't trust me.' His brows knitted together. He sounded hurt, not angry, but certainly not forgiving.

Marnie swallowed as they stood facing each other like two torn lovers in an opera. They eyed each other, looking for answers, for reassurance. 'I opened my heart to you, Harry. That's difficult for me,' Marnie offered.

'And I to you … gently and without expectation. I knew you had a life, a family somewhere else. But then I started to feel more. You must have realised that. You helped me, Marnie; I learnt to focus, to feel alive again and appreciate all that I've had and have. At the same time, you stole my heart.'

Harry's eyes darkened as he dropped one hand to his side, the other raking through his hair. Marnie took a step back, at a loss at what to say. She knew she would think of a hundred replies later. Harry reached out, gently brushing strands of her hair out of her eyes. She hadn't even noticed they were there.

'But there has to be trust. I was brought up to trust and to be trusted. It has gone against me on many occasions, particularly with my brother, as I shared with you. But I believe a relationship has to be two-way, that people must be able to talk directly to each other. I'm sorry that you didn't feel we could discuss any problem beyond a couple of accusations over a drink.'

Harry put his finger against Marnie's mouth, silencing her

reply. 'I know many people in the business world have called me naïve but that's their call, and this is mine. This is how I want to lead my life and my career. With honesty and no external judgements. I'm done with all that. I'm sorry you hadn't realised that.'

She had been such a fool, but had it really been all her fault? 'Harry. I wasn't wholly to blame, you know. I was caught between Libby and Whimsy and trying to do the right thing. Then when it looked like you had other things on the agenda …'

Harry half turned, staring out over the water. Marnie wavered, but went on, '… which I know now weren't true, then I … Oh, Harry, it wasn't really you I didn't trust. I think it was me I didn't trust. You know? I was so confused that I presumed I had been lied to. Again. I didn't stop to think, to feel. I didn't fully appreciate what we had. I know that now.' She looked earnestly at him.

The party and the universe rotated around them, offering a gentle breeze to whisper through Marnie's dress. It seemed an eternity before Harry spoke again.

'Here's what happened, Marnie, so we're perfectly clear,' he said seriously, shuffling his feet in the sand. 'My feelings for you, our relationship, are uppermost in my thoughts. Every day, in fact. But let's do the business side of things first, shall we? Starlight Enterprises has grown from the company my brother Lewis and I started a long time ago. It now has a structure made up of a lot of diverse businesses. Over the years we disagreed on so many points. He is totally ruthless and can only see the end dollar figure which makes good business sense, particularly in tough trading times. But I just didn't want to play that game day after day. So I stayed on as an advisor and board member. I wanted to make sure

Starlight kept the same community ethics as it had in the beginning.'

'Harry …'

He held up a hand, halting any further interruption, and took a ragged breath.

'I need to explain all this to you, Marnie, although it's an odd place to be doing it. I can think of other more intimate joys we could have been enjoying on such a beautiful evening. Anyway, let me continue.'

Marnie nodded, linking her fingers in front of her to give them something to do.

'Lewis partly bought me out and a remaining component of that was Petrie Island. I had always loved that place more than he did so I made it a priority. I also inherited the tastes of one of Lewis's stylists or mistresses or whatever she was. But that's not important.' He shrugged.

Marnie recalled a passing reference he had made during their fleeting hours on the island. She wished he would get to the relationship part to get that off his chest.

'The payout also enabled me to concentrate on my love of sculpture and to buy Pocket and, luckily for me, it included the access to the beach we visited.'

In the soft moonlight Marnie thought she saw him smile warmly. She hoped it was due to a memory of their time there together.

'Whenever the company makes a decision on the property development side of things I try to be involved. Our parents were adamant about giving back and not to take more from the land or a community than is rightfully ours. I believe that too, but keeping tabs on such aspirations in the business world is very difficult. It makes you play your cards close to your chest. I tend to try to change things behind the scenes, such as with Sandypoint.'

He paused while a couple strolled past, hand in hand. 'So you returned to Melbourne. And now you'll be heading overseas. You've done a lot of planning in a very short time.'

His voice hardened. 'I'm sorry if you think I did something wrong, but I know in my heart I haven't. If you think I lied or misled or tricked you in any way, then you are mistaken.'

Marnie's thin excuses floated away on the waves. She tried to bring them back, but nothing came. She strengthened her voice and held his gaze. 'I'm sorry, Harry. Truly I am. I apologise for doubting you and for not listening properly. I did try to phone you after Libby told me it had all been a mistake, but I could never get through. That's the truth. I needed to apologise but didn't quite know how to. I did send you a long, wordy text that probably jammed your inbox.'

A frown creased Harry's forehead. 'I went away for a bit, back to Mitchelton's Run to clear my head. I left my phone there which will come as no great surprise, and then it got lost. I changed the number.'

Marnie's heart gave a leap. At least he now knew she had tried to apologise earlier, even if her attempts had petered out. Tears threatened as she said, 'I miss you.'

Muffled calls of goodbye, happy birthday, great night drifted to them across the sand. The party was ending, lanterns were being turned out and guests were heading home. They both turned as Jake came running toward them.

'Hey, Harry. We're heading back to the island. Are you coming with us on the boat?'

Harry gave him a wave. 'I'll be right there, Jake. I'll just find the keys.' He glanced back to Marnie, patting his pockets.

'Mum's got them, remember?' Jake laughed as he waved and sped off again down the beach.

Marnie cleared her throat as she reached for his hand. She knew she had been judged and had, most likely, not come out well. His respect and opinions mattered so much to her, but she could only wait, annoyed that she wasn't better prepared. That he wasn't allowing her more time.

Harry placed his other hand over hers. Marnie knew that if she lifted it to her lips, she would feel its rough warmth, taste its saltiness.

'I'm sorry I didn't get those messages, but it turns out I'm not a very patient man, Marnie. I've thrown myself into my work, sweating out my frustrations, I guess. There's a lot on the horizon which I have to be excited about and grateful for. Ours would have been a great partnership on all levels.'

He bent and kissed her, his lips lingering on hers. One arm curved her body against his own. Then he turned and walked back along the dark beach, his hands digging deep into his pockets. Marnie watched him go, her words to stop, to come back to her choking on the sting of her tears.

CHAPTER FORTY

MARNIE LAY in bed as a distant farewell from Libby echoed through the cottage. Her sister was being picked up by a friend and dropped into Figtree Street. There would be too much traffic to risk not getting a carpark, so Libby's car was still in the garage. Marnie was too exhausted to follow. It had been a night of tossing back and forth under the sheet, turning the fan on then off and thumping her pillow into different shapes. At one point she had got out of bed and gazed forlornly through the shutters and across the undisturbed river. It was so humid – but peaceful, the only sounds the lapping of the water and rustle of nocturnal wildlife.

She ached with a yearning for Harry's strong arms to be wrapped around her.

Her dreams came and went but they all focused on Harry's wounded feelings intermingled with his steely frown. They verged on nightmares as the waves had crashed and the wind howled around them like in a horror movie. Their clothes had whipped around their bodies, words stolen by the wind never to be returned nor understood. Now, in the light of day, she was so tired and remorseful she couldn't recall half of their conversation from the previous evening. She certainly didn't know where she stood with him, despite her late apology.

Except she did remember him saying, "Ours *would have been* a great partnership on all levels." And he hadn't offered her his new cell number.

She wished she had booked a return flight for that day instead of the following evening. Harry had obviously moved on and she should do the same as soon as possible. New Year's Eve was looming, a night she had never really looked forward to. Surely this was the perfect year to go out with friends, kick up her heels and toast to new beginnings; to make dozens of New Year resolutions, then break them. She certainly was feeling bah-humbug.

She needed to lean into her dreams. That's what she had been missing, wasn't it? The wine appointment was waving a great opportunity under her nose, and the travel it would entail surely would satisfy her wanderlust. She might even be able to fit in a trip to see Ollie while he was overseas, and maybe Claire would like to come with her. The prospect of a new home would also be cleansing. Onward and upward would have to be her new motto on life.

So why wasn't she feeling wonderful and ready to take on the world? Maybe she didn't want to take on the world anymore. Was that being lazy or wrong or just a cop out? Maybe she just wanted, as Claire would say, to do her own thing, to be content with nurturing the creative side of life. What was so wrong with that?

Unable to untangle her thoughts, Marnie leashed Beebs and set out from the cottage at a cracking pace. She was worried to see how dry the foreshore had become; the region desperately needed the summer rains. To be refreshed, just like she needed to be.

When she first arrived in Nautilus Cove, she had to remind herself it was still spring. The heat and humidity were already having their way, particularly on her as a southerner. She had come to think of that entire time as being summer.

'My summer in Nautilus Cove,' she had said to Dee before her friend had set her straight. That summer in Nautilus Cove, when everything changed.

Before she realised it, the marina came into view. *Starlight* was moored as if it was waiting for someone to just jump on board and take off to somewhere magical. Marnie wished it could have been her.

The busy season had certainly begun in Nautilus Cove with every road and shop crammed with holidaymakers. Marnie headed back to the cottage for a shower, with the plan to head in via the ferry to help Libby. It was the sisterly thing to do.

As she approached the front door, Marnie saw something small and round on the door mat. It was olive green and didn't move. Hoping it wasn't a coiled snake, she shooed Beebs aside. One of Harry's little brass turtles sat waiting for her. It was tied with a piece of string, a note tucked under its belly: *You know what to do.*

Harry! A broad smile broke across Marnie's face, her heart skipping like a happy stone across a lake. He had remembered her love of that particular little sculpture. But what about his message? She pushed aside her overthinking gene and accepted now was the time to experiment with that messy life idea. Even if Harry rejected a future together, Marnie knew her life had to change. She only hoped that the little turtle brought the promise of its maker being a part of it.

GIDDY WITH ANTICIPATION, Marnie set the car in the direction of Pocket. It seemed years since she and Libby had first visited the studio; so much had happened since that day. She tapped the steering wheel, impatient for endless surfers and families to cross to the beach. Despite No Standing signs, cars were parked all along the cliff road, many dangerously close to the edge. As she drove under the arch of fish she blew out a breath of relief, then reverse parked into the clearing in front of the studio. If she had misinterpreted the note and things got awkward, she wanted to be able to leave graciously. Straight out. No looking back.

Marnie didn't know what to expect from Harry, but she was tired of second-guessing herself. She had made a firm decision and couldn't contain her happiness as she stepped out of the car into the sticky heat. Not even the resident kookaburra's raucous laugh could break her resolve.

She nudged the door open and stepped inside. It was as cool and gorgeous as ever, as if the space was welcoming her home. A dozen large, wooden baubles, lit from within, hung low around the gallery, sprigs of mistletoe bursting below each one. A single Christmas tree stood in a corner near the panoramic windows, its lights twinkling in merriment.

As Marnie's eyes searched for Harry, she registered a few changes to the exhibition. He had obviously sold a number of pieces over the Christmas period, these being replaced with several of the bird sculptures she had seen at his workspace. A few turtles were still in the corner, nestled in sand. Her eye was drawn to the counter where a little pair of pewter angel wings sat atop a polished cedar block. Marnie's stomach clenched at the memory of his angels, of her joy photographing them, of the storm and their intimate time together.

An inspection of his works wasn't why she had come, and she ventured farther.

Harry's deep, smooth tones drifted to her, followed by a woman's voice. Marnie quietly moved through the space, just catching their conversation.

'I'm not sure I'm familiar with what you mean, Mrs Dobney,' Harry said.

'But I thought you must, because when I saw your *Milky Way* wall sculpture at Cecilia Anderson's house, it reminded me of the hare and the moon. I don't see why you can't …'

They both turned as Marnie approached. She smiled toward Harry, then spoke directly to the woman. 'Excuse me, I overheard you. Do you mean The Moon Gazing Hare? It's a part of mythology. If you see a hare – not a rabbit, it has to be a hare – gazing at the moon, it brings good fortune and renewal. Fertility, if that's what you want.'

Marnie took the moment to look at Harry, now embarrassed about butting in unasked. His expression was of surprise but his warm smile gave her the answer she was hoping for. 'Sorry to interrupt. It comes in many forms. Drawings, stories, decorations and, I guess, sculptures.'

The woman turned to Harry. 'There you go. This lass knows what I'm on about. You should keep her on. I don't see why you can't make me one. A hare sculpture.'

'I'll do some drawings for you, Mrs Dobney, but there should be no problem. Thank you for coming.'

Harry was obviously trying to usher his visitor along and luckily she left, not suspecting a thing.

Harry and Marnie locked eyes as the woman's footsteps faded across the floor and out the door. Marnie had been so focused on Harry when she had arrived, she hadn't noticed another car parked to the side of the studio. They both winced as they heard crunching gears and skidding tyres.

'A *Milky Way* wall sculpture?' Marnie asked, unsure how to proceed.

Harry shrugged, offering her his cheeky boy grin. 'I'm adaptable.'

The silence wavered between them, unsure whether to stay or flee. Marnie took in Harry's body, tense with uncertainty. She couldn't take her eyes off him.

'I, um, found the turtle. I wasn't sure what to do, so I came here. Was that what I was supposed to do?'

'Marnie.' Harry quickly stepped towards her, placing his finger on her lips. 'Ssh. Never think you are "supposed to do" anything. I was hoping you would come, and you have. Thank you.'

Marnie eased back. 'You don't have anything to thank me for. I'm so sorry, Harry, for doubting you. Trust is so important to both of us.'

'As am I. But at least you did try to phone. I'd better give you my new number, hadn't I?'

Harry gathered her in. She smiled as he embraced her, placing his forehead against hers. 'I like this,' he whispered.

'Having Mrs Dobney talking about hares?' she joked.

'No, having you in my arms, Marnie Fawkner. I've missed you.' Harry kissed her long and hard.

He took a step back, holding her fingertips with his own. 'But I do have to say something.'

His steadfast gaze unnerved her.

'Are you heading overseas to live? Is there any way you could rethink your plans and give Nautilus Cove a go? Give us a go? I rabbited on last night about what's important to me, but I didn't listen to you. It kept me up all night.'

Marnie nodded. 'I came here to say I want to stay. I haven't thought all the details through but I'm trying desperately to become more of a dandelion.'

'A what?'

Marnie laughed and shook her head, waving away her Libby-style decision to live in the moment more. Harry didn't push it, and Marnie hesitated further when she saw his frown hadn't disappeared.

'I have to be sure that what we could have here is better.' Harry paused as if trying to find the right words. 'No, more important is what I mean. That it's more important to you than what you returned to Melbourne for. That your family wouldn't suffer. Would you really be happy to come with me on my journey?'

Catching her breath, Marnie raised her hand to shield her heart, warning Harry she needed to voice what was on her mind. 'Harry, it would be my journey too, don't you see that? Absolutely my journey too. And that doesn't exclude Ollie and Claire – I would never risk losing them. It's the same as the relationship you have with Jake.'

Marnie paused, willing their hopes and desires to meet somewhere between them, like putting all the right ingredients together for a delicious multi-tiered cake with icing and sparklers.

'I thought about what you said, Harry. You know, about how I'd helped you. Well, I agree it's a two-way thing like you also said. Helping and supporting. You've made me – well 'made' isn't the right word, but it will do for now – you've made me think about self-respect and confidence and focusing on what's important. I don't feel like putty anymore, to be moved around at everyone else's whim. If you have to think about what you'd pack to pursue your dream, then I'd pack you.'

'Sorry?' Harry asked, clearly lost by another of her hazy references.

Unaware, she continued, 'You believed in me. I think I have a different outlook on life now, and …'

Harry raised his eyebrows. 'Really? That sounds rather a lot for one man to have done. I've obviously been busy. In fact, I am pretty busy now.' He turned to look around the studio, not meeting Marnie's eyes.

Marnie felt her cheeks flush. She edged away, uncertain. She turned and walked towards the window, willing the bush to swallow her if he asked her to leave.

'You see,' Harry said, the hint of a smile behind his words, 'I need to find someone to take some amazing photos. Someone who could stay with me on my island so said person wouldn't miss a moment of my incredible creative passion, whilst fulfilling her own.'

Marnie turned, tossing her head. 'Creative passion? I know someone who might be interested in passion. You know, general passion, not just the creative kind.'

'Do you?' He was in front of her in a couple of easy strides, holding her close, searching her upturned face. He wound a wayward curl of her hair around his finger. 'I wouldn't have given up on you, Marnie.'

'I know that now, and I missed you too,' Marnie replied. 'And that's why before I came here today, I sent off an email letting the wine group know I wouldn't be taking up their offer. That I will be pursuing other interests interstate. Heavens, even Claire might take on the sale of my house for me.'

The studio cocooned them as they kissed. Harry caressed Marnie's body as if he couldn't believe she was wrapped in his arms. As a tear escaped from Marnie's brimming eyes, he gently wiped it away with his thumb. Taking his hand in hers, she kissed his palm and for a long second, let her lips linger before whispering, 'They're tears of happiness, Harry.'

CHAPTER FORTY-ONE

DEE'S TEASING tone filtered through the phone. 'Am I right if I picture you and your Island Boy lazing on recliners under a thatched umbrella, Pimm's in hand, a soft breeze curling around your caftans?'

Marnie laughed. 'If only. No, Harry and I are hard at work – I heard that snort, Dee! Mind you, Petrie Island is a pretty amazing place to be. It's so beautiful and tranquil. A boat goes by every now and then, and there are lots of bush animals and birds making noises, but my thoughts are my own here.'

'You're not overthinking again, are you, my friend?'

'Well, it's a big step. I mean, I've packed up my house and sold it in record time with no further meddling from Philippe, put most of my life into storage and moved to Queensland. Who knows for how long. I've left behind my children …'

'Ah, not true,' Dee interrupted. 'Oliver is couch surfing around Europe somewhere and Claire gave you her, well, we'll call it her blessing for want of a better word. Or has there been some backtracking from her?'

'No, she was happy for me to go.' The gap was definitely narrowing, and Marnie was confident their future relationship would be sound. 'When are you coming to visit?'

'When it cools down up there. Do you still feel like a wrung-out rag all the time?'

'It is still summer so yes, it is humid. Thankfully there haven't been any cyclones here this season. They all seem to have been up north. But there is a rather magical pool to cool down in, you know.'

'I did see the photos and it all looks divine, but have you got your swimsuit wet yet? Oh wait, you're in love. You and Harry probably just float around naked.' Dee hooted.

Despite her friend's over-the-top interpretation of a life in Nautilus Cove, Marnie had to admit that it was pretty idyllic, with and without clothes. She couldn't believe how quickly she had moved north and then moved in with Harry. She'd presumed she would live with Libby until she found her feet, but had lasted only a few days at the cottage. They had been floating along the river in *Starlight* when Harry had pulled the boat into a little sandy cove.

'Marnie …'

The nervousness in his voice cut through the laziness she had been enjoying. A crow flew overhead, its call rasping against the river's solitude. Marnie's heart had missed a beat – was Harry having second thoughts about being with her? Silently she waited, trying to find clues on his handsome face.

'I think you should move to Nautilus Cove. Now. And not just for a little while, which I suspect is at the back of your mind, but permanently. I want to be with you, to meet your family, to be a part of your life and for you to be a part of mine. I want to introduce you to Mitchelton's Run.'

'To live together, Harry? We'll be working together too,

so don't you think we should …' But Marnie bit off the words she didn't want to say.

Harry had moved to sit beside her, to take her hands in his as *Starlight* rocked gently in the shallows. 'I can come to Melbourne with you to meet your kids first if you want,' he added, looking cheekily over his sunglasses. Then in a more serious tone, he said, 'I want to have you by my side every day.'

'And night?' she had teased.

'Never in doubt,' Harry had whispered as he squeezed her to him. He wasn't aware of the secret smile Marnie was holding in, in recognition of that phrase; it was one she used often with Ollie and Claire. Libby would surely think it was a sign.

And that had been that. They had spent the afternoon strolling along the sand, picking up tiny shells and sharing more about their lives. They would have made love right there in *Starlight* if they could have, but instead they had felt hustled away by a couple of innocent teenagers and their fishing rods.

'It's like Bourke Street,' Harry had muttered as he started the engine.

Marnie laughed. 'Hardly. You obviously need a trip down south to remind you what a crowd looks like.'

Marnie had chosen to return alone for her-tidy up visit to Melbourne. She had enjoyed a couple of fun farewell drinks with girlfriends and dinner with Claire, who seemed to approve of the move. There had even been no more mention of Scandinavian glass. But Marnie found her thoughts constantly bouncing back to Nautilus Cove. She had made her decision and was eager to start her new life.

Libby had raised an eyebrow when she had first visited

Petrie Island. 'If I hadn't gone to Hong Kong …' she had begun.

'Oh, Libby, please don't try to take credit for my relationship with Harry,' Marnie had sighed. 'Of all people, I would have thought you would have been the first to say "It was meant to be" or some such mystical thing.'

'Well, be careful what you wish for,' Libby replied cheekily. 'One little word leaked from me about this island and you'll have Mum and Dad parking their Winnebago in a corner of bush as quickly as you can say Grey Nomad. Oh, they wouldn't be able to get it over here, would they – clever you!'

There were still times when the sisters circled each other warily, but Marnie was relieved that their relationship was on more steady ground.

Harry made it clear he understood that, on some level, it was still a big step for her to take. He took great delight in sprinkling little surprises to welcome her, from scattering tealights down to a romantic candlelit dinner on one of the island's jetties to buying her a little runabout.

'But Harry, I don't have a clue about boats!' she had exclaimed. And she wasn't sure she really wanted to. But when Harry explained that if she was to live on an island, she had to know how to get off it if she needed to, she realised his gift made a lot of sense.

'I can't see you stand-up paddling all that way, and I thought it was a bit miserly to buy you a row boat,' he had said. 'I'll give you a couple of lessons. It's easy, and then you can get your boat licence. How else are you going to get to yoga and Nest or head off to photograph whatever you want, whenever you want? You need your independence.'

Nathalie and Eleanor couldn't hide their amusement, and often called out *ahoy* when seeing her around the Cove.

Marnie couldn't blame them. After all, she wouldn't have believed it of herself six months ago either.

HARRY'S FOCUS and passion for his craft sent tingles throughout her body; she loved watching him give himself to his creations, always striving to find a better result.

She would relax at the door of his workshop, watching every move his muscular body made. The high level of physical input his work demanded seemed exhausting. It wasn't a matter of just soldering a couple of bits of metal together, but heaving heavy blocks of stone and repositioning works in progress. Despite the fans, it was still hot in his studio and his body reacted with glistening sweat and strained muscles. Even the geckos chose to find a cool spot instead of scurrying across the warm walls.

His energy never faltered even during the hours he spent bent over sheets of designs. Marnie would stand, massaging his shoulders, and witness his ideas for various sculptures unfold onto paper.

'How do you expect me to concentrate when I can smell your fragrance right behind me?' he'd asked before scooping her into his arms. 'But what a delicious distraction you are.'

Marnie threw herself into her photography. She had already taken a few portrait and artist-in-action style shots for his promotional material when an unexpected email from Samantha, Harry's New York contact, arrived.

Heavy rain had emptied onto the coast as though heaven had opened its catchment gates, so they had retreated inside the villa to catch up on emails and paperwork. In true style for a Queensland summer it was hot and sticky, the overhead fans providing little relief. Marnie knew she would have to give in soon and turn on the air conditioning.

'Wow,' Harry said. 'There has been a gallery cancellation and Samantha is urging me to pick up the space.'

'But you already have space at Little Lucifer Gallery in Brisbane,' Marnie replied vaguely. 'Gosh, that rain is really coming down now.'

She moved to close the window and scoop in one of the billowing curtains which was already saturated with warm rain. The veranda was soaked despite its deep awning, but Marnie couldn't resist leaning against the doorway and scanning the garden. Hefty palm leaves were no match for the torrent as they bent towards the earth, the pool and lagoon were potholed with raindrops as though a thousand needles were puncturing its surface. Her view of farther down the property was hampered by a grey shield of rain. She knew she would never tire of the pungent smells of the wet bush nor the sheer force of nature.

'The gallery Samantha is referring to is called Lucifer and is in New York; it's Little Lucifer's head gallery. I would be exhibiting there during their late autumn season. Marnie, come and look at this.' Harry beckoned to her.

'This year?' Marnie jerked, possible timetables and to-do lists instantly jumbling around in her head. 'There's no way to be ready. And what about Brisbane?' She could hear how negative she was sounding, particularly when she saw the spark of excitement in Harry's eyes.

'Damn, where did I put my pen?' Harry frowned, anxious to investigate the details.

Marnie picked up the pen from the sideboard and silently handed it to him.

'So, Samantha is suggesting we postpone Brisbane and

take up the opportunity in New York instead, because and I quote "you only get a chance like this once in every few years, Harry".' He reinforced the comment by nodding and tossing the pen onto the laptop.

The remaining details of the email jumped off the screen as Marnie leaned in. Samantha asked – demanded, really – many more images and in different formats. She planned to swamp New York in the lead-up to the exhibition with very different designs and themes from those Marnie was already putting together for Brisbane. She had even suggested photographs of Mitchelton's Run as a 'country boy makes good' idea.

Marnie's agitation grew in momentum with the pouring rain, until finally she had to come clean to Harry.

'I'm not ready,' she said, clasping her hands in her lap.

'Good lord, Marnie. It will be fine. I already have enough stock from Brisbane – I only have to add a couple more pieces. It's more the transportation of it all, but Samantha is looking into shipping and says it can be done in time if we commit immediately.' Harry leaned back, crossing his hands behind his head, and smiled at the ceiling.

'I said I'm not ready. What she is suggesting is the polar opposite of the direction I've been heading in. Surely you don't want to go along with the Australian country boy thing?'

'Marnie, stop judging yourself. I love what you've done. The portrait shot makes me look way hotter than I am. What's that saying – If you're not in over your head how do you know how tall you are?'

'I don't need another bloody quote in my life,' she said.

Harry laughed and strolled away to brew more coffee.

Marnie's frustrations grew at Harry's dismissive attitude.

She slipped into her old habit of having to have all her lists completed, items ticked off, and a proper plan in place, having weighed up all possible options. In her mind, her work wasn't good enough for a grand New York exhibition.

Her mood simmered around the room. Harry returned to the couch with two mugs and shuffled across the couch until their legs touched. He gathered her hands into his and tilted his body in front of her.

'Look at me. We already know our theme and design and that's not going to change no matter what Samantha wants; we just have to adapt it to the other gallery's layout. It's the same as Brisbane, only New York. All you have to do is take a few more photos soon. I don't know, do you email them or tube them over, or have them developed there?'

'That's what I'm saying. I don't know. I mean for some reason it all seems overwhelming. What if I can't …'

He took her into his arms and held her tightly, planting gentle kisses into her hair. 'We'll work it out. I have every confidence in you,' he whispered. 'But I think we should give Samantha the go-ahead to book Lucifer for autumn.'

And people say I'm the stubborn one, Marnie thought.

With the New York exhibition being all systems go, Marnie found herself almost frozen with doubt as she desperately tried to steal some of Harry's creative drive. She could see the images that were needed in her head, but her camera stayed quiet in her grasp. The confidence, stamina and sense of adventure that Harry displayed just wouldn't be summoned. She was thrilled at the amazing career opportunity the exhibition offered Harry and was determined not to let him or herself down. They were a team.

Despite the humidity, Marnie set aside time every morning to walk around the island. She needed to pace like she had with Beebs when she first visited Nautilus Cove, when problems with Claire and her own future wouldn't leave her alone. She needed to regroup and figure out how to attack the job she was supposed to be doing. For Harry, and for herself.

Surprisingly, it had been a call from Libby that spurred her on.

'An exhibition in New York is really something, Marnie. Harry's career will shoot through the roof,' she had said.

'I know. I'm so proud of him. I only hope I can hold up my end.'

'What do you mean? You're a great support and it's not as though it's your solo exhibition, is it? I mean, don't get me wrong, I'm sure your marketing skills are in overdrive but …'

Marnie had smiled at her sister's habit of being painfully blunt. 'Samantha seems to be covering that side of things. But she is still insisting on a different direction for some aspects of Harry's branding.'

'Pfft,' Libby had replied instantly. 'It's what Harry and you want out of the exhibition that's important. You two are living it, feeling it and know instinctively what you need it to say. Come on, sis. Trust yourself. I'm sure Harry does.'

The quote on Libby's dream magnet flashed before Marnie's eyes again as she thought about their conversation. She slowed and raised her camera and clicked off shot after shot of whatever presented itself. She adjusted her depth of field settings and kept going, loosening up and finding her rhythm between showers. The temptation to review what she had accomplished was ignored and before she knew it, she had done a full circle back to the workshop.

Marnie eased open the door. As a gap in the clouds released a wavy beam of sunlight through the window, a tiny rainbow reflected off the copper angel's wing that Harry was working on. With a click of the shutter and a pinpoint focus on the rainbow and wing, Harry's hands and the angel's shoulder softly blurred out of focus. Without looking at the image, Marnie knew in her heart she had captured everything she wanted to.

EPILOGUE

NINE MONTHS LATER.

Opening night of the two-month exhibition of An Angel's Kiss in Autumn at the fashionable Lucifer Gallery had arrived all too quickly.

However, Samantha had proved to be worth more than her weight in gold bullion when she had secured the exclusive New York gallery and schmoozed New York's creative elite. The transport of already completed pieces earmarked for the Brisbane exhibition had started immediately, but the lead-in had still been extremely tight. Yet here they were.

Harry and Marnie had arrived in The Big Apple nearly a week before the exhibition opening to finalise the displays and for Harry to fulfil promotional interviews. Samantha had stressed how hard it would be to crack the city's buyers, so every opportunity was vital. Much to Harry and Marnie's relief she had moved on from many of her conflicting ideas once they dug their heels in on the direction they wanted their story to take.

Harry had insisted on a shopping trip as soon as they arrived, to find perfect outfits for the opening night. Marnie had wanted a simple black cocktail dress and, on Dee's insistence, high altitude black stilettos. She found just the right dress quickly, amused at the relief that had swept across Harry's face.

Marnie now paused at the gallery's entrance – she wished Harry success with every bone in her body and was proud to have played her part, albeit a minor role. She glanced again at Lucifer's window which flaunted one of the oversized sets of angel wings. The installation was dark and moody, interrupted by a sultry spotlight that filtered down through the feathers. It was stunningly evocative.

As they walked through the door, Harry took Marnie's elbow and swung her around. 'Marnie,' he said, his frown startling her.

'Harry?'

'I hope I've done the right thing,' he said, searching her eyes. 'I mean, when I asked you if you had a favourite photo, you said it was the one you had taken in the workshop, and when I then asked if you thought it was as good as you could make it, you said yes. Am I right?'

'Yes, but what …'

He guided her through the crowd to the main gallery, and there it was. An enlarged print of her photograph, suspended on rods in the middle of the space – a rainbow and an angel's wing, Harry's hands and the angel's shoulder softly blurred out of focus.

Marnie gasped. She remembered the moment she had captured the image, the tingles it had sent through her body. A gentle enhancement of the rainbow's colours and the wing's metallic hues eased into the blurred black and white background. 'Oh, my goodness! How …?'

'Samantha had it hoisted after we left yesterday, so you wouldn't see it. Is it okay that I did this? I mean, you just had to be a part of Lucifer. There isn't any stupid copyright thing or creative boundary I've crossed, is there?'

Marnie remained glued to the spot, mesmerised at her photograph. It looked amazing – powerful and intriguing. She had wanted it to symbolise creativity, of bringing the artist's work to life, and she knew she had achieved just that.

'It's perfect. Isn't it?' she whispered, tears brimming.

'Yep. I reckon it's perfect. I'm so lucky. Thank you, Marnie,' Harry replied, taking her hands in his.

Her stomach had churned with excitement when she first thought of ideas for the exhibition, then when Harry had whooped with joy at her insights and stuck by them, she knew it would be a true team effort. She knew that he had fallen in love with not only Marnie the woman but with her work. His inclusion of her image was living proof.

Billed as being *Enthralling, Captivating, A heavenly collection of works in full flight*, no one seemed surprised when the vast industrial space quickly filled with creatives from New York's Lower East Side. Except for Harry and Marnie; nothing had prepared them for the overwhelming reaction. Reviewers – and hopefully buyers – continued to arrive.

Marnie's eyes followed Harry around the gallery. Her handsome Island Boy was dressed in a loose deep charcoal suit and crisp white shirt. She knew his tanned skin, muscled physique and dancing blue eyes were the centre of every woman's attention, but it was toward her that his wink was directed if they drifted apart. She fingered the rose gold and diamond bracelet he had given her on the eve of their departure from Nautilus Cove.

'Hello.'

A fellow had sidled silently up beside her; instantly she put on her smile of welcome. 'Are you enjoying the exhibition?' Marnie enquired of the short man who was dressed in head-to-toe black. He wore a felt hat, called a cow pat hat in Australia Marnie thought fleetingly, but she presumed it had another loftier name in New York.

He nodded. 'Intriguing.' He didn't try to hide his appraisal as he looked Marnie up and down. As their eyes met, she was relieved to see a distinct twinkle rather than anything more disturbing.

Marnie held out her hand. 'Marnie Fawkner. All the way from Australia.'

'Benny Benbow. All the way from three blocks away,' he replied. 'So, Australia. I went there once to visit my sister. So darn hot. How can you stand it?'

Marnie laughed. 'Oh, it snows in Australia too. Did you know that?'

'No, I didn't,' he said, frowning. 'And I'm not sure I believe you. My sister has had the last visit from me, so it doesn't matter anyway. How did this collaboration come about?' He waved his hand around in circles, encompassing everything within the gallery walls.

Marnie wasn't sure how to respond, particularly as he seemed to be confident in calling it a 'collaboration'. How had it come about exactly? And if she could be honest about that answer, would she want to share it with a stranger? Benny hadn't taken his eyes off her, seemingly amused at her hesitation.

'Well, Benny. Harry is an incredibly talented sculptor who I just happened to come across during a holiday in Queensland. It was a meeting of, um, minds.'

'Ah, I get the impression it was a lot more than that.' He

winked. 'I've inspected his magnificent angels and your installation and photo, and I venture to say that they go hand in hand. I can't imagine one without the other.'

Marnie's Angels in Autumn creation was a roped off installation displaying dozens of miniature wings suspended from the roof, with metal feathers and leaves scattered across the floor below. Her premise was to stimulate stories and for guests to read into it what they wanted. For her it spoke of the cycle of life and seasons – change.

Marnie started with pleasure. 'Are you a collector, Benny, or from the media?' she asked tentatively.

'A lover of art. A sort of mini Saatchi, let's say.' He giggled at his own reference, and wandered away, leaving Marnie none the wiser but extremely hopeful.

The exchange had done nothing to settle the unruly butterflies in Marnie's stomach. Her relief that the exhibition had come together at all was overwhelming.

Inside the gallery guests mingled and clinked glasses to a backdrop of tunes by The Teskey Brothers – their nod to an Australian band. Harry's angels slumped in corners or rose from the concrete floor, each one informing an emotion. From sultry to shy, erotic to angry, Harry's skill shone through in each potent sculpture. Bronze cherubs squatted on top of plinths; small copper angels dotted the floor throughout, some serene with wings folded, others sullen or ready to fly. Guests couldn't help but run their hands down the smooth metal, as if willing the feathers to ruffle or the muscled messengers to emerge from their silence.

Harry's pieces still sent a shiver of joy and pleasure through Marnie's body. She couldn't help but marvel at how the hands that created such powerful art forms could be the same as those that could stroke her body as if it was a fragile dove. She recalled his comment from the previous night. They had just made love and she was lazing in bed, admiring his nakedness as he stood at the window of their hotel suite. His arm muscles were taut as he pressed a hand against the glass, his legs firm as they stood slightly apart, his tan lighter on his firm buttocks.

'We've come a long way, haven't we,' he had uttered, almost to himself.

And now, in this 'pinch me' moment in a gallery in New York, Marnie whispered to herself, 'Yes, Harry. Yes, we have both come such a long way.'

For days Marnie's cell phone had beeped endlessly with messages of Good Luck from Melbourne and Nautilus Cove, as their friends extended heartfelt support. She had wished that their respective families could have been by their sides; particularly Libby who Marnie knew would have absorbed New York with gusto. But the timing just hadn't allowed it. 'Next time!' they had all promised. A tub of flowers had been delivered from Angie and Jake, another from Ollie and Claire, with a note saying, 'So proud. Xx'. Harry and Marnie couldn't wait for them all to get together on Petrie Island when they returned from New York.

Marnie's manicured nails tapped against her hardly touched champagne glass – she didn't dare take a sip until after the formalities. As the gallery owner started her speech, Samantha quietly shared that she had already taken offers for several of Harry's works. Marnie quickly glanced around the crowd, her attention caught by a short man in black who, looking directly at her, saluted her with his catalogue.

She sensed that even the normally laid-back Harry was nervous, his leg jiggling against her body. He reached around her shoulder, pulling her to his side and gently kissed her forehead. Holding her close, he thrust his other hand into his pants pocket, starting with surprise. Marnie kept her attention on the podium but couldn't resist a quick, loving glance as he realised that, at the bottom of his pocket, sat a tiny smooth shell nestled in a few grains of sand. Queensland sand in a pocketful of dreams.